# Benefits Included
### Erin Lisbeth

Copyright

All rights reserved. No part of this publication may be reproduced, stored or transmitted in any form or by any means, electronic, mechanical, photocopying, recording, scanning, or otherwise without written permission from the publisher. It is illegal to copy this book, post it to a website, or distribute it by any other means without permission.

This novel is entirely a work of fiction. The names, characters and incidents portrayed in it are the work of the author's imagination. Any resemblance to actual persons, living or dead, events or localities is entirely coincidental.

Erin Lisbeth asserts the moral right to be identified as the author of this work.

Erin Lisbeth has no responsibility for the persistence or accuracy of URLs for external or third-party Internet Websites referred to in this publication and does not guarantee that any content on such Websites is, or will remain, accurate or appropriate.

Designations used by companies to distinguish their products are often claimed as trademarks. All brand names and product names used in this book and on its cover are trade names, service marks, trademarks and registered trademarks of their respective owners. The publishers and the book are not associated with any product or vendor mentioned in this book. None of the companies referenced within the book have endorsed the book.

First Edition 2025

Copyright © [2025] by [Erin Lisbeth]

Dog art created by Paige Moreland (@Ipm_draws)

Editing by: Sarah Pesce at Lopt & Cropt Editing

Author photo by Bella Mia

*Also by Erin Lisbeth*

The Dating Debacle
Sugar Cookie Kisses
The Witch's Knight

**To all the lovely readers who are wandering aimlessly, may you find a place that feels like home.**

*Author's Note*

This book may contain subjects that could be triggering to some.
-Explicit sex scenes
-Swearing
-Dog attack (off page)
-Death of a parent and grandparent (off page)
-Sexual harassment

# Prologue

## The Wedding

My red-bottom heels echo as I walk towards the altar to marry a man that I've never met.

I inhale a deep breath.

I've been in the city less than twenty-four hours, and I'm about to become a missus.

Who would have thought?

Granny always said I'd amount to something. I don't think she meant I'd be mounting on top of this handsome businessman before bedtime tonight, a stranger I met online only a few weeks ago. If she's watching me from heaven right now, I know she'd be rolling her eyes and waving a tired finger at me. But it's not like I'm really doing anything wrong, per se; I'm just not marrying for love.

And since I feel like part of Granny's purpose in the afterlife is to now watch over me and my questionable decisions, I glance towards the ceiling and silently apologize for this behavior she definitely would not condone.

Anyway, I'm about to become really, really happy, because no matter what anyone thinks, money does buy happiness. I might not have love, but I will soon have money.

And a husband—for now, at least.

This is just a temporary arrangement. Within a year, I will have everything I need to finally start my real life.

I step up to the altar, careful not to step on the satin train of my dress. My eyes widen when I place myself before my groom and meet his eyes up close for the first time. Time freezes, and it feels like the walls are closing in around the two of us. I'm lost in his warm brown eyes, which give me hot-chocolate-on-Christmas-morning feels.

I knew Jaxon was attractive from his pictures and our videochat a few weeks ago, but this up-close-and-personal Jaxon is next-level hot.

He clears his throat, distracting me from my thoughts, then nods at something behind me.

I turn my head, and there's a woman holding out her hand, signaling for me to pass her my bouquet.

"Oh," I say, and hand it over.

When I turn back to Jaxon, the officiant speaks.

"Please take one another's hands."

His hands envelop mine, covering them completely, warm to the touch.

I take a quick glance around the room nervously to find the space mostly empty. There are a few witnesses, and our driver, Henri.

We have a *driver*. And not just an Uber driver. A man in a suit with dark glasses covering his eyes despite the cloudy day, type of driver. He looks kind of bad-ass, like he's the getaway driver in an action movie.

My attention floats back to Jaxon—Jaxon Baker, my *fiancé*—and I flutter my eyelashes, knowing the light gold eye shadow I'm wearing will make my eyes sparkle. I've never been one to wear much makeup, but today definitely called for it. That, along with pale rose lips and long curls cascading down my back.

I wink, and I'm met with a blank expression. He shifts from left to right, as if he's in a hurry to get this over with. I'd be lying if I said I didn't feel the same. I don't want to chance him changing his mind now that I'm here and I've already kissed my shitty job and dead-end town goodbye.

This is the door I've been waiting for. The opportunity for a better life, and I can't risk Jaxon bailing before we lock lips as husband and wife. The contract's been signed, but it will only come into effect after the ceremony.

I wiggle my toes, and bite my lip, a habit I've had for years, and I see him frown, his gaze dipping towards my mouth. Forcing myself to stop, my lip stinging, I smile again, only half listening as the officiant speaks.

Jaxon is gorgeous, built broad and thick, tall and handsome. My gaze drifts down his pant line, and I'm left wondering if it's true what they say about big feet.

But I can't let myself get attached. This is a business deal of sorts. Plus, I haven't caught Jaxon checking me out once. He's a millionaire, for God's sakes; he is probably used to being around gorgeous women who throw themselves at him on the daily.

The gold bracelets that circle my tiny wrist clink together as I shift. I'm outwardly keeping my cool, but on the inside, my nervous system is like a volcano ready to erupt.

He might not have checked me out, but he is staring deep into my eyes, and when I smile this time, I notice he returns it with the slight crook of his lips.

"I promise to cherish you always, in sickness and in health, in poverty and wealth."

My beating heart kicks up a notch. We signed a contract. A marriage contract securing me and my future after this marriage inevitably ends. He wouldn't have lied about everything, would he? He paid for my one-way plane ticket and a room at The Cartier last night, and I did find him on a millionaire site. One that seemed pretty legit. I guess I could wake up tomorrow with more debt than my own, or worse, I could find myself missing a kidney in a bathtub full of ice cubes.

I shake my head. I refuse to think the worst. We have a contract, and Jaxon will live up to his end of the deal once we exchange vows and sign the marriage license.

Plus, Jaxon paid the attorney fees for us both after he had the contract drawn up. The young lawyer in the oversized brown suit, the one I hired to check if the contract had any hidden clauses, told me I was safe. He specifically said that once we were married, Jaxon would have to pay up. It was all part of the negotiations.

Clearing my throat, I push those thoughts away and plaster my people-pleasing, customer service smile back on my freshly powdered face.

He's legit, this is real, and I will not lose a kidney tonight. We may have this deal between us, but it doesn't change the fact that this is a huge leap of faith.

I've been treated like a princess since I stepped foot into first class. Or at least like the outcast loner turned popular girl in a teenage romcom.

"Do you take Jaxon Baker to be your husband?"

"I do," I say more confidently than I feel.

"Do you take Quinn Cameron to be your wife?"

"I do," Jaxon's husky voice agrees.

# PROLOGUE

We exchange rings and then the officiant declares, "By the power vested in me, and by the power of your commitment, I now pronounce you married. You may kiss your bride."

Jaxon's lips meet mine in a soft, pillowy touch, and when we pull apart, my fingers graze my mouth, and I watch his eyes darken.

I'm in trouble.

# Chapter One

*Quinn*

*Three weeks earlier*

"Grab my ass one more time," I threaten, a hiss between my teeth. I dart my eyes around the rest of the table, setting my hands on the wet surface, leaning in. Three sets of eyes are watching me, waiting for me to lose my shit so they can call me crazy.

Chuckling, the blond puffs his chest out. "Whoa, come on. Relax."

I point my finger directly at him. "Don't you know, you're never supposed to tell a woman to relax?" I don't let him answer. "Finish your drink and get out."

"You can't talk to me like that. I'm a paying customer."

"Wanna bet?"

I straighten the apron that's cinched around my waist, and I wipe my hands down the sides. Turning on my heel, I head towards the staff room. Making my way to the mirror that's hanging on the wall, I pull out a bobby pin and adjust the hair that's fallen out of my ponytail.

I've been working at this bar since my early twenties, and some regulars seem to be getting a little too comfortable with the servers.

"Quinn, what the hell was that all about?"

Rick, my boss, is glaring at me from the doorway, or he would be if his eyes weren't hooded with an alcoholic haze.

"The table you were waiting on is stirring up some trouble, saying you're kicking 'em out," he slurs.

"Yeah, they can't keep their hands to themselves." I walk towards the door, but Rick doesn't budge, blocking me in.

"And?"

I place my hands on my hips. "And what?"

"They mean no harm."

"It's not okay, Rick."

"Suck it up and get back on the floor, princess. No one's getting thrown out."

"You can't be serious." My cheeks flush, heated.

Rick takes a toothpick out of his shirt pocket and sets it between his teeth. "Yeah, I am."

Infuriated, I take a few steps back towards the lockers, and I reach for my purse. I dump the tips I've been carrying from the day into the wide opening of my knockoff designer bag.

"What do you think you're doing?" Rick pushes himself off the door frame, teetering on his toes, the scent of whiskey heavy between us.

I shove my dirty apron into his hands. "I quit."

Quickening my step, I push the front door to the bar open, and I'm hit with a blast of cool evening air.

I start my beater car and let myself sink into the worn leather bucket seats.

I need to get my life together.

Twenty minutes later, I'm sitting at my kitchen table eating leftovers and scrolling job ads on my laptop when a pink banner blinks at the top of my screen. *Want to date a millionaire?*

Chewing the last of my deep-fried pickles, I hover the cursor over the banner wondering if I'll get a virus if I click on the ad. Will my webpage be overridden by porn and scam ads?

A man all suited up is staring deep into the eyes of a young brunette at the bottom of the page. They look happy. I'm not naïve; I realize that it's a fake picture, but it's hard not to notice their smiling faces. It's been a long time since I've let myself fall in love. My focus has been on paying the bills Mom and Granny left behind.

I click the ad before I can stop myself, and a pink website comes to life. Elevator music spills from the tiny laptop speakers, filling my apartment. After reading over the terms and agreement and browsing the five-star reviews, I start the application process.

This isn't your average dating site.

This is a matchmaker bringing people together, some of whom just happen to have money, and a lot of it.

I scroll through questions from shoe size to ring size, debt amounts, dates of my last physical, and a copy of a criminal record check. I just so happen to have had a record check done last year after applying for a job. A job I didn't get.

It takes me a while to upload proof of all the requested information, and I shake my hair out of its elastic, my blonde curls dancing around my shoulders, the weight of the ponytail leaving a lingering ache.

I can't believe I'm doing this.

Once the form is complete and I'm happy with my bio, I change out of my work clothes and into a cropped soft pink sweater and leggings. I fluff my hair and apply some lip gloss, and then prop my phone up against the toaster in the kitchen. I press the button for the timer and focus on getting my pose just right before the three seconds are up, and the flash flares, blinding me.

I glance over it while spots hover in my sight and hit submit.

My fingers play with the bottom of my fuzzy sweater as I contemplate what I've just done.

Why am I even seeking a man with money?

Maybe because I've been struggling as long as I can remember. I've been working since I was twelve, delivering sale flyers before school. Once I turned sixteen, I got a job as a hostess at a diner, which turned into a waitress position, which led me to working at the bar for Rick. I wonder what it would be like to sit back, relax, and enjoy a weekend off, to not be thinking about money every hour of the day.

A notification pops up, and I read that it can take anywhere from twenty-four hours to three days for my account to be reviewed and approved.

Job searching is what I should be doing right now, but I've been playing the good girl, rule-following, debt-paying daughter and granddaughter for years, and I'm exhausted.

It's time for a little adventure. I just hope this isn't too good to be true.

# Chapter Two

## *Jaxon*

"Fuck. I'm fucked."

Lester moves swiftly out of my way as I pace the floor in my office. "No, you're not."

"I'm *fucked*," I repeat, then stop to face the floor-to-ceiling glass windows overlooking the bay. I place my hands on my hips, legs spread in power pose. Edward had us take some bullshit self-confidence course at last year's retreat, and this is what stuck.

But I don't need confidence. What I need is a *wife*.

"You work hard," Lester says soothingly. "Edward will see that."

I roll my eyes. "When Edward has a thought in his head, he runs with it. If he wants a family man for CEO, he'll get a family man for CEO."

Edward is closing in on sixty and wants to take a step back from Edward Rummens Watches, the company he built from the ground up. Three weeks ago, he announced he wanted someone he could trust to protect his baby and keep it growing strong.

Everything was fine until this watercooler bullshit. "I've been here the longest." I count out my strengths on my fingers. "I take my job seriously. I develop and implement leading strategies for marketing and customer retention. I produce and execute every task."

Every. Fucking. Time.

I frown, a dull ache settling deep into the middle of my forehead.

"I understand." Lester nods. "You can't always trust office gossip, though."

Lester's been my protégé for the last year. He's a great sounding board, always upbeat—honestly, a bit too happy and positive for my serious demeanor—but he puts up with my bullshit. Lester's a good kid, really. He's sitting upright in his crisp button-down shirt from Marshalls, willing to do whatever it takes.

I was him once.

I walk around settling in on my black leather ergonomic chair and roll up my sleeves.

"Go find out." I nod towards the closed door.

"Me? How am I going to do that?" His voice takes on a higher pitch, one that sneaks out when I challenge him.

"You're friends with the women in this office. Go chat them up. Find out where they got this information from while I figure out what the hell I'm going to do about it."

Standing and pushing his glasses further up on his nose, he walks towards the door.

"Close the door on your way out," I order, and wait for the click of the latch.

I've spent my entire adult life so focused on work that relationships were always off the table. There's been no one since Claire, not even the slightest situationship.

She and I met at university. We were in love, or so I thought, but during those last hours of graduation, Claire made her intentions known. I had just been someone to pass the time with, a study partner, until her real life started. The heartache left a sour taste on my tongue, and I decided then and there to put work before everything else. To climb the corporate ladder so that I could be in charge of my own destiny.

Everything's been going just fine until now.

I pick up the contract I was reviewing before I went to the kitchen to grab a coffee and overheard the busy bees talking about this year's retreat. It's the same goddamn thing every year.

Everyone is invited.

No, let me correct myself: everyone is *encouraged* to attend.

Wrong again.

Everyone is *voluntold* to show up at the corporate retreat. Forced socialization. Forced meals with coworkers who I couldn't care less about and forced proximity with Brodie.

Brodie fucking Mullin.

A stick-up-his-ass boss's pet.

Brodie started working for the company about five years after me, and from the moment he got here, he made sure I recognized his intentions to surpass me in ranking in Edward's eyes. We all knew that wouldn't happen, Edward included, but now with this new promotion, I bet he's dying to slither his way past me as vice-president and go straight to CEO from head of client relations.

## CHAPTER TWO

If the rumors are true, the only thing Brodie has going for him is the one thing I don't: a family. He's a suburban dad with a teacher for a wife and two kids under five. A picture-perfect family.

Brodie will *not* be CEO.

It can't happen. I won't let it.

I just have to think. Opening my bottom drawer, I pull out a bottle of pain reliever and pop two small white tabs into my mouth, swallowing them with a swig of my leftover morning coffee.

I've spent my entire adult life in a business suit, making my mark.

I don't date. I have my needs met from time to time, but I haven't woken up with a woman in my bed in years. Do I spend too much time alone? One thousand percent. Do I think about how it would be waking up to someone nuzzled into my neck on a Sunday morning? Sure, I'm not a total robot.

But a wife? I wouldn't even know where to find one.

I rack my brain, running my hands through my hair.

A knock on my glass door catches my attention, and I glance up in time to see Brodie himself opening the door without my consent. Fuck.

"Yeah?" I nod my head in greeting when he's a few steps closer than I'd like him to be. We get our work done and work together when we have to—and well, might I add—but it ends there. That's surface-level bullshit. Brodie hates me, and I hate Brodie. For no other reason than I'm his competition, and he's mine.

"You have the Carter contract?" he asks, surveying my office. I watch as he looks out the windows towards the bay, and a part of me radiates inside knowing he's jealous of the size of this space. Who wouldn't be? I've got a corner office, and what does Brodie have? A view of Foxholme Highway, concrete and traffic jams.

I pick up the folder I was just browsing and pass it to him, eyebrows rising, silently questioning him. "The numbers were off."

"Thought so," he says, glancing through a few of the pages.

"They're good now. This collaboration should go off without a hitch."

"Great."

And that's the end of that. He closes the file. "Mind if I look through?"

"Be my guest." I turn to my laptop, my back towards him, signaling that this conversation is over, and he's headed to the door when I hear his footsteps stop.

"Hear about Edward's wish list for CEO?"

Is this motherfucker really rubbing it in my face? Did I really expect anything less?

Before I can make a remark, Lester is back, and Brodie briefly acknowledges him by name as he exits.

Lester closes the door behind him and sits back down in his chair, the one closest to the window.

"Tell me you have good news," I all but plead, rubbing at my temples.

"Sally told Maggie that she had heard from Jenny..."

"Get to the damn point, Lester."

Hesitation crosses his face. Poor kid. I understand that I'm hard on him, but life is hard, and business is harder. He needs to be tough.

"Edward wants a CEO with a family."

"I'm thirty-six! It's not like I'm a fifty-two-year-old bachelor. And what would be so wrong with that, anyway? What does a family man have that I don't?"

## CHAPTER TWO

"A family." I roll my eyes, and Lester shrugs. "He wants someone who will care for his business like a man would care for his family."

"He needs someone with a good head on their shoulders, one with strong and innovative event concept execution."

"I'm just relaying the information that Jenny..."

"Jenny who?"

"Brodie's assistant, Jenny."

I'm shaking my head in disbelief. Fifteen years working with Edward. I was *his* protégé, for fuck's sakes, and now I'm going to be passed on this promotion because I put work ahead of women all these years?

No. I won't let this happen.

"I haven't worked my ass off for Edward just to lose a promotion to Brodie. All I need is a wife."

Lester sits upright in his chair. "You haven't got much time to find someone. Six months at most."

My mind is churning. "I can't waste time on a random dating app." I consider my options. "I need someone who will take this seriously. If Edward wants a family man, he won't settle for a bachelor dating online. I can't get the whole family all at once, but I can start with finding a wife."

Or my whole life will have been a waste.

# Chapter Three

## *Quinn*

I squint at the sound of Alysha's voice. Her long hair shines platinum in the sun coming through the slats of my mini-blinds.

"Girl, I need your car."

"Ugh, why did I ever give you a key to my apartment?" I mumble, pulling the covers over my head.

She sits on the edge of my bed. "Come on, I need to drive into Fairfax this morning." She pauses, and I can hear her biting her nails. "What time do you work tonight?"

"I don't. I quit," I answer, my voice muffled under the thickness of the duvet. The memories that I've tried hard to block the past few days come floating back whether I want them to or not.

She pulls down the covers, and I immediately sense the impending freakout. "You *quit*?"

"Yeah," I say, rolling onto my side.

"Rick... he do something to you?" I can hear her concern, and I feel bad for making her worry. Rick's been an ass since

I first started working at the bar, and she knows all about it. He's as bad as some of the drunks. Heck, he *is* one of the drunks.

"No, nothing like that. I just can't do it anymore. The groping, the late nights. It was time. I just want more, you know?"

"Yeah, I know."

Alysha and I have been neighbors for a few years now, two single girls living in the same building. We look out for each other. I have her spare key, and she has mine. She just started a new job earlier this year as a substitute teacher, so she's got her shit together a little more than I do.

"Okay, well, I'll grab some snacks when I'm out, and we'll watch some reality TV tonight. There's a new episode of that housewives show you like. You can fill me in on everything." She pats my knee over the duvet. "Keys?"

"Fine, take them. They're probably in my purse," I say, motioning towards a few piles of clothes that are scattered on my floor where I discarded my purse a few nights ago "But I expect the usual," I demand, knowing that she is well aware that I need both sweet and crunchy when it comes to snacks.

"You got it." She stands and grabs my purse, shifting through the contents.

I haven't left my apartment since I got back home after throwing my apron at Rick. I've been back and forth from my couch to my bed for three days, in a slump of TV and takeout. The keys rattle in her hands as I roll onto my back, staring at the ceiling, wondering what will become of my life. I trace the flowers in the stucco ceiling with my eyes, something I do whenever insomnia hits at three in the morning and my room is lit up by the streetlamp outside. I could probably draw the entire design with my eyes closed.

"Be back in a few hours, babe," she says, the keys jingling in her hand. "We'll find you a better job, one without a Rick in it."

"Take care of Carl."

"He's in good hands."

Granny always said if you name your car, he'll take care of you. No one ever disagreed with Granny. And Carl is the only man that's always had my back.

Balancing my glass of orange juice and a plate of avocado toast and eggs, I make my way to my laptop. It's still sitting on my coffee table, so I let myself fall onto the living room sofa with a humph. It's time I get myself out of this funk. Plus, I'm going to need money, and soon.

It's been difficult finding a job that interests me. Saying this town is small is an understatement. That, and my lack of a degree, has me at the bottom of every pile of résumés. Sometimes, when I'm up late at night after my shift at the bar and I need to unwind before bed, I scan the web and imagine myself going back to school or working in some fancy job that I'm excited about. If funds weren't a concern, I don't even know where I would begin, or what I would want to do with my life. I just know that leaving this town would be at the top of my list. I'd miss Alysha, sure—she's the closest thing to family that I have—but every cell in my body wants more than this.

I set myself up and take a large bite while I watch the screen come to life. Pink hearts float about, and elevator music bursts out of the tiny computer speaker. Has Cupid taken over my life?

I chase my toast with a gulp of orange juice, and it all comes back to me. How could I forget that I signed up to be matched with a millionaire? I blame stress and a lack of sleep.

Curious, I click on the pink envelope indicating I have a welcome message.

I spend the next five minutes reading about how I'm going to be matched with one millionaire at a time. If I choose to decline my match, a new match will reappear. Interested, I click agree and let my eyes scan the page trying to find the tab of matches.

Once I spot it, I see that this match will expire in twenty-four hours. I click without hesitation, excited at what's behind door number one. The thought of dating a millionaire seems more and more appealing as I stare at the stack of bills on my counter.

I rub my hands together, heat building from the friction. I've only ever been on a dating app once before, and it wasn't for me. But this is playing at another level. Plus, it's not a dating site where I will be overwhelmed with an inbox full of random messages, half of them only looking for a hookup. This is classy. This is a matchmaker that will find me a successful man with a good head on his shoulders.

Hopefully.

The entire purpose of this site is to help successful people meet someone who might be their soulmate. To help busy professionals who want a serious relationship. It connects people to someone they wouldn't necessarily have the opportunity to meet. It goes beyond your friends' circle, or someone's divorced cousin, or people you might meet during happy hour.

A picture pops up, along with several others beneath it, followed by likes, dislikes, dreams, goals, and expectations.

I read through and click on each picture, staring into the eyes of this eligible bachelor who just happens to be a millionaire.

I close my laptop and let my head fall into my hands, my elbows resting on my knees.

What am I doing? Am I actually going to go through with this? I'm not a gold digger.

But…

The back of the couch cushions me as I press my back further into the pillows, opening the screen once more.

I stare into his eyes.

Jaxon Baker.

Tall, dark hair, rich chocolate brown eyes that are giving a seductive demeanor even through my screen.

Alysha would call these "fuck-me eyes."

The seconds tick by, maybe minutes. I'm analyzing the angle of his jaw and imagining myself running my fingers through his thick dark hair when a sound erupts and an envelope pops up over his picture.

One new message.

Letting my head fall back, I look at the ceiling, as if waiting for a sign, and it pings again.

Two new messages.

Wow, ask and the universe shall deliver. I take this as my sign and click on the envelope.

Jaxon Baker

> Hello Quinn, Jaxon here.

The second message pops up once I've read the first.

## CHAPTER THREE

**Jaxon Baker**
> Are you there?

**Quinn Cameron**
> Hello Jaxon.

I try to match his reserved tone, like I've got my shit together.

**Quinn Cameron**
> I'm here.

**Jaxon Baker**
> Good. I've reviewed your profile and according to the agency, we're a match. Let me get right to the point…

I log off, my eyes blurred, and my head swimming. We've discussed all topics we would normally not discuss at the beginning of dating. But this isn't just regular dating. This is a millionaire looking for a wife.

A *wife*.

Jaxon made it clear that he doesn't want a hookup or a girlfriend—he wants a ring-wearing, vow-taking wife.

He didn't hesitate to put it all out there for me to see. I have to give it to him—he's unapologetically himself, no beating around the bush.

I'm not sure what I was expecting, but marriage wasn't something that crossed my mind when I signed up for the site. I hardly had the time or strength to even date before quitting my job a few nights ago.

What if I can't live up to his standards? A small-town girl is all I've ever been.

We agreed to chat again tomorrow morning at nine a.m. He wants to leave me with twenty-four hours to process his terms and what he laid out as a mutually beneficial agreement. I rub my temples while I think and process this. No more hospital bills; he'll take care of that. And a life of luxury—or so it sounds. Corporate retreats, dinners with clients, and the like.

In return, I'd be his arm candy. His housewife.

But I'd have to move across the country and leave everything I've ever known behind, something I was thinking about only moments ago. Something I've wished for late at night.

I peer around the familiar room and note the faded floral wallpaper, the closet door that doesn't shut all the way unless you slam it, and the outdated brown carpet that lines every room except for the kitchen and bathroom.

I've been caretaker, waitress, and bill payer, and nothing more. My life has been hollow and full of heartache, and I'm realizing that it's possible I let a part of me die with my mom and my grandmother. Escaping these four walls wouldn't be the worst thing.

And a husband who looks like that—could I really ask for more?

Perhaps it's time I let someone take care of me for once.

# Chapter Four

## *Jaxon*

I'm sitting at the kitchen island in front of my laptop, my leg bouncing in anticipation. Something that annoyed my parents growing up.

It's Saturday at 6:54 a.m. my time, 8:54 a.m. her time, and I'm waiting to log on to the matchmaking site and talk with Quinn.

My parents have been traveling since I left for university. We video chat once a week, and they visit a few times a year, but in between those times, I'm on my own.

And I'm just fine with that.

My childhood was pretty great. I had a lot of friends—that is until I was mauled by a dog that left me with a scar that covered a good portion of my face. Overnight, my friends were too cool to be seen with me.

This was only the beginning of years of bullying.

I run my hand down my face at the memory, stroking the short coarse hair on my jawline, my index finger landing on the deep scar on the left side of my face, mostly hidden beneath the thick layer of dark hair edged with one or two whites. I've learned my lesson in trying to pluck those out—hurts like a bitch, and I couldn't even grasp the white ones in the sea of brown.

I already swam my laps, showered, and now I'm watching the clock on the bottom right side of my screen.

Anxiously, I watch as another minute passes by: 6:58 a.m. my time, 8:58 a.m. her time.

*What in the actual fuck am I doing?*

Am I really offering to marry a woman I know so little about? One who lives a 30-hour drive away, or a four-and-a-half-hour flight. I know this because I searched the internet high and low yesterday to find everything I could about her. Lester did a rush background check on Quinn Cameron, and nothing came up. This is a gamble, but I'm desperate.

Lester suggested the millionaire matchmaking site to step it up a notch from regular dating apps. So, here I am. I'm highly aware of the gravity of such a legal partnership, and I need to follow through with my gut. The same way I handle my business. Logic of course plays a role, but my gut never lies.

Lester asked if I knew anyone who could set me up, but I've been a loner most of my life. I could get a hobby, meet someone with similar interests, or kick off my evenings by going out for happy hour, but I don't have time to waste sitting in a fancy club waiting to find the future Mrs. Baker. I just need to find a decent woman who I will get along with and who is willing to sacrifice her current lifestyle for a better one.

At thirty-six, I know what I want. I want to succeed, so I'm hoping that a woman in her mid-thirties will think the same, one who I can maybe offer something currently out of

## CHAPTER FOUR

their reach. I've worked hard to get where I am and to have all the things that surround me.

It turns out Quinn lives clear across the country, and at first this put me off, but if she's willing to move, I don't see why it matters. This woman has made it clear she's stuck with hospital and medical bills from the passings of both her mom and grandmother.

She's recently unemployed, which at this moment is ideal, since I need to find a wife who isn't attached to her location, home, or job. She told me she hadn't thought of the idea of marriage, which is why I'm bouncing my knee like a teenager waiting for school to finish on the last day before summer vacation. I've got a good feeling about her and how we can make this work. This is a quick decision, but time is of the essence. If I'm going to convince Edward that I'm in love with my wife, we're going to need some time to manage the bumps that will no doubt present themselves.

The time changes on my screen. I log on to the site and can see her active status by the little green dot at the base of her picture. I message her immediately. When she doesn't reply right away, I click on her main photo.

Quinn Cameron has wavy, dark blonde hair and eyes the color of the ocean. I find myself lost in them when my laptop pings.

Quinn Cameron

> Good morning!

Jaxon Baker

> Morning, Quinn. I hope you slept well after considering my offer.

I sound like a businessman about to sign a contract—but I *am* a businessman, and this *is* a contract. The entire purpose of marrying Quinn is so that I can get that damn promotion.

> **Quinn Cameron**
>
> I've honestly thought of nothing else since. But I'm curious about you.
>
> **Jaxon Baker**
>
> Okay. Do you have any specific questions for me? I gave you a lot of information yesterday, and I'm sure it was unexpected. I assume you were on the site looking to find love or a future with a partner?

This could be a deal-breaker.

> **Quinn Cameron**
>
> I'm not exactly sure what I was looking for. I signed up for the site in the heat of the moment after quitting my job the other night. But I'm sure I can come up with some questions for you.
>
> **Jaxon Baker**
>
> Hit me.

# CHAPTER FOUR

**Quinn Cameron**
> How many women have you proposed this offer to?

**Jaxon Baker**
> Just you.

**Quinn Cameron**
> I'm your first match?

**Jaxon Baker**
> No, I've been at this about a month now. I've spoken to multiple women, but none felt right.

**Quinn Cameron**
> So, you're saying I felt right? ;)

I'm at a loss for words, but luckily another message pops up before I can figure out how the hell I'm going to come up with an answer to that probing question.

**Quinn Cameron**
> So, we would be man and wife, legally. Does that mean we share a bed, do couple things together, or is this only for show?

> **Jaxon Baker**
> You will have your own room. This marriage is for work purposes, so yes, couple things, as you say, would be required for work events.

> **Quinn Cameron**
> What would my day look like? Would I get a job? I've been working my whole life.

> **Jaxon Baker**
> Your job would be to be my wife.

> **Quinn Cameron**
> Hmm. I'm not sure what I would do with my day while you're at work. Wouldn't I get bored?

> **Jaxon Baker**
> Well, I would expect you to be a housewife, and do, you know, housewife things.

I don't even know what I'm saying. What are housewife things? God, I'm going to fuck this up.

> **Quinn Cameron**
> Housewife things, ok.

## CHAPTER FOUR

Uh-oh. This isn't going well. I can sense her hesitation by the dots that appear and disappear in the chat box.

> **Jaxon Baker**
> Anything else you're curious about?

> **Quinn Cameron**
> Do you have any pets?

> **Jaxon Baker**
> Pets, no.

I never even thought of asking Quinn if she has any pets. My palms start to sweat at the thought, pulse quickening and breath shallowing as I wait for the dots on the screen to turn into another message.

> **Quinn Cameron**
> Me neither.

Thank. Fucking. God.

> **Quinn Cameron**
> What type of music do you listen to?

I'm thrown off by her line of questioning. I was expecting much more serious questions. What does music have to do with getting married?

> **Jaxon Baker**
> Country, top 40. I listen to pretty much anything.

**Quinn Cameron**

Same. I love music. I have it playing while I get ready in the morning from the time I take my shower until I'm dressed. Where do you stand on shower radios?

**Jaxon Baker**

Every shower in my house has one.

**Quinn Cameron**

How many showers do you have?

**Jaxon Baker**

I have six bathrooms altogether. Three full, two powder rooms, and one in the pool house.

**Quinn Cameron**

A pool house, oh my. I've always wanted a pool.

**Jaxon Baker**

It's an infinity pool, and there's a hot tub. You would have access to everything on the property.

**Quinn Cameron**

Would I have my own bathroom?

## CHAPTER FOUR

*Jaxon Baker*
> Of course.

She sounds tempted. Tempted by the luxury that I can provide her. Not everyone needs love. Money buys things love can't always provide.

Can she go through the next few years without love?

Can I?

I've gone without it up to this point, and you can't miss something you've never had. But what if she decides that she wants love or falls for me during this fake ordeal? What if I fall for her? This sure will change life for us both. I'm used to a quiet, peaceful house.

But how much noise and chaos can one woman bring?

It'll be fine.

I wasn't expecting to have hesitations myself now that I've found someone and offered marriage, but this is a huge commitment. I'm asking this woman to spend the next few years with me just so I can get a promotion.

This is next-level, bat-shit crazy.

I run my hand over my face when a ping sounds.

*Quinn Cameron*
> Ok, I'm in! You had me at infinity pool. :)

*Jaxon Baker*
> You're in?

> **Quinn Cameron**
> Yes! I'm in!

I'm flabbergasted, astonished, and bewildered at this outcome. I guess on some level I didn't think that this would work.

I'm getting fucking married. For a promotion.

Fuck me.

> **Quinn Cameron**
> On one condition.

> **Jaxon Baker**
> What is it?

> **Quinn Cameron**
> We need to set up a video chat. I'm not moving across the country to marry someone who's catfishing me.

> **Jaxon Baker**
> Not a problem. When's a good time for you?

I casually peek through her photos while I wait for her to reply. She's hot as fuck with her girl-next-door appearance. That won't hurt the living situation or make it difficult to be the doting, loving husband at the annual retreat and client dinners.

But how the hell do I portray a doting, loving husband when I haven't had a girlfriend in years?

# CHAPTER FOUR

I'll figure it out. I always do. This will just be another project that I need to excel at, and I always excel when I put my mind to something.

I clasp my hands behind my back and stretch.

A sound pings.

> Quinn Cameron
> **How about now?**

I sit up, my back erect, and glance around the empty room. I guess there's no better time than the present. Might as well get this thing going.

I crack my knuckles, easing the tension that's trying to settle in.

> Jaxon Baker
> **Sure, why not?**

Before I can think twice about it, my laptop is ringing, and I see that Quinn is calling me through the site's video chat feature.

I click on the green icon that says accept, and Quinn's face appears in front of me. Words get caught in my throat. I take in the beautiful face peering back at me, the ear-to-ear smile, the blue eyes piercing through me. I swallow the lump that's threatening to choke me.

"Hey!" she says, her voice echoing out my speaker.

I push the laptop a little further back on the counter so the camera can capture more of me.

"Hello, Quinn."

"Well, you look like your pictures, that's a relief." She sighs softly. "So, what happens now?"

Her shoulders are raised close to her ears in excitement, but I'm struggling to break eye contact, mesmerized. She's fucking gorgeous.

I clear my throat trying to get my act together.

"I'll have a lawyer draw up an agreement, a contract," I tell her. "You'll need to have one look it over before you sign it."

"Oh."

"Is that a problem?"

Her smile twists into something I can't describe. "I can't really afford a lawyer," she reveals, and I now understand the change in her demeanor.

"They can bill me directly. I'll take care of it."

"What's this contract going to say exactly?"

I watch her expressions change with each passing thought, intrigued. A complex woman with thoughts and opinions, something I'm not used to in my quick meetups with a lover here and there.

"We need to confirm a timeline, expectations, and of course the financial aspects of it."

"How long will we be married exactly? I mean, I don't want to upend my entire life for just a few months. What are you thinking?"

"There's a corporate retreat in a few months. I should find out about the promotion around that time. But I'll need to maintain this relationship—um, marriage—for some time after, for appearances."

"Of course."

"Does eighteen months work for you?" I ask.

Lester and I came up with a few points on how this will all work, so thankfully I'm somewhat prepared for this spur-of-the-moment negotiation.

She nods. "Yeah, that could work. What happens after the marriage is over?"

## CHAPTER FOUR

"Well, like I mentioned yesterday, I will pay off all your outstanding debt after the ceremony, and of course, I will be providing you with a good amount of cash for you to do what you wish with after this marriage dissolves."

She's nodding, and I can see her processing the situation.

"What if you don't get the promotion? What happens then?"

Fuck. I run my palm down my face. I hadn't thought even for one minute that I wouldn't get this promotion if I could secure a wife. That's all that's missing from Edward's wish list for CEO. Wife equals promotion—it's as simple as that.

"That's a non-issue."

Her eyebrows knit together. "How are you so sure it's yours?"

"It's mine."

"Okay, but what if it's not?" She crosses her arms and leans back in her chair.

"I can assure you the promotion is in the bag with a wife on my arm." She shakes her head, and I think I might be losing her. "Okay, let me think."

I'm trying to come up with a solution, but her squirming around in her seat has me distracted. She's wearing a light purple sweater that has the blue in her eyes appearing lighter than in her photos. The sweater dips just low enough to leave me wondering what the rest of her looks like. She runs her hands through her hair, and I watch as the curls bounce around as they settle back around her slender shoulders.

I squint and rub my temples. "Okay, so if I don't get the promotion, the amount drops, but you're still obligated to endure the terms of the contract and fulfill the entire length of the marriage. I don't want this getting out, that I lied to get ahead."

"Wait, why would I get less because you couldn't land a job?"

Goddamn, she's sassy, and I fucking love it.

"Do you have any idea what it's like as a woman to leave the workforce and come back with a hole in her resume at thirty-four years old? No, thirty-six by the time our marriage ends. It might not be that easy to get a job after a gap year. I can't exactly put *wife to millionaire* as work experience." Frown lines appear at the sides of her light pink mouth.

I might have just met my match.

"You'll have more than enough to get by."

"I'm moving across the country. I don't want to just *get by* after you get everything you want out of this."

"Let me remind you that I'm paying off your debts. You'll start with a clean slate when you leave this place. Plus, you'll have no bills for eighteen months, living rent-free." Her frown lines deepen. I want Quinn to be my wife—for business purposes. She's clearly smart with a good head on her shoulders, just who I need on my arm at the retreat. I need to lock this in before she changes her mind. "Fine, you'll walk away with the same amount, promotion or not."

The lines around her mouth start to curve upward.

"What about sex?"

Fuck, she's straight to the point, something I've always admired in the people I work with. No sense beating around the bush and wasting valuable time.

We both agree we'll be celibate during the course of our marriage, and then we spend the next three hours diving into everyday questions. She's easy to converse with. Quinn has this spark to her, an excitement that reveals itself through all her expressions and energy. And in the end, we settle on an amount we both agree to.

## CHAPTER FOUR

We exchange contact information, and I tell her I will send her a one-way plane ticket. We settle on three weeks to give her enough time to sort out her things and decide what she's going to take with her. If anything needs to be shipped out, she can pack it up, and I'll take care of the cost.

By the time I close my laptop, I let out a sigh of relief. This is all going to work out.

I will get that promotion, and Brodie can go fuck himself.

# Chapter Five

## *Quinn*

"I'm getting married!" I almost yelp at Alysha. The missing light inside me is now glowing, brightening every inch of me. It could just be the adrenaline—I'm about to do something crazy—but it feels electric.

I think this might actually be fun. It's going to be a huge adjustment, but one I can handle. I spent the rest of yesterday researching everything I need to know. That and the fact that I've been watching *Social Circles and Secrets* for years, I know what is expected of a housewife to a millionaire. I also know that Jaxon is in a time crunch, and that I couldn't let him hold all the power. I know my value and what I'll bring to the table, and if his boss wants him to have a wife, he needs me.

Despite all of that, when the dollar amount slipped out of Jaxon's kissable—not that I was noticing—lips, I was shocked. Never in my lifetime did I dream that kind of money would fall at my feet. At least not to this extent. I can't *not* take that offer. This will literally change everything for me.

I'll have eighteen months to figure out what I want to do with my life, and what better way than to spend it lounging poolside and drinking cocktails? Besides all of that, I know that I can help Jaxon. I've worked shitty jobs my entire life with a smile on my face. I can be charming, happy, doting, and with Jaxon by my side, it won't be too difficult at all. I will not be the reason Jaxon doesn't get that promotion.

Bonus? That man sure is something to look at, and that was miles away and through a camera on my laptop that is nearing the end of its life.

I'm dancing around the room, trying not to trip on boxes.

"Have I been in some strange time warp? When the hell did you get a boyfriend?"

I roll my eyes, laughing. Alysha closes the door behind her.

"Girl, seriously, what are you talking about, and why are you packing up your stuff?" Her hands come to her hips.

I plop down on the sofa and grab the muffin I was eating earlier. "Want one?"

"No, thanks. Now quit stalling." Her long blonde hair sways as she sits on the hand-me-down chair beside me, her eyes boring into me. She takes the worn red pillow and places it on her lap, resting her arms in front of her.

"So, um, I signed up on this app..." I start, then stop to take a bite of the muffin. "Oh my God, this is so good."

"Quinn!"

I quickly swallow my bite. "Yeah, so, the other night when I was browsing jobs, this ad popped up for a millionaire matchmaking site, and you know, fresh out of a job and bills piling up, I'm not sure what I was thinking, but I matched up with this man, Jaxon. He's flying me out to marry him."

"Quinn, this is *insane*. You know that, right?" Her eyebrows reach new heights across her forehead, causing her skin to wrinkle.

I shrug my shoulders. "I mean, I get what it sounds like, but I'm dying here, Alysha." She's watching me carefully, waiting to hear the rest of it. "This is a new opportunity for me. To start fresh. All of my bills will be paid, and I'll be in a new city full of opportunities."

"Honestly, that sounds great, Quinn, a dream, really. Things are tough here for you, but you don't need to run away to marry a stranger. And why marry anyway? Can't you just date, do the whole long-distance thing?"

I tell her all about Jaxon and his need for a wife. She listens patiently, but I can tell she's skeptical. And I get it. This is crazy. But excitement has been running through me since I agreed to Jaxon's offer. It's like all the years of financial burden weighing me down have been lifted. There's a light at the end of the tunnel, finally.

"I'll be fine," I insist. "It's only for eighteen months."

I tell her all about the police check and information the site gathers from their matches.

"Be happy for me?" I plead, begging her like all I'm asking for is a cookie before dinner and not her blessing to fly across the country and marry a stranger.

"I don't know, Quinn." She shakes her head and stands, walking towards the kitchen, undoubtedly heading for a muffin.

When she's back on the chair beside me, I try again. "Let me show you his profile." I drag my laptop across the table and open it up to Jaxon's main photo.

"Damn, girl."

"I know, right?"

"Okay, I'll hear you out. Tell me everything."

# CHAPTER FIVE

Quinn Cameron

> I can't believe we're doing this!!!!!

Jaxon Baker

> And yet we are.

I've been sending Jaxon messages on and off for days, and I'm getting the impression that he isn't much of a texter.

His responses are short and to the point, but I'm sure he'll lighten up when I get there.

I send him a dress emoji before typing.

Quinn Cameron

> What am I going to do for a wedding dress?

Jaxon Baker

> I'll take care of that.

Quin Cameron

> Do I get to pick it out myself?

Jaxon Baker

> Send me your measurements.

I've never in my life sent my measurements to a man before, and I find it's a bit odd to have the groom pick out the dress. Before I can tell him about my concern, he responds, and the worry that began showing up dwindles back down.

> **Jaxon Baker**
> I will get a few options for you to choose from with the help of my assistant.

> **Quinn Cameron**
> Okay :) What if it needs to be altered?

> **Jaxon Baker**
> I will make sure they all fit to your size.

I send my weight, height, and measurements to Jaxon. I never really thought about what I would want to wear on my wedding day, because I never actually dreamed that I would get married. I trust Jaxon will pick out something nice. I'm not picky, plus Jaxon's probably got connections. He sounds like he's always in suits for work, and he's probably aware of what's stylish or at least has people who know.

> **Quinn Cameron**
> Yay!

## CHAPTER FIVE

The next few weeks pass in a blur. I still haven't broken through Jaxon's serious side, and he has yet to use a single emoji in his texts, but I don't let that stop me from sending them. I've gotten to know a little more about where he lives and his lifestyle. It seems all the man does is work. He likes to swim laps and work out. He's a fan of thriller movies and reading, and his favorite meal is lasagna with garlic bread. He told me all about the book he's currently reading by Alyssa Milani called *Who Did It* and said that I could borrow it when he's finished.

I looked up the book after we finished our conversation, and there's a few from that same author that intrigue me. Maybe I could join a book club or something once I'm settled in my new home.

The boxes are piled high in my living room, leaving little space to move around. Alysha has been helping me go through stuff, and I gave her a ton that I didn't want to take with me. I'm also giving her Carl, which she gladly accepts. My beater wouldn't make it across the country, and Jaxon says I won't have to worry about one when I get there, so he probably has an extra car or something.

I hear my phone ping, and I jump to it, smiling when I see his name.

I guess my room is ready for me. Jaxon claims that I don't need to bring anything but my clothes and any memorabilia I want to keep. He tells me that I will be able to go shopping when I get there and spruce up my wardrobe for when we dine with clients so I can look the part as his wife. I'm completely okay with a shopping spree. I don't think I've officially had one of those since ninth grade when Mom won a hundred dollars on a lottery ticket and took me to Target.

The text is just Jaxon reminding me of my flight. I smile and send him an airplane and bride emoji.

Three weeks have flown by, and I can't believe today is the day. My flight leaves in a few hours.

Jaxon is paying my last month's rent, since I didn't have two months' notice to give the landlord. Goodwill is coming by to pick up these boxes, and Alysha's agreed to let them in when they come. She'll also hand in my key to the landlord at the end of next month.

I hear the door open as I'm bending over a box.

"You just about ready?" Alysha calls.

We've talked a lot over the last few weeks, and she doesn't completely understand why I'm doing this, but the relief and the excitement of starting over is enough to keep me moving forward with the offer. It just feels right—like I was meant to quit my job, open my laptop, and meet Jaxon Baker. I can only hope that this ends like a rom-com and not some true-crime murder podcast.

"Yeah, just about."

"I can't believe you're really leaving." She hugs me when I turn towards her.

"I know. I'm going to miss you."

"Babe, I'm going to miss you too, so much," she replies, a little teary.

A lump forms in my throat, but I swallow it quickly. "We will chat all the time, and you can totally come visit me once I'm all settled in. I'm sure Jaxon won't mind, and even if he does, you're still going to come."

"I will take you up on that. I need to meet this man who is flying my girl across the country, but until then, you have to promise to keep in touch. Actually, hand me your phone. I want to track your location."

She sends herself a link to my location once I slide the phone into her hands.

## CHAPTER FIVE

I take one last walk through my apartment, grab my purse, and flick off the light before closing the door behind us.

When we arrive at the airport, I hand the keys over to Alysha. "He's all yours."

"Carl, it's just you and me now, babe," she says, patting the faded red roof of the small car.

We say our goodbyes, and I turn one last time to wave to Alysha before walking towards this new future I've chosen.

"Let me show you to your seat." The flight attendant's red lips part as she smiles at me.

I walk the aisle and notice the large leather seats.

So, this is first class.

She shows me to my seat by the window, and I let myself fall in and accept a glass of wine from another flight attendant who passes by a few minutes later.

I watch the buildings below get smaller and smaller.

In less than five hours I will be landing in a new city and meeting my fiancé.

My eyes close shortly after sunset, and before I know it, I jolt awake as we're descending. Brushing some of my hair out of my face, I peer out the window as the plane comes into contact with the pavement. When it's time, I stand and thank the flight attendant before stepping through the passenger boarding bridge.

This is it.

Time to meet my millionaire.

My toes dig into the soft rug as I step out of the large claw-foot tub, suds still slithering down my body.

It's my wedding day.

For someone who never dreamed of getting married, I sure jumped on that bandwagon pretty quickly. I'm floating around like a lovesick teenager today.

When I got off the plane yesterday, there was a car and a driver waiting to take me to The Cartier Hotel.

I was a little disappointed that Jaxon wasn't there to meet me, but I guess it is bad luck to see the bride before the wedding. Jaxon went all out, though. A large clothing rack lined with wedding gowns sat in my room, along with matching shoes for the big day.

I wrap myself in a large, soft bathrobe and twirl my hair into a matching towel, walking towards the gown I chose.

A gorgeous floor-length dress with beading throughout the corset hangs at the end of the rack. I've paired it with a beautiful pair of sleek, white, four-inch pumps.

The hotel concierge informed me that a hairstylist and makeup artist would be arriving this morning for me. I'm not used to being pampered or wearing more than winged eyeliner and mascara, so this will be a treat.

I'm still pinching myself, checking that I haven't been transported into some magical world where I'm a princess, about to meet my prince.

# CHAPTER FIVE

The morning passes quickly as I get glammed up, and I have to remind myself a few times that this is a fake marriage and that I should just enjoy the ride.

When the time comes, the driver, Henri, picks me up and takes me to city hall. I walk up the steps to the large double front doors and head inside.

Within moments, I'm walking down the aisle, and my eyes finally fall on Jaxon at the altar.

# Chapter Six

*Jaxon*

I pull away, my lips still warm from our first kiss as husband and wife. Quinn is a beautiful woman, but I can't let the physical attraction get the better of me.

But up close and personal, Quinn is even hotter than I expected.

She's scanning me with a small, shy smile on her face. This is a business deal, I remind myself. I will not fall for her quirky personality, her charming smile, or how I think it's sweet that she sends me way more emojis than anyone should ever send in their lifetime. The fuck would I do with an emoji, but with her, I picture her face bright as she scrolls trying to decide which ones to send, and it makes me smile—on the inside.

I chose the dresses myself—well, with help from Lester. I don't know a goddamn thing about dresses. He said she needed options, and I think we did a good job, because she looks phenomenal. He's the only one who is plugged in about this fake marriage.

Oh shit, this is a real marriage now.

Quinn is my wife.

I have a wife.

I push down the slight ignition in my stomach from that kiss.

I managed to keep a straight face throughout the ceremony despite her winks and cute smile. This is business, and I need her to understand that. And I need to remain neutral, but I don't doubt that I will in fact manage.

For now, though, my focus is on getting this promotion and making this marriage work until the role is mine.

We clasp hands and walk down the aisle, and she's chattering away, so much so that I can barely catch a single word she says.

"Oh my gosh, I can't believe we just did that!" Her eyes are wide, the blue of them bright as we step outside of city hall. She turns to me, and I nod, saying nothing. She is so petite next to me. I could pick her up and throw her over my shoulder, and she'd have no say in the circumstance, no matter how much she wiggled and thrashed around in protest.

She's waiting for a response from me, and I have nothing. I'm not the most sociable person. I'm awkward at best, even though I know people perceive me as a shark in business. I just don't do women. Well, that's an incorrect statement—I just don't know how to *be around* women, with all their fluttering and gossip and emotions.

I need to say something. This is my wife, and I need to be doting and attentive.

"It's nice to finally meet you, Quinn. Thank you for making the trip down here. The room was all right last night?" I haven't yet answered her questions or acknowledged what she just said, but I'm hoping this will distract her from the fact that I wasn't paying full attention.

"All right?" She claps her hands together. "It was amazing, thank you." Her smile is wide, and she's playing with the bracelets around her wrist.

She's as bright as the sun, and it has me squinting.

"So, what now?" she asks, and I watch Henri drive up in the black sedan.

I open the car door. "Let's take you home."

"My stuff is at the hotel," she says, glancing through the tinted window and then back to me.

"Henri went and picked it up. You don't need to worry about it."

"Oh, okay."

She lifts the bottom of her dress to fit into the back of the car, and I can't help but notice the little sliver of gold wrapped around her ankle, and her toes painted in a light pink shade. I close the door when she's in and buckled, and I walk around the car and get in on the opposite side.

Quinn turns towards me, her eyes sparkling. "So, you have a driver?"

"*We* have a driver. Henri will drive you anywhere you need to go," I reply.

"Will I get to drive? I'm used to driving."

She sounds disappointed, and my heart does something knowing that. I push the feelings away and look at her.

"Traffic is crazy in the city. You might not want to get stuck driving in this."

"I can handle traffic." There's an edge to her voice as she folds her arms, challenging me. Quinn is obviously an assertive, confident woman, a mix of sunshine and a tropical storm.

"Okay, let's see how things go. If you still want to drive after trying it out with a driver, we'll look at getting you a car."

"Okay."

"Give it a week, and we'll reconvene."

"Reconvene?" Her eyebrows lift.

"We'll discuss it." She seems to accept that answer. At this point, there's no use telling her about the sports car I have in the garage. It's a stick anyhow—not that I want to keep her locked in or anything, but like I said, we'll reconvene, and if she needs one, I'll get her her own car for while she's here. Something a little safer than the yellow beast that's sitting lonely in the garage.

When we pull into our neighborhood, she turns her body towards the window, hands resting on the ledge, the window down. I watch her hair blow chaotically around her as she takes it all in.

"These homes are beautiful."

We live in a gated community. The lawns are always well manicured by the gardeners and groundskeepers, the pools always crystal blue, the flowers always blooming and bright. I like my privacy, and the fact that none of the neighbors can see into my backyard where I like to barbecue or swim laps was a huge selling feature when I purchased this after my first bonus at the firm.

Henri pulls into the driveway, and a high-pitched shriek fills my ears, causing me to wince.

"Jaxon, this is it? This is my house now?" She turns to me with eyes wide, like she didn't fully believe I was a millionaire. I smile at her innocence, but I don't let my guard down. I'm not a complete moron. Not everyone gets to live like I do, but I won't be distracted by this fresh face full of wonder that's stirring up something below my belt.

"Yes." The car stops, and she's out the door before Henri can turn off the engine. I nod at him to bring in the bags, and I step around the car myself. "How about you get changed, and then I'll give you a tour."

She hikes up her dress, revealing that glittery anklet and heels that could kill a man if used as a weapon, or stop a man's heart, if he was willing and naïve. She walks towards the house. "No need, I can walk in my dress."

"Your heels are going to sink into the grass."

She glances down. "You're right, I hadn't thought about that. Okay, I'll get changed."

We walk in after Henri, and she lets out another loud gasp.

This is going to take some getting used to.

"Come, this way," I tell her, and motion towards the staircase.

She seems to float across the marble floor as if she's always belonged here. I'm waiting for her at the top as she makes her way up, holding onto the banister to steady herself on her high heels. Halfway up, she pauses, lifts her dress, and takes off the shoes, dangling them from her pinkie.

"Much better," she says, laughing, standing next to me on the landing, her petite frame shrinking another four inches. "Which way?"

I turn towards the hallway to the right, and when I pause in front of one of the rooms, she walks past me and in, straight to the floor-to-ceiling windows.

"Wow."

I notice the curve in her backside as she leans on one hip. Her head turns towards me, a sparkle in her eye.

"Will this suffice?" I ask.

"Suffice? Oh my gosh, yes. Obviously."

"There's the en suite that way, and your closet is behind here." I motion towards the floating wall behind the large bed.

Her hand caresses the duvet as she walks towards the space that's half hidden, and she gasps. "Jaxon, are you freaking kidding me?" Her suitcases lie in the middle of the space. "Where's all your stuff?"

"My stuff?"

"Yeah, isn't this our room?"

"This is your room."

Her eyebrows crease together. "Oh, yeah. I forgot about that. But you're my husband—shouldn't we share a room if we're going to be playing husband and wife?"

"I wasn't sure if you would be comfortable jumping right into my bed." Before I can change my wording, I see her blush, and for fuck's sakes, there's that pull again below the waist.

She fidgets, pulling at her dress. "I mean, I don't know. I guess I'll be fine in here."

The last thing I wanted for tonight was for her to feel like I paid her way for a good fuck. This is business, a marriage of convenience, and she'd best remember that.

"We can discuss how things go. Let's take it slow."

"Ha! Take it slow? Do I need to remind you that I'm now Mrs. Baker? How in the world can we take it slow?"

"This is new to both of us. Let's just talk things out as we go." I nod at her bags. "Get changed, and I'll meet you out back."

# Chapter Seven

## *Quinn*

I've died and gone to heaven.

I pull out my phone from my bag and take pictures to send to Alysha, so she knows that I'm okay and that I have not disappeared off this earth. And also, because this room… I have no words.

There are decorative pillows lined up in a row over the thick sky-blue duvet. A soft throw in a cream color spills thoughtfully over the end of the bed, and two bedside tables on either side hold reading lamps that will be perfect to read late at night when I'm not busy seducing my husband. I know we said we'd be celibate, and we wouldn't date or have sexual relations outside of our marriage, but we're only human and I know Jaxon must be expecting something. I did take on this giant one-eighty to have a little adventure of my own. It's not like he's buying me for sex. It's business—he needs a wife to advance his career, and I get to benefit from that by living here for free with a beautiful infinity pool, a closet that would make any shopper swoon, and a man who appears to hit the gym seven days a week.

This marriage definitely comes with benefits.

Anyway, Jaxon didn't buy me for sex, because I am not for sale, technically.

It can just be a bonus for the two of us. A sort of forced proximity minus the sharing of a bed.

I never really thought about marriage, but now that I am married, I feel kind of light and free. Which is odd—don't you usually have less freedom when you're married? Or maybe it's the fact that Mom and Granny's debt will soon be taken care of and the weight of that will no longer be holding me down like two large sacks of potatoes.

Mom went first, and my heart was shattered. She had cervical cancer with no symptoms early on, so by the time she found out she had it, it was too late. Mom had been in menopause when she started bleeding for no reason, or that's what she thought at the time. Confused by the changes her body had been going through, it was difficult for her to tell anything was wrong at the age of fifty-one. She was told it was menopause and that her symptoms were normal, but when the pain intensified, and the constant fatigue and general discomfort of being unwell overtook her, she demanded answers.

But it wasn't caught in time.

I had so much anger after seeing what Mom went through. Losing her was the hardest thing I have ever gone through.

Granny, on the other hand, took her last breath in her sleep. She was a fighter. She held on through the passing of her husband, the love of her life just six years before, and the passing of her only daughter, two years later. I saw life's hardship and grief overcome her, hollowness settling in below her once-bright and shiny blue eyes that matched mine. Aches and pains took over where vibrancy and spunk had been before. And when it was her time to go, she died peacefully in her sleep. And just like that, the family I knew was gone, and I was alone.

I silently tell Mom and Granny I love them as I always do when I think of them.

The lights are bright when I turn them on in the walk-in, and it takes a moment for my eyes to scan over the space as I change out of my wedding gown and hang it up in the closet. When I've finished looking at every square inch of the bedroom, I walk back to the large windows and catch a glimpse of Jaxon outside.

He's in the same pants he wore for our ceremony, but he's lost the jacket, and the sleeves of his shirt are rolled up, showing off his tanned forearms that are surprisingly covered in ink. I turn to go meet him for my grand tour.

The coolness of the banister under my hand calms me slightly. When I reach the bottom of the stairs, I turn to the left where I find the patio doors that have been pushed open, creating an indoor-outdoor living space. I step out into the warm air and bright sun, and it's like I'm walking out of Barbie's dream house. The grass is a bright green, the pool water looks inviting, and Jaxon is standing there, his eyes dark, watching me.

"Quinn." Jaxon nods, a serious expression on his handsome face.

I notice the rose and thorns tattoos that trail down his forearms to his wrists. My mind is spiraling about what else might be hidden under the reserved exterior of Jaxon.

Snapping out of it, I scan the back yard, and I'm hit with more awe. I can only assume that for the next few days, this is going to be my new normal. I am going to see things I've only ever wished to have or have seen in the movies, and I am going to have to pinch myself to see if it's real. If this *temporary* new life is real.

I have to keep reminding myself of that.

"This place is incredible," I say again, but holy cheese balls, I can't help myself.

"You've mentioned that."

Okay, now I feel stupid. I should act cool. I've watched dozens of hours of *Social Circles and Secrets* to know how I should behave, and I've researched core differences between our two classes, to know what's expected from a wife of a millionaire. It must be the fact that things are changing so fast and I have all this energy running through me, like a child getting a puppy on her birthday. I need to play the part, like I spend every other weekend at the golf course and I eat lobster, truffles, and caviar every Sunday. I need to make this work.

"Yes, of course," I reply, taking my excitement down a notch.

"Is something wrong?" His eyes scan over me with concern.

"Is something wrong with you?" I poke my finger at him and accidentally jab at his firm, hard chest, harder than I meant to. "Oops, sorry about that."

I glance up at the sky. Kill me now.

He grabs my hand, and I'm pulled back to his gaze.

"Come on, let me show you around."

Okay, so sweeping stuff under the rug is his thing. I can pretend I didn't just sprain my finger against his chest.

He guides me onto the soft grass that from afar appears fake. I want to kick off my sneakers and let each sliver of grass slide between my toes and cushion my step. I'll save that for another day, one where Jaxon will be at work, because I don't think rolling around on the grass is on the list of acceptable millionaire wife behavior.

"The pool," he says, guiding me towards the shimmery blue water. Tanning chairs line one side, while lemon trees surround the rest. "There are pool inflatables, sunscreen, towels, and anything else you would need in the pool house over there." He's pointing at a cute little house with floor-to-ceiling windows that match the home behind us. "There's also a bathroom in there with a shower."

I nod, still attempting to play it cool at the top of my list. I don't want Jaxon sending me off before we've had a chance to make a go at this.

I think I'm sort of confused about who the real me is. The downtrodden bartender with loads of debt, the shiny, golden girl from my youth before I realized how hard life is, or this adventure-seeking chatterbox that seems to come out around him. Maybe I'm a bit of all three. Only time will tell.

"There's a tennis court down that way." I follow his gaze, but all I see is a paved path leading through more trees.

"Are you going to show me?" I ask, playfully bumping his arm with my shoulder, and adding a wink for good measure.

His eyes do that thing where they grow darker as if trying to read my soul. Gosh, I'm going to have to work on this whole wife-flirting-rich person thing. Maybe I should be matching Jaxon's resting dick face with my own RBF that helped me get through long hours at the bar and the perverts that came to drink there. I'm just having a hard time trying to figure out who I'm supposed to be here.

When he's shown me the rest of the grounds and we're headed back into the house, I tell him that I will need some swimwear when we pass the pool again.

"Not a problem, you can update your, um..." He looks me over, and I can't tell if he's questioning my style or pondering something nice to say about my ten-year-old skinny jeans, canvas sneakers, and a plain, baggy top that does nothing for my figure.

"Thanks," I respond before he can finish his sentence, releasing him of having to come up with a compliment.

When we spoke on the phone about our terms, Jaxon mentioned I would need to look the part. I told him I didn't have the cash to dress to his standards, and he assured me that he'd take care of it, along with those hospital debts from Mom and Granny.

I can't say it's not a little weird accepting the debt payments or the new clothes and lifestyle. Although I guess not any different from marrying a man I barely know. But still, I've always worked hard for everything I've had, which, to be honest, wasn't much. I tell myself to allow him to dote on me and treat me like the princess my granny always claimed I was. But it will take some getting used to.

"Let me show you the rest of the house."

We finish the tour, and then Jaxon tells me that he wants to get right into my debt, so I give him all the outstanding bills I have. When dinner rolls around, Jaxon suggests we order in.

He's just clearing up our plates, and I disappear back up to my room to take advantage of the claw-foot tub and some bath salts. Jaxon said he had a few things to take care of and that he'd see me before bed.

Damn right he'll see me before bed. I want to seal this deal. We're going to consummate the shit out of this marriage.

When I've buttered my skin with my coconut body soufflé and put on the pastel blue lace thong bodysuit I splurged on for our wedding night, I crack open the door to my room.

I don't bother covering up. We're husband and wife, and he's expecting this, I'm sure. That's why he said he'd see me before bed. It's my duty to perform, and I'm not complaining by any standard.

After the tub finished draining, I heard Jaxon walk by my room. Earlier on, at the end of our tour, he mentioned his room was at the end of the hallway, beside the guest washroom.

I'm tiptoeing, light on my feet, until I reach his open door.

Peering in, I have a moment to watch him before he notices me. He's wearing reading glasses and holding a book. Hm, I never thought reading was hot, but this is actively turning me on. It might have something to do with the reading glasses he's wearing—big DILF energy.

I clear my throat and lean one elbow against the doorframe in my best *honey, I'm home, come do me* pose.

And I'm thinking it's working when I watch his mouth drop open.

# Chapter Eight

*Jaxon*

Ten seconds pass, maybe a minute. I'm not sure how long it takes me to close my mouth and snap back to reality. My mind is lost in a sea of blue lace, and I can't seem to make words fall out of my mouth.

Good Lord, my wife is hot.

I slide my reading glasses off and place them on the table beside me on top of the book I was reading before Quinn blessed me with the blue lace barely covering one third of her body.

My eyes dart to the dip between her breasts, trailing down to her hips where the lacy one-piece sits high on each side. I can only imagine the backside of her. If the material is sitting that high on her body, this one-piece sea of blue lace has got to be a thong, perhaps even a G-string.

Fuck me.

I stir on my chair, not getting up, for more than one reason. Thoughts are pulling at me from two different directions.

One, I want to spin her around and take a look at the fine ass that I know is split into two with a thin piece of lace threading her center.

Two, this isn't what I flew her here for.

This is a marriage of convenience, and I need to keep reminding myself that spinning Quinn around and bending her over until her ass aligns with my crotch is not in the cards tonight.

Now, because I have yet to utter two syllables to her, Quinn takes my silence as approval to enter my room.

"Fuck me," I utter under my breath, but not low enough.

"That's why I'm here," she says, eyeing me seductively.

I run a hand through my hair and let out a sigh.

If this woman only understood that she doesn't need to put on this show for me. I could see her on our tour this afternoon, trying to impress me, downplaying her quirkiness. But it's too late for that. She's been texting me emojis and slang that I don't even understand and have to search the internet for their meaning. She can't fool me; I can see right through her. It's one of the reasons I went for this fucking fake marriage deal with her in the first place. She's real. I wouldn't be able to hold up my end of the marriage if I was going to be living with a pretentious, stuck-up know-it-all.

With my pants fitting a little tighter, I stand. Quinn steps right up to me, leaving only a few inches in between.

"Quinn, this isn't..."

"You don't need to say anything, Mr. Baker," she responds with a wink. "We're husband and wife, it's only normal if we... you know." She tilts her head and peers at me from under her eyelashes.

Her hands glide up my arms, and this time I have a view from above as I tower over her. My eyes fall between her breasts, darting to her hard nipples pressing through the lace.

I run a hand down my face and take a step back, not realizing the distance between me and the chair I just stood up from. Landing with a little more of an impact than I would have liked, I wipe my palms on my thighs while Quinn laughs lightly.

"Am I making you nervous?" I watch her hands trail up her sides until they stop on her hips.

Her legs are spread shoulder-width apart, and now that I'm sitting, I can see every inch of her, the lace leaving little to the imagination.

It's probably best that I've fallen back in my chair because if I were to stand up right now, I wouldn't be the only thing standing at attention.

Before I can reply, her knee presses down into the soft leather between my legs.

I lightly place my hands on the sides of her waist.

"Quinn, wait," I say.

Her expression changes, and it does something to my insides, twisting and turning in my stomach. I'm not a complete jerk, and embarrassment is the last thing I want her to endure. Her knee slowly slides off the chair, and she's standing with her arms folded over her chest. I can see she's waiting for me to speak.

"This isn't why I brought you here." I'm unsure how to approach the subject without hurting her pride. "I don't want you thinking I married you just so you'd have to..." I wave my arms around foolishly as if trying to portray the act of sex and motion to her chosen lingerie. Which I couldn't ask for a better selection, if the time called for it. Quinn is stunning.

"I just thought..."

"You're here to help me get a promotion, that's it," I say maybe a little too firmly, and immediately regret it.

Before I can utter another word, she turns on her heel and heads towards my door. And it's in that moment that I can fully claim that I am a giant asshole as I watch her leave. Instead of soothing her or explaining my thoughts on the matter, I watch her full bottom bounce, and I no longer have to wonder if it's a thong or a G-string.

The door to Quinn's room was still closed tightly when I woke up early to get in a workout before sunrise, but when I walk past again an hour and a half later, the door is wide open, and Quinn is nowhere in sight.

I shuffle faster to my room, shower, and dress for work. I was hoping Quinn would sleep in and we wouldn't have to cross paths so soon after last night.

I don't do awkward, and this is going to be awkward as fuck.

"Oh my God, tell me more."

I hear a voice I don't recognize echo through the kitchen. I stop at the entrance and watch as Quinn adjusts her position on the stool at the island. She has her feet on the edge of the dark wood and her arms wrapped tightly around her bare legs. Her phone is propped up against something, and a face I don't recognize is looking back at me.

"Uh, Quinn, behind you," the voice tells her, and she spins around, sitting upright. Her feet dangle down from the high stool, that sparkly gold anklet making itself known in the morning sun.

Who would have thought that I'd be so enthralled by a goddamn ankle. I tear my gaze away from Quinn's bare legs and start walking towards the kitchen.

"I better call you back." Quinn picks up the phone before her friend can respond, and the screen goes black. "My neighbor, my best friend back home," she tells me, shrugging her shoulders. Her gaze doesn't quite meet mine, and she's back to picking at some fruit on her plate.

"Mornin'," I say, coming around the island and helping myself to a cup of coffee. "Thanks," I tell her, lifting up my freshly poured cup towards her.

"Yeah, no problem," she replies.

I glance over at her as she takes a bite of a strawberry, and it takes everything in me not to stand and watch her lips wrap around the red freckled fruit.

Lord help me. This is bad. This is really bad.

I'm fucking hooked, obsessed, spiraling over Quinn, and her goddamn ankle, her lips, her hips, and her ass. All of it.

My new wife has been here less than twenty-four hours, and I want her. In my bed or on this island—either one would suffice.

Shaking my head, I grab an apple from a basket and take a seat at the island, leaving an empty stool between us.

Business, this is business. I've got to get my shit together. I will get that promotion, and Brodie will go fuck himself.

"How did you sleep?" I ask, after enough time has passed that it makes the awkward silence even more unbearable.

She stands up and walks to the dishwasher. "Fine."

"Was there anything missing in your room?"

"Nope, I'm good."

And it's in that moment that I know that she's not good.

"Look, I'm sorry about last night." I need to have this conversation with Quinn. Get it out of the way so that we can both move on. "This is a business deal." I say to her. "We need to remember that."

I need to remember that. I will not catch feelings.

"Yup," she replies, and I'm aware that I am fucking this up, royally, but it is what it is.

"You're my wife, yes, but it's not real. Is this going to be a problem?"

And there it is, jerk Jaxon is back. The giant asshole from last night.

"Not a problem, Mr. Baker." She's now facing me, her jaw set, and I can see her shoulders sitting a little higher than they were yesterday. There's a fire in her eyes, but a very different fire than the one that bored through me last night when her knee was resting between my thighs and my dick was twitching.

"Jaxon," I insist.

"Not a problem, Jaxon." She turns and walks away, and I listen as she makes her way back upstairs.

Fuck.

# Chapter Nine

## Quinn

I let my body fall onto the pillowy bed, that, if I'm being honest, felt like heaven last night. But it wasn't Jaxon's body, and my embarrassment did not dissolve into thin air as I slept.

And had Jaxon not showered as rapid as wildfire, I could have been back up in my room after finishing breakfast and avoided that whole kitchen island fiasco.

Last night wasn't really me. I think that's why I'm embarrassed. I want to live a little more on the wild side, and my first attempt was a giant flop.

I groan into the soft duvet before turning onto my back. Staring at the ceiling and the chandelier hanging over me, I wonder what I'm going to do today, now that I'm a lady of leisure.

My phone buzzes, and I see that I have a message from Jaxon.

We've been married one day, and we're already at the stage of texting to avoid a decent conversation.

That's okay. I'm okay. I just need a bit more space between us before I can pretend last night never happened and get on with this business deal, which he so kindly reminded me of minutes ago.

Speaking of being a lady of leisure, wife of a hot millionaire, arm candy, one may say... I need a glow-up.

I turn back to my phone and open the text.

> Jaxon Baker
>
> I'm heading out to work. I've left a list for you on the fridge.

A list? I wonder if it's because he wants me to update my style. Maybe we're more compatible than I thought, and he was reading my mind on the glam-up.

> Jaxon Baker
>
> I've left a credit card on the counter for you. Henri's number is also on the fridge if you need a ride anywhere, just text him.

Bingo. Makeover it is, and soulmates in the works. It's only a matter of time.

> Quinn Cameron
>
> Have a great day at work, hubby ;)

The winky face is my first attempt at pretending last night never happened. I jump out of bed with a newfound excitement. I have never had a makeover in my entire life, not unless you count when Macy Adams over-tweezed my eyebrows in the eighth grade.

## CHAPTER NINE

Ignoring my message and winky face, I get a reply.

Jaxon Baker

> Text me if you need anything. I'll be home for dinner at 6.

I get up and toss my phone on the cloud that is my bed. I pass the large window that takes up one wall of my bedroom and looks over the grounds. I can see a gardener tending to the flowers by the pool. What a difference a few days make. Only five days ago, I caught a stray cat playing with a dead mouse outside my window. This is a much better view to start my day.

Once I've gotten dressed and found my purse, I nearly skip down the steps to the fridge and the list from Jaxon, but when I get there, I don't see anything but a list of chores for the maid.

I find the credit card and Henri's number and send him a text. I guess I'll need him to drive me around until I get a car. While I wait for my ride, I spend a few more minutes trying to find the list Jaxon left for me. I even get down on my hands and knees to check and make sure it hasn't fallen under the fridge, but I come up empty-handed.

Oh, well, perhaps he changed his mind and threw it away. I scan the list for the maid, and I'm suddenly appreciative that we have one, because with the size of this house, those chores would take hours to finish.

When there's a knock at the door, I rush to answer.

"Hey, Henri." He nods, smiling at me, and returns to open the door to the back seat of the sedan. "Oh, can I sit up front with you?" I ask nervously. I'm not sure if this is appropriate, but it doesn't sit well to be in the back when he's up front all alone.

"Mr. Baker would probably prefer you to sit in the back."

"Um, but I'd much rather be up front with you so we can chat and you can help me find where I need to go."

He smiles, and I notice a small dimple in the older man's left cheek. "Of course." I wait for him to open the front passenger door, because he seems to take his job seriously, and I thank him once I'm in and buckled.

We head out of the driveway and down the windy road to a gate that appears to magically open as we exit the gated community and onto the street.

"Where to, Mrs. Baker?"

"Um, so I need clothes, but I think I want to get my hair done. Is there like a Main Street with boutiques?"

His dimple reappears. "I know just where to bring you." We pass rows and rows of large homes, tennis courts, pools, and gardeners working diligently at plucking the smallest of weeds. Although the temperature is dry and hot here, not an inch of grass is burnt by the sun.

"Wow, everyone's grass is so green, and the flowers all look so perfect."

"Perfection can be overrated."

"You're right, but it does make for beautiful things to look at."

"Sometimes we need to appreciate what we have in front of us for what it is and see the beauty in that."

I wonder if Jaxon's driver is a retired motivational speaker-turned-getaway driver. I laugh lightly at his last comment. "You're wise."

He returns the laugh, his eyes crinkling at the edges. "It comes with age."

A bustling street comes into view as we take a left turn. I open the window and let the warm morning air tickle my face, and that's when I see it. A shiny gold sign. "Here, stop

## CHAPTER NINE

here," I say to Henri in a rush, afraid to pass by the shop. The gold sign has bold pink lettering, and I read it once more.

*Make Me a Blonde, B.*

The traffic is bustling, and I scan the block as Henri turns down a side road, back tracking to find a parking spot. When we've neared the shop again, after circling the block, I point a finger at a spot. "Right there." He parallel parks with precision. "Do I just text you when I'm done?"

"I'll wait a few minutes to make sure you can get an appointment, and then I will stay close by."

"Thanks, Henri!" I pop open the door before he can get out and open it for me. I wave through the open window.

I stop in front of the gold sign and peer through the front windows. This ain't no small-town parlor with women setting their curls for the week.

Once inside, I approach the large front desk, and I'm greeted by a perky blonde.

"Welcome to Make Me a Blonde, B. How can I help you?" she asks with a customer service smile—but unlike mine, hers might actually be genuine. "Do you have an appointment?"

Suddenly nervous, glancing around at all the shuffling, chatter, and noisy hums of blow dryers, I hesitate. "Um, no, I don't. Do you take walk-ins for color and a cut?"

"We're pretty full, but let me take a quick peek."

"Thanks." I look through the open double glass doors. There must be about a dozen stylists in there.

"You're in luck, Nicky had a cancellation. His client's pup is ill."

"Oh, okay."

"I'll tell him that you're here. Your name?" She stands, grasping a bedazzled pink cane propped up against the ledge of her desk.

"Quinn. Quinn Baker."

She nods and turns on her heels. I watch her walk slowly but confidently towards a back room, her long ponytail swaying left to right across the open back of her sleek dress.

Fiddling with my ring, I choose a soft bucket chair next to the large window. This really is something else. The sidewalks are packed with shoppers, and I think I'll take a walk after my hair is done and explore a little. Nerves mix with the excitement at my new life. I still can't believe I'm actually married. I stop twisting my ring to notice all the diamonds circling my finger and how they're sparkling under this lighting.

"Excuse me, Quinn? Is that you?"

I stand and walk towards the man who seems to be around my age. "That's me."

"Nice to meet you. I'm Nikolas, but everyone calls me Nicky." He leads me through the open double doors and into a thick black leather chair.

Nicky ties the black cape around my neck and runs his hands through my hair. His eyes meet mine in the mirror. "What can I do for you today?"

"Make me housewife blonde," I demand, clasping my hands together under the thick cape.

"Girl, I got you."

He cards my hair between his fingertips. His lips are in a tight line, and I can tell he's thinking. Plotting, maybe.

"Let me go mix that up." Nicky leaves me to my thoughts. Minutes pass, and then he's back with the mixture. "You new around here?"

"I am actually. I sort of ran away from my hometown."

"Don't we all at some point," Nicky says drily as he separates my hair into sections.

## CHAPTER NINE

I haven't told a soul about my fake marriage—I mean, except for Alysha back home—since Jaxon had me sign a nondisclosure agreement. He was really adamant that no one can find out about our contract, as it could ruin everything. I don't think friends were included in that. I mean, I need to make friends, and if I find trustworthy friends, like Alysha, it's only fair to our friendship that I'm honest and open with them.

"How long have you lived in the city?" I ask, curious about Nicky and the casual statement he just made.

He begins to paint thick white goop on my golden strands. "Well, I guess since your stuck in my chair for the next three and a half hours, considering the length and thickness you have here, I might as well tell you my story."

I try to get comfortable in the black cape with my arms by my sides, all tucked in for the sake of becoming a true housewife.

"I was just a boy with a dream..." Nicky starts, and I spend the next hour listening intently through the sounds of dryers and gossip alike. It turns out we're a lot more alike than either of us could have predicted. Nicky left his hometown searching for a sense of belonging. I can definitely relate to that.

"I'm so sorry you went through all of that," I tell him.

"Was years ago, it's fine. Look where I am now."

Nicky tells me he'll be back after he rinses his bowls, and I stare at my reflection in the mirror. My head is heavy with foil, and my stomach growls, telling me I'm about to miss lunch.

"Hey, are you hungry?" Nicky asks as he walks back up to my chair, as if reading my mind.

"Yeah, I am." I laugh as the sound from my abdomen reiterates the fact that I am starving, actually.

"I pre-ordered lunch knowing I had a full day today. Come share with me in the lounge."

"There's a lounge?" I ask, standing, and taking a second to adjust to the added weight on the top of my head.

"Yep. It's quiet back here, and you can read or scroll on your phone until your thumbs ache, or you can have lunch with me."

There are chairs along the sides of one wall with a footrest each, and a few tables in the center of the room.

"I'll be right back," he tells me.

I pull out a pink chair and have a seat at one of the tables, taking in the soft rose walls and the simple design of the space. Nicky returns with a brown paper bag that's been stapled shut.

"This is my longest day of the week when I work open to close, so I always order a lot of food."

"Well, I don't want to eat your leftovers for dinner."

"Girl, I've got enough food here for days."

I find myself liking Nicky. He comes from a small town just like mine. He's been through it, and with no family who respects him, he followed his dream of living in the big city. We dive into the cardboard containers of food, and I find myself wanting to disclose my secret to him. "So, when I said I ran away from my hometown, what I really meant was that I flew here to marry my husband. I'm a newlywed."

I wait and let the information settle in, as he swallows a bite of food.

"I was wondering when you were going to explain that giant rock on your hand." He puts down his fork and takes my hand in his to inspect the ring, turning my hand side to side.

"My husband is a big-time corporate guy."

"Sounds like you lucked out."

## CHAPTER NINE

I lower my voice. "I met him online only three weeks ago," I reveal, my cheeks blushing, and I watch his eyes widen.

"What do you mean you met him only three weeks ago?" He stops eating. "Spill. Tell me everything."

"I met him through an agency, like a matchmaking site." He leans in waiting for more. "Okay, so it was more of a millionaire matchmaking site." I cringe, a little embarrassed.

"Honey, why in the world would you marry him, though?"

I tell Nicky everything and swear him to secrecy.

He smiles at me and squeezes my shoulders. "Well, your housewife blonde is in the works"—he motions to the foil—"and you've found your big-city stylist and your new best friend, all in one afternoon."

I feel like I've suddenly hit the jackpot with this new life.

Hopefully, with time, my new husband will feel the same.

When Nicky's finished my hair and I've paid with my brand-new card, we exchange numbers and I promise to meet him for drinks later this week.

I can't believe I've already made a friend. Besides Alysha, I haven't really ever had time to make friends outside of work. But this is the new me. I glance in the mirror at the entranceway. I'm a lighter shade of blonde, with a new cut, and I'm ready to make the effort and do what I can to help Jaxon get his promotion.

Outside of the bedroom.

After Nicky finished styling my hair, I found a department store, got a little lesson on makeup application, and bought everything the salesgirl put on my face. Between that, the hair, and the new clothes I found, I'm barely recognizable, but in a good way. I look like I belong here in the big city, and I'm not just some imposter.

I walk into the kitchen and set my shopping bags and iced coffee down. Walking the busy streets today sort of took it out of me. Three weeks not working and waiting tables every day, and my body is suddenly a bit achy.

I walk up to my room and let myself fall onto the bed, but this time I'm smiling and happy, wondering if Jaxon will like my new style.

# Chapter Ten

## Jaxon

"Jaxon, have a moment?" Edward is walking into my office and sitting across from me before I can answer him.

"Of course, Edward." I close the file on my desk and lean back in my chair.

He clicks the pen in his hand a few times, and the sound makes me cringe. I wonder why he's here paying me a visit on the fourteenth floor.

"I guess the rumors aren't rumors after all."

"Excuse me?"

"Did my wedding invitation get lost in the mail?" His eyes are narrowing in at me and my left hand, and I can't tell if he's pissed or testing me. He unbuttons his black suit jacket as he sits back.

How the hell did news travel so fast up to the eighteenth floor? It's barely noon.

Lester. It must have been Lester.

"No, sir. There were no invitations. Just a little ceremony down at city hall, that's all."

"I wasn't aware that you had a girlfriend, Jaxon. I thought we were closer than this." He frowns in disappointment.

Shit, I hadn't thought of this.

Did I just make things worse for myself?

I need to turn this around, and fast.

"Quinn, my wife, she's a bit on the shy side." I ponder where to go from here. "As you know, my family are always traveling, and Quinn, well, her family has passed, so we decided to keep it small, just the two of us. Make it special, more romantic." I shrug my shoulders, but I can tell that he isn't buying my explanation. I'm barely buying it myself. Sounds like an excuse for a shotgun wedding.

Edward stands, so I peel myself off the chair and wait for his reply, not wanting to show a hint of self-doubt.

"Two things, Jaxon. One, there is nothing romantic about city hall."

He's right. Why the hell did I say that?

"And two, you have to know that I'm your family. You're like a son to me, Jaxon. I'm a little upset, if I'm going to be honest, that you never mentioned anything about this Quinn."

Fuck me.

"It all happened somewhat quickly. I meant no disrespect, sir. You know me—I come in, keep my head down, work hard, and leave personal shit at the door where it belongs." I try to distract him. "By the way, that watch looks great on you." He's wearing one from the newest collection, a 34 mm diameter on grade 5 titanium with a satin-brushed rotating bezel, and the deep rich brown upper flange.

Edward glances down at his watch and smiles. "They really grasped my vision on this one," he says, tapping at the glass plate. "The phoenix blue would make a great addition to what you already own." He makes his way towards the door.

"Yes, sir." I study the stainless steel and platinum watch that circles my left wrist.

I'm following him when he clears his throat and turns back towards me.

"I hope this Quinn will be at the retreat in a few months. I'd like to meet the woman who finally stole Jaxon's heart."

I laugh. "Yes, sir, she'll be there."

The door closes behind him, and I'm trusting that I didn't just screw everything up by marrying a stranger I found online without inviting my boss, the man who took me under his wing.

The whole fucking purpose for this last-minute marriage.

I'm just leaning back in my chair when Lester comes in.

"Lester." I nod. "What can I do for you?"

"I saw Mr. Rummens walking out of here. Does he know?"

"Tell me that wasn't you spreading gossip?"

"I just told Betsy. I figured you'd want the news out, get you back in the running for the promotion."

I close my eyes, thinking about this a moment. "You're right, good idea." Lester's always on top of shit. I couldn't ask for a better assistant. "Best to let it sit with Edward for a while before the retreat so he knows I'm serious about my life. He'll get over not being invited to the wedding."

I'm tapping my hands on my desk. This whole situation has me out of sorts.

"Now, are you going to tell me about Quinn? Does she look just like her pictures?" He settles into one of the chairs.

Now I can see why the women in this office have no problem spreading rumors and gossip to Lester. He's just as bad as they are.

I smirk. "Even better ." And I leave it at that, thinking about Quinn in her one-piece blue lacy thing.

"What is this?" My brows knit together, my fingertips pinching the bridge of my nose.

I left her alone for *one* day.

One goddamn day, and the kitchen island is covered in shopping bags. The bags aren't even the worst part of it. Condensation is dripping down from what I can only assume was an iced coffee drink, which has left a caramel-colored ring on the white marble countertop.

"What's what?" Quinn walks into the kitchen, looking at the piles of bags, ignoring the plastic cup I place back down, which quickly forms a second ring.

"This mess. Why are there shopping bags everywhere?" I throw my arms up in the air.

"I don't know, I got tired and went up for a nap. What's the big deal?" she replies nonchalantly, shrugging her shoulders. "Henri took me out, and I got my hair done and did some shopping. Check out the shoes I bought." I watch as she twists her ankles right and left, oblivious to the rings forming on the white island. My eyes trail over her, from her shoes to her hair, but not before I catch a glimpse of that same thin slice of gold wrapped around that tiny ankle.

## CHAPTER TEN

Sighing, I cross my arms. "Did you do any of the chores from the list I left you this morning?"

"Chores?" She folds her arms, unconsciously matching me.

I turn to the stainless-steel fridge, motioning to a piece of lined paper being held up by a magnet.

She places her hands on her hips. "I saw that list, and I figured it was for the housekeeping staff."

"Did you even read it?"

"I glanced over it when I was looking for the list you said you left me, which I couldn't find, by the way."

"This was the list I left for you."

"Jaxon, I thought you wanted me to look the part of your wife, so that's what I did." She turns her head, her soft highlighted blonde curls bouncing around her shoulders. Fuck me. Quinn is absolutely stunning.

She grabs at the bags on the island, and the half-drunk coffee.

"I'd appreciate if you'd do your part, and take care of the house, keep it tidy. None of this..." I'm motioning at the sleek countertops where her bags were only seconds ago, my voice rising slightly.

Her eyebrows raise. I can see she's annoyed, teetering on resistance.

"You wanted a wife. I'm your wife. I will be your arm candy, the polite, agreeable woman on your arm nodding and laughing at all your jokes—if you're even capable of making any—but I won't be your maid," she says, standing erect, as if all 5'4" of her will intimidate me.

"Maid, no. Housewife, yes."

We're standing face to face. Well, face to chest. She's tiny next to me, but she doesn't back down, and there's a spark of gold in the blue of her eyes. She pivots to the fridge, drops her bags on the floor, and yanks at the edge of the list I left her this morning until it tears from the magnet, leaving a corner still stuck to the fridge.

I lift the magnet and take the small piece that was left behind as she studies the scribbled note. I ball up the tiny edge and roll it between my fingers.

"Make the beds? Seriously, you want me to make your freaking bed?" Her baby blues roll. "I'll make my own bed, not a problem, but yours? Come on, you can make your own bed, you're a grown-ass man." Her cheeks are starting to turn pink, an angrier shade of rose as she continues to scan the list.

Okay, I might have gone a bit overboard with the making of my bed since it's not like I haven't been doing it myself for years. I can honestly say I don't know what the fuck I'm doing here. I took a stab at it, thinking I needed Quinn to have a *job*, to be a *housewife,* but all I really need is her here with me, to be my wife.

"Clean the toilets, empty and fill the dishwasher, do the laundry, dust...." She continues through the rest of my list, and I watch as her pink cheeks grow darker and darker. Okay, I've definitely gone too far. "Jaxon, you said it yourself, you have housekeeping come in once a week." She slams the list down on the counter and balls up her palms into fists, resting them on her hips once more. "I'm not cleaning the toilets. Where did you get this list from anyway?" she demands.

"The internet," I offer meekly, embarrassed.

"Who has done your laundry until now?" she asks.

"The housekeeper."

"So did you hire me as a second housekeeper, or as a wife to help you get a promotion?"

Fuck, she's right, but I dig in further. "You need to contribute to the house. I pay the bills, and you take care of this stuff." I regret my words seconds after they roll off my tongue. What the fuck am I even saying? I need a wife, not a housewife, I remind myself. But this mess, these bags everywhere, and that fucking coffee ring that's growing in my peripheral vision. I shake my head, feeling distraught.

"Fine." She stamps her right foot so hard I fear it'll chip the flooring. "I will take care of the dishwasher, and if I leave a mess, I will clean it up, but that's it."

"Thank you." I listen as she continues.

"But let me make one thing clear."

Oh, fuck. If looks could kill, I'd be one dead man right now.

"I might have married you to climb myself out of debt, a dead-end town, and a shit job, but you will *not* control me. You might be some hot-shot deal at work, and obviously that works for you, given your financial situation"—her hands wave around the room—"but I'm an independent woman with a mind of my own, and you're going to have to accept that."

I don't answer her for a moment, and she's watching me, waiting for a reply, but all I can focus on is the pulse in my pants.

Fuck, I'm a prick.

"You about done?" I ask, willing her to come at me again, enjoying the sexual tension that is rising between us.

"Don't be a dink, and I'll be the best trophy wife you will ever have," she says with a sliver of arrogance.

"A dink? Really? Did you really just call me a dink?"

"Yeah?" she replies, her voice rising like she's the one asking me the question.

I laugh. I can't help it, she's so hot and so cute. When I've managed to settle the dirty thoughts, I turn to face her. "I'm not used to living with someone, and I like things a certain way." I pause, thinking. "What about making my lunch?" I try to joke with her now, raising my eyebrows with a smirk.

"Jaxon!" she shouts.

"I'm kidding."

She grabs at her bags once more, and I can tell that she didn't appreciate my little joke.

"Yeah, you better be."

Okay, so I might not be her favorite person in the world at the moment.

"We'll discuss things as they come up," I say a little louder to make sure she hears me.

She turns with a humph, and I watch her hips sway as the bags crash against her thighs, her heels clacking loudly throughout the open space. When she turns the corner and I can no longer watch her walk away, I'm left wondering if this whole marriage thing will be worth it.

# Chapter Eleven

## Quinn

Ugh, this man is *infuriating*.

I've known him for almost twenty-four hours, and I haven't seen him smile once.

Not once.

And now he has the audacity to let out a chuckle at me for calling him a dink?

Not even a smile at our wedding. Okay, well, there was that moment where he grinned at the altar. Barely. I think it was more of a smirk. If I weren't so aggravated, I might just find my cheeks warming at the thought of this six foot three man, dark and handsome, grinning at me.

He barely appeared happy yesterday, and he definitely didn't in the kitchen today until I uttered the only insult I could muster up, but then five seconds later, back to Mr. Stick-Up-His- Butt Baker.

I unload all the bags onto the floor of my walk-in closet.

I pace, my insides boiling. I thought I had left all drama behind when I heard the doors to the bar shut behind me the night I quit.

He wanted me to look the part, and now he's pissed because I left a few bags on the counter? And he left me a list of chores, like I'm some kind of maid. My fists clench at the thought. He found me on a matchmaking site, not one for cleaning services.

I let myself fall onto the floor next to my bags, legs sprawled out in front of me. I hate to admit that as much as Jaxon pissed me off by wanting to make the next Stepford wife out of me, this brooding, bossy man in control has me so fired up I'm seeing stars.

Seeing him, hair all tousled, his thick arms under his dress shirt, has me needing a release.

Unclasping my new shoes, I slide them off and rub at my soles before sinking my feet into the soft plush area rug beneath me and letting all my pent-up energy around Jaxon dissolve as I take some deep breaths.

I thought I was done being the caretaker. Maybe that's what this is all about. I thought this journey would be a carefree one, full of fancy dinners and relaxing, floating on an overly giant swan in a pool I'd be calling my own.

The closet is decorated in soft blue tones to match the bedroom. The walls are pale, with white shelving, and blue hangers waiting to be filled with elegant clothes. I take the shoes into my hands and bring them to the empty hollow, propping them into their position as art, as if they're to be admired and not worn. These shoes cost more than a month's worth of rent, and the guilt had followed me from store to store. As much as I'm trying to embrace this new lifestyle, it just doesn't feel natural to spend someone else's money. But I chose to do this, and doing this means living up to Jaxon's standards.

The island in the middle of the room is filled with drawers, and I open each one, knowing that they're all empty. I quickly realize that my cotton bikini briefs and my sports bras are going to seem out of place here. Once cocktail dresses, tailored pants, and whatever else will give me big rich energy are dangling from the abandoned hangers, the space will come to life, I'm sure.

But is there even a point in trading in my comfies when I was so loudly rejected last night? Jaxon's lack of interest was as clear as a bright summer day. The disappointment in my chest from last night returns at the memory. What if I can't live up to the idea Jaxon was hoping for? I mean, we now know that I'm not the housewife he wanted after the whole kitchen argument, but is he even attracted to me? Will he even be able to pretend to be in love with me at the corporate retreat? I guess I wasn't really sure what was going to happen. I don't usually sleep with men I just meet. Hell, I don't usually meet men.

I go to the bathroom and turn on the taps to the walk-in shower, letting warm drops slide down my wrist, landing on the white-tiled floor. When I'm satisfied with the temperature, I close the glass door and turn to face myself in the large mirror over the vanity. My blonde hair loose around my shoulders, my plain blue T-shirt spotted from drops of my iced coffee, and my cropped jeans, landing right above my ankle. Fancy has never been my middle name, but I wanted an adventure. To experience an incredible night with my new husband, all inhibitions out the window. And God help me, it would have been so easy to slide into Jaxon's bed. So, why do I feel like I'm already failing so miserably on day two?

I twirl my hair into a bun on top of my head so that it doesn't get ruined so soon after my trip to Make Me a Blonde, B.

Thirty minutes later, I emerge refreshed and optimistic.

Who knew a rain shower could have that kind of power to turn my day right around and let me forget about the gnawing rejection that's slivered itself in my chest? Or maybe it's the fact that my showers for the last ten years have come from a drippy faucet that was most likely installed at the same time as the pink tub and matching vanity were. One whose water pressure soared from heavy to light, depending on its mood and the neighbors' water use, and whose temperature never quite reached hot enough.

I towel-dry the bits of my hair that I couldn't manage to keep dry. Knowing that my blow dryer is still in my suitcase, I walk back out to the closet to find it. While crossing the bedroom on my way back to the bathroom, I stop short when I notice movement outside. I spot Jaxon doing laps in the pool, and I find myself mesmerized by the clean sweep of his arms, the muscles in his back rising and falling. His mouth opens as his head turns, catching a breath quickly before disappearing back into the crystal-clear water. Seconds pass as I stand there in a trance when he comes to a stop, one hand grabbing at the edge of the pool, the other one pushing the small goggles from his eyes to his forehead. He suddenly glances up towards my room, and our eyes lock.

Shit, here I am standing naked in front of the window. I let my body fall to the floor to hide from being caught. It's only after I'm crouched down that our eyes meet once more and I realize what an idiot I am. On day one, I show up in his room in a lace bodysuit, and then on day two, he catches me gawking at him, naked in front of floor-to-ceiling windows. Apparently, I just bare it all for anyone to see. Turning my body back towards the direction of the bathroom, I abandon my suitcase and quickly crawl on hands and knees, tits dangling, and try not to think how Jaxon can still see me.

Later, there's a light knock at my door. I can't help but still be a bit peeved at what he wants me to be, but I manage a smile and open the door, shoving our first argument and the two embarrassing moments under the rug.

*Never happened*, I tell myself, choosing to live in denial so it pains me less.

"Jaxon," I greet him.

"Dinner's ready. Please come down to the dining room." I watch as his eyes trail down to my bare feet and back up to my eyes.

"Dinner's ready? As in you cooked for me, after all that debate about me being the housewife?"

He turns towards the hallway. "No need for the attitude. Come on."

"It smells amazing." I follow him through the main floor towards the dining room, and I can see that two spots have been set, with Jaxon at the end, and me to his right.

"I hope it's okay that I've set your spot next to mine. It'll be easier to talk than if you were at the other end of the table."

"You set the table?" I ask.

"My wife didn't," he responds, and for a moment I want to whack him on the arm until I see that smirk tugging at the side of his lips.

"Very funny. So, do I add this to my list of housewife duties?"

"Yes, that'd be great."

Setting the table is the least I can do. I mean, he paid off mountains of hospital bills, and as much as I don't want to admit it, I do kind of owe him. It's probably best not to let my guard down too much and keep him at a distance.

"Let me go grab our meals."

"Do you need any help?" I follow him to the kitchen before he can answer.

He passes me a plate and keeps one for himself.

"Our meals are prepared daily and dropped off. All that's needed is to heat them up. I'm not much of a cook. You want a burger on the barbecue, I got that, but chicken parmesan, I don't."

"Noted." I smile, softening up a bit as we both sit down at the table. This is nice. Who knew Jaxon had another side to himself besides being big ol' bossman asshole?

"I'll share the app with you after. I have a list of favorites, and I've scheduled the meals I want for the next month. You can go ahead and see if there's anything you would like to add or change if there's something you don't like. I will eat just about anything."

My taste buds explode from the flavors. "This is the best chicken I have ever had," I tell him, reveling in the tender pieces covered in cheese and a rich tomato sauce.

We eat the rest of dinner, and I have never been so satisfied by a meal in my entire life. This might actually be enough to distract me from the parts of me that are so clearly unsatisfied. The conversation throughout went well as Jaxon and

## CHAPTER ELEVEN

I continued to get to know one another, and I have to say when he's not being so rigid and uptight, he's actually decent to talk to. And to help matters, it seems Jaxon has shoved my naked gawking under the rug as well, so that's a relief.

I help him clear up the table after I've blown out the candles. When we get to the kitchen, I tell him that I'll clean up the rest.

"Thank you, Quinn." A smile forms on his face, and I gasp. "What, what is it?" he asks.

"You can smile?" I ask. "Your face can actually form a smile. I literally did not know it could do that, especially twice in one day." I'm laughing now as I finish my sentence, my cheeks hurting.

"You think you're so funny," he responds, and a light sound escapes his lips, sending a wave of heat through me.

I place our plates in the dishwasher as he walks around the island. I can see he's about to leave the room, so I rush around to meet him.

"Wait," I say.

I stop right in front of him, ready to abandon all anger and awkward moments from the past twenty-four hours, no grudges to be had. Without my four-inch heels, I can't quite reach him.

I tilt my head upwards, gazing into his dark brown eyes, and I place my right hand on the back of his neck, bringing him down towards me so that I can plant a kiss over the stubble of his cheek.

"Thank you for dinner." I say into his ear as my lips part from his skin.

That's when I notice the scar on his left side, protruding out from his perfectly coiffed facial hair. I run my finger over it lightly, my eyes questioning him. He stands tall, obviously startled at my touch, and clears his throat.

"You're welcome, Quinn. Good night."

And with that, I watch him walk out of the kitchen and up the stairs, wondering what happened to him.

# Chapter Twelve

## Jaxon

"We need to utilize these client insights to drive customer loyalty to Edward Rummens Watches," I tell Ashley, who works closely with Brodie, the head of client relations. I gather my things as she closes her laptop. "When can we expect to hear from our global client relations and event team?"

"We should have a reply by the end of next week at the latest."

Accepting the answer, I walk towards the door to the boardroom, and Ashley and Brodie follow closely behind. Before I can open the door, Lester comes in and gathers up the half-drunk water glasses and napkins.

I hold the door open as the three of us spill out into the wide corridor and walk towards the elevators.

"This new launch and rebranding are going to be dope," Brodie says, and I cringe at his choice of vocabulary in the office.

"Ashley, if you can reach out to the team mid-week next week, make sure they're on top of things," I tell her, and she nods, shifting her bag on her shoulder. Turning to Brodie, I say, "Send me your sample strategies for the rebranding."

We pile into the elevator, and when the doors close, Brodie and Ashley discuss what they're working on, and my phone vibrates in my pocket. I take it out and look down to see a text from Quinn.

The elevator dings when we've reached our floor, and Ashley and Brodie wait for me to step out. I motion to the cell phone in my palm, and I tell them I need to get back to my office.

It's not until I close the door behind me that I swipe my screen to life, and when I see her name, I can't help myself but think of that soft skin, perky tits, and bouncy ass that I had the pleasure of watching through the window from the pool the other day.

Quinn Cameron

> Hope you're having a great day at work, Hubby ;)

Even though she's always awake before I leave for work, she still sends me these messages at some point during the morning. I check my phone, wondering what to reply when I notice her name at the top of the string of messages. Quinn Cameron. My wife. I still can't believe it. And in a few hours, I have to break the news to my parents that their only son is married, and that they weren't invited to the wedding.

I called last week, but it took them a week to get back to me, and by text message at that, to say we'd talk on our scheduled call this afternoon. Figures—you can't always rely on people just because they're blood related.

## CHAPTER TWELVE

I'm not sure what to expect when they hear the news. I think they'll be fine, to be honest, since they aren't exactly present in my day-to-day. It's been a week since the big day, and things are running a little smoother. Besides some things that Quinn would say I'm nitpicking her on, I think she's settling in.

I click on the contacts app on my main screen and find Quinn among the sea of marketing agents, managers, clients, and Mom and Dad. Now's as good of time as any to change her name, so I click on edit. Typing in Baker, I hit save as another message pops up on my screen.

Quinn Baker

> Just want to let you know that my BFF is coming over for a swim later. Margaritas and tanning. That ok?

BFF? Where and when did she have the time to make a friend in the time she's been here? Oh, well, I'm happy for her. If she's setting down roots, then maybe, just maybe she won't take off at a moment's notice like the others.

Jaxon Baker

> Thank you, Quinn.

> BFF?

I don't mean to come across as possessive. It's not like that, I'm just curious. I've managed to keep everyone at arm's length, not having any close friends by choice, but for some reason, I'm a bit envious. It's been all work and no play my whole adult life. I enjoy my own company, I have a routine, and plus, no one really sticks around anyway, so why make a fuss just for someone to leave?

My fingers graze the scar across my jawline, a habit that's been with me since childhood. One of the reasons on why I keep everyone at a distance.

I was twelve when it happened. Riding bikes with four of my best friends, boys I spent my entire childhood with, when the dog came out of nowhere. I had just finished my first jump off the small ramp Matty's dad had built for us. Matty was the first friend I had ever made, as far as I can remember. I was on a high, fist-pumping the air, jumping up and down as I let my bike fall on its side getting ready to watch Matty next. Matty's mom was just coming home from walking the family dog, and she was crossing the street towards us when we all heard the growl and rapid barks of a dog fast approaching. What happened next changed the rest of my childhood. I run my hand down my face. A neighborhood dog had gotten loose and came running at Matty's golden retriever out of nowhere, and my first instinct was to jump in between Matty's mom and Bruce, the dog, just as the large dog lunged. I ended up with a broken nose from face-planting on the pavement and twenty-two stitches from where the dog's teeth met my face. By the time summer ended and we were starting grade seven, I'd become the kid with the messed-up face. A face no girl wanted to look at, and a face too mangled to be cool. No one wanted to be around me, and I can't blame them. Fear followed me everywhere, and I stopped riding my bike and walking the neighborhood like I used to.

Shaking my head, I clear my thoughts and blink away a small amount of moisture that is threatening the corners of my eyes. I take a breath and open Quinn's string of

## CHAPTER TWELVE

texts again, letting the past melt away, replaced by Quinn's curves.

Less than a minute later, her response comes through.

> Quinn Baker
> **Nicky, my hairstylist.**

Her hairstylist. Okay, so she must have met this Nicky her first day out of the house when she went and did all that shopping and left that coffee ring on the fucking island, which, by the way, I finally managed to get it out.

> Jaxon Baker
> **Sounds good, help yourself to the pool house. The key is in the lock box in the cupboard in the kitchen.**

> Quinn Baker
> **Thanks!**

She sends me a kiss emoji, and I turn my attention back to her name.

I hate to admit, but it's kind of nice seeing my last name on her. The emojis are even growing on me. Despite the fact that I've only felt her lips on mine one time, I get excited at the thought that maybe another opportunity might present itself one day.

"You did what?"

I'm in my office, and I've just told my parents that they now have a daughter-in-law.

If anyone was going to be upset about missing out on my wedding day, I figured it was going to be Mom, but surprisingly Dad is the one who's losing his shit.

"I got married," I reveal with little to no emotion, as if I'm saying nothing more than confirming that, yes, today is in fact, also a Tuesday.

It's funny, but having Quinn around, all spunky and bright, I'm actually starting to like her, as a person, more than just the woman I want to fuck and stare at all day. She's smart, capable, and sassy. There are still the random squeals that pierce through my ears when she gets excited about something. But there's also the humming sound she makes when she takes a bite of something that she loves, one that begs to have those pursed lips on my skin.

"Jaxon, are you telling me you got married and your mother and I were not invited?"

I sigh. "We got married at city hall. No one was invited."

"Dear Lord," Mom says. "City hall?" She rests her hand over her heart, and I shake my head.

"It's no big deal," I reply.

I've spent the last week at the office getting more attention than I have in years. Lester let everyone in on the fact that I got hitched, which is turning out to be a bigger deal than I had anticipated. The women in the office are asking too many damned questions for my liking. But everyone is congratulating me. Everyone except Mom and Dad.

Mom appears sad when Dad starts back up again. "You never told us you were serious about a woman, Jaxon." He crosses his arms.

## CHAPTER TWELVE

"It's not like you're around to notice," I mutter under my breath, a bitterness I know all too well landing in my chest.

"Well, we're going to have to plan a trip back home," Mom says.

"Not necessary," I reply. I sit back in my chair and cross my own arms behind my head, leaning my body weight into the leather.

Mom's eyes widen when realization hits her. "Why aren't you on a honeymoon?" Another question I get asked at the office, and I keep finding one reason or another to dodge it.

"Work is busy right now. I'll take her somewhere when things settle down."

"Jaxon! First you get married at city hall without telling us, then you don't even take your wife on a proper honeymoon. Is this how we raised you?"

"Come on, it's fine. Quinn is fine with this."

Quinn and I have not once talked about a honeymoon. Why would we travel the world, staying in fancy rooms with champagne and roses fluttered across the bed when this is purely business? She seems plenty happy with the accommodations she currently has at the house.

"We'll check out the flight options and let you know when we'll be in the city." Dad leans closer to the camera.

I'm not worried. My parents hate traveling back here, and this will just be something that I'll have to face eventually, but not anytime soon.

"Sure, Dad."

We disconnect the call after another fifteen minutes and a few more dissatisfied head shakes and a story about how they couldn't get to town this morning because a bunch of goats were blocking the road in their small town just outside of Collaston across the sea.

I finish my day at the office, pack up, and head home, wondering how Quinn's day has been.

I'm constantly wondering what kind of mess will be waiting for me when I get home. Tidiness isn't her forte. I've been contemplating getting our housekeeper to show her a thing or two, although I know that might not go over so well.

The way she stacks the dishwasher is truly unbelievable—not a single dish in its proper place. I've told her countless times, but she blatantly refuses to think of it as a problem.

I can hear a thump of bass from outside as the car pulls into the driveway.

Henri's just opening the door to let me out when it's clear the bass is coming from my own house. Henri and I exchange glances, but he gets back in the car and drives off, leaving me to find out what the hell is going on.

# Chapter Thirteen

## Quinn

"Quinny, this place," Nicky says as I open the door to greet him. He's looking around, taking everything in, and I smile.

"I know, right? I still can't believe I live here most days," I admit.

"Can I move in?" he asks, turning to me, taking my hands in his as he pleads. "Seriously, I can be your full-time stylist."

"I don't think Jaxon would go for that," I reply with a laugh.

"Fair. Well, what are you waiting for? Let me in." We drop hands, and I close the door behind him.

His eyes wander just as my own did on the day I moved in with Jaxon.

"Do you want me to show you around?" I ask.

"Yes, please. Show me your castle," Nicky jokes, and I laugh again.

It feels so good to laugh. There's *joy* in my life now. I think I've smiled more in the last few weeks than I have my entire adult life, which doesn't say much for the life I was living.

I was living under a rock. A great big boring grey boulder.

Not anymore.

Now that I've had a taste of life, I want to live. Thrive, even.

We walk through the house, and Nicky tells me I need to have a date night with Jaxon, but I don't think Jaxon would go for that, not yet. Plus, we have dinner together every night, just the two of us, so how would it be any different?

"Quinny, come on, you deserve to be wined and dined."

"I am wined and dined," I persist.

"Out on the town, under the city lights." He's swaying his arms in the air, looking at the

imaginary lights twinkling above us.

"You've been watching too many rom-coms."

"There is no such thing, take that back." He puffs out his chest and lifts his chin up and to the side, looking away from me.

"Maybe one day we'll get there. But I plan on making him dinner tonight."

"I thought you said it was your job to make him dinner every night. Isn't that what you're already doing?"

"Yeah, it is." I think about this. "Well, I mean he's not forcing me to, I agreed to take on some of the responsibilities. I mean, I am living here for free, the least I could do is heat up dinner."

"You do not want to get complacent. Yes, take care of your man, but taking care of your house is also for you. Remember that when you feel like you're doing this all and only for him. This whole charade you chose to live is for you too. And you know what they say?"

## CHAPTER THIRTEEN

"Who says?" I ask.

"People, Quinny, people." His cheeks puff up in a wide smile. "They say, keep your home, head, and heart clear."

"People don't say that," I scoff.

"They do. Anyway, this is the first time you've gone without a job, right?"

I nod.

"So, now is the time to take care of you and where you live, where your head is at, and your heart."

We walk towards the backyard, and I push open the sliding doors.

"You know what?" I push my hip out, locking the door in its place. "You're absolutely right."

"Well, of course I am."

I've been thinking about this whole thing as a job, a duty, and wanting to rebel when told by Jaxon to do something. But taking care of this house and him is for me too.

I've never had to cook for anyone before. And I can't really say I've been cooking for Jaxon when all I've been doing is reheating items that have already been prepared.

"Hey, could you help me cook something for Jaxon tonight from scratch? I'm going to make a lasagna. It's his favorite."

"Do you even know how to make a lasagna from scratch?" He places his hand on his hip, leaning into his left side, waiting for me to answer.

"No, but it can't be that difficult." I think about the items I've seen in the pantry, the ingredients I have to work with. "I'll make lasagna, salad, and garlic bread."

"Sure, girl. I got you."

I can't wait to see the expression on Jaxon's face when he finds out I made him dinner from scratch. Granny used to say the way to a man's heart was through his stomach. I honestly believe it's the other way around. Buy your woman the right snacks, keep them ready and at hand, and she'll love you forever.

I grab Nicky's hand and pull him towards the pool.

"But first, pool time." We run towards the pool as if we're in a race.

We slip off our clothes until we're standing in our swimsuits. I drop my sundress on the lounge chair facing the pool.

"Cannonball?" He wiggles his eyebrows.

"Um, no."

I watch as he eyes one of the floating rings in the pool that I blew up and placed in the pool before he got here.

"I think I can jump right into that ring."

Piling my hair high on my head, twisting it into a bun and wrapping my thick blue scrunchie around it, I look from him to the floatie. "You'll never make it."

"Have some faith." Nicky takes a few steps back from the edge of the pool and surveys the distance to the floatie. He moves from side to side as if calculating the angle that he needs to jump at. He's placed his left leg forward and shifts his weight back and forth. "Watch and learn."

The water is cold and sends shivers up my legs as it splashes me. Nicky makes it right into the floatie as predicted.

"Okay, okay, nice jump," I call out to him, my hand shielding my eyes from the sun. "Want your sunglasses?"

"Yes, please."

I grab my own and his from the lounge chairs and slowly enter the pool by way of the steps. When I reach the second floatie, I sit myself in the giant hole, legs dangling over edge. I paddle my way towards Nicky and hand him his glasses that were perched on my head.

## CHAPTER THIRTEEN

We spend the next hour chitchatting about everything under the sun, and when my stomach grumbles, I offer some snacks and drinks to Nicky.

We hop out of the pool and make our way to the kitchen.

Nicky suggests I prep the lasagna now while we're out of the pool so that we just need to pop it in the oven before Jaxon's due home.

We search the internet for the best and easiest way to make the lasagna, and when we're done, I suggest margaritas.

"Grab my drink, will you?" I ask as I pick up the tray of veggies and dip, tortilla chips, and salsa, and we head back outside.

Nicky reaches into his Make Me a Blond, B tote bag for his reusable water bottle and takes a sip after a helping of nachos.

"I brought us something," he announces.

My eyebrows raise. "What is it?"

I watch closely as he takes out a small box that's covered in three different shades of blue. "I am going to give you an oracle card reading," he says, shimmying his shoulders in excitement.

"What does that even mean?"

"Oh, Quinny babe, you've lived such a sheltered life."

He's not wrong.

He removes the cards from the box, and I lean forward trying to catch a glimpse of the front of the box while I dip another carrot in ranch dressing. On top of the blue box are multiple animals.

"Is this like a psychic reading?"

"It's a reading, but the animals on the cards will help us discover what's going on in your life. They'll tell you what you need to know."

"Got it. But it's not, like, real, right?"

"Quinny, girl, yes, it is. Now stop trying to analyze and just do as I say, alright?"

I watch as he knocks on the stack of cards. I don't question him, as to not break his concentration, because he honestly seems to be really zoned in.

"Okay, I'm going to do a three-card spread," he says as he shuffles the cards. "I want you to clear your mind and think of a question. You can tell me the question. Like, you don't have to, but I want to know. But, also, don't feel obligated." I laugh, and Nicky shushes me. "Concentrate."

I do as he says, and I close my eyes. When I've settled on my question, I say it aloud.

"Will Jaxon and I be together forever?"

"I forgot to mention, your question can't be a yes or no question."

"Huh?"

"Let me try to re-word it for you." He closes his eyes as he continues to shuffle the cards. "What do the cards need Quinn to know about her relationship with Jaxon?"

He places the cards down on the lounge chairs, and fans them out, telling me to choose three cards.

I pick three cards, turning them over as instructed.

"Oh, look, your first card is a spider."

"Ew, I hate spiders."

"Spiders are good. Okay, let me read the meaning behind it."

"Can't I pick a new one?" I ask, wincing at the hairy legs of the spider.

"You have the power to manifest your own destiny. As spiders weave their web, you are now in a position to create a life you want. You are in a time of building connections and co-creating a new beginning."

"Shut up," I shout at him.

"Seriously, Quinn, the cards know. Let's check your second card."

I lean back and rest my body against the raised back of the chair. I let my legs slide down so they can feel the warm sun.

"Okay, for your second card, you chose the owl. This card represents what you need to release and let go of."

I close my eyes and listen to Nicky's voice.

"The owl is known for its key abilities in seeing in the dark and beyond surface appearances. You are now in a time where it would best serve you to tap into your own wisdom. Let your intuition guide you as you release old patterns and judgments."

"Fuck," I say. "These hit so close to home."

Nicky goes on, ignoring my current revelation.

"Your third card represents what you need to focus on. The dolphin's energy can help release trapped emotions through joy and finding balance in your life. They are intelligent creatures known to be playful. The dolphin encourages you to find love, connection, and positivity."

"Wow, I can't believe how much these cards relate to my life."

"That's a pretty good reading you got, so now it's your job to listen to them. Here, keep these cards as a reminder for now, but I will want them back."

"Thanks, Nicky." I take the three cards and notice the spider one again. "You can keep this one." I try to hand him back the card, but he shakes his head.

"Nope, you need to remember these. Keep it."

I tuck the spider card between the owl and the dolphin and hold them to my chest.

"First things first, you heard the dolphin. You need to have more fun in your life. The last person in is a rotten egg."

I laugh as Nicky beelines towards the pool, landing in a belly flop. I wince, covering my own stomach at the pain he probably just felt.

"Get in here!"

I place the cards down beside the snacks, and this time instead of taking the steps one at a time into the pool, I run and jump into the deep end.

Maybe the cards are right. There's nothing wrong with having a bit more fun.

# Chapter Fourteen

## Jaxon

I walk into the house and go straight through to the back patio. "What the fuck?" I mutter and open the back patio door. The sounds of country fill the air and the laughter of a man who's far too close to Quinn for my liking.

A BFF, she said. What does she think I am, a fucking fool? I never should have let anyone into my home, my life. People will always disappoint you, no matter how hard you try to believe that they won't.

Fake wife not excluded.

Her head is back, face to the sun, legs spread across the tanned ones of a man whose face I can't see as she floats on a ring. He's floating on his own, holding a drink in one hand and resting the other on Quinn's ankle.

"What the fuck is going on here?" I ask. I'm instantly ignored due to the high level of bass coming from the pool house, and the fact that neither of them have yet to notice me since the rings have turned them to face the back of the yard.

My heart is pounding.

How fucking dare she?

I'm walking slowly up behind them, and I can't help but notice her tiny frame barely covered in small white triangles attached to a thin white string tied around her neck. If I wasn't so royally pissed right now, I'd stop and stare at how the sun is warming her skin, making it glisten. Or how tiny water droplets cover her arms and legs, and I can see faint goosebumps where the breeze is warming the drops caressing her skin.

But I'm not going to stand here and stare at my wife being just a bit too cozy with this stranger she's let into my home.

I pace for a few seconds behind them, and when the song comes to an end, I take the opportunity to make myself known.

"Quinn!" I holler and startle them both. They crane their necks, and I watch as the man uses his feet and hands to paddle himself around to face me, while Quinn is smiling at me, doing the same, eyes covered in large, oversized sunglasses, and nipples pressing against the thin fabric of the so-called swimming suit she must have bought with my fucking money. "Care to explain what you're doing?" I ask her again now that she is aware of my presence.

She raises her hand to her ear to let me know that she has not heard a single word that's come out of my mouth now that another song is piercing through the air from the pool house. I stomp angrily towards the sound and shut off the music. I'm about to ask if she's lost her goddamn mind bringing a man into my home when I hear her laugh and splash in the water.

"Jaxon, come meet Nicky," she yells out across the crystal blue water. She's let herself out of the ring and is swimming towards me.

Nicky.

Nicky, the hairdresser.

Nicky, the BFF.

You've got to be kidding me. She wants to introduce me to the man that she is so clearly into, who she was draping her legs over, who was touching her soft skin—skin I have yet to touch myself?

I stand at the pool's edge as she comes right up under me, placing her sunglasses on top of her head. She peers up at me in a way that has me wondering if this is what she'd look like down on her knees. Fuck, I'm being a giant pervert when I should be raging in anger right now, but the way her nipples are hard against the white triangles and her mouth open slightly and wet, her sun-baked shoulders dripping with water, I can't ignore the thoughts that are popping up in my head. "What is going on?" I ask, my voice hoarse. I cross my arms waiting for her to reply while my eyes narrow in at this *Nicky*.

There's a shift in both of them at my tone, and I can see him glance from her to me.

Damn right, you better be concerned.

"My God, Jaxon, cool it. This is *Nicky*."

"I can see *Nicky*." I nod at him. "But why the hell were your feet in his lap and his hands all over you?" I ask, throwing a death stare in his direction.

"Oh my god, dude, chill. I'm gay," Nicky tells me.

The tension in my jaw dissipates as shame, embarrassment, and guilt begin to gnaw at me. "Fuck me," I mutter, turning away from them.

The sound of water splashing around behind me has me wondering what's going on, but I'm not quite ready to face either of them while I'm standing here like an idiot trying to find the words to correct this situation.

When I finally turn, Nicky is coming up the ladder and walks right up to me in his canary-yellow swim trunks, which, as he gets closer, I notice have bananas scattered across them.

"I apologize," I begin.

He's dripping water only an inch from my oxfords and he puts his hand out at me, smiling awkwardly.

"Nicky, Quinn's new BFF, and also a hairstylist at Make Me a Blonde, B," he says. I pause before clasping hands and giving it a good shake. Before I can respond, he starts speaking again. "Quinn told me all about this." He waves his other hand between Quinn, who is still holding onto the pool ledge, and me, who is still standing here looking like a donkey.

I shake off the water from my hand and turn to Quinn. "If what you're referring to is that we are newlyweds, Quinn is right, we're fresh out of city hall." I answer, not wanting to reveal our marriage of convenience if Quinn hasn't unloaded her deepest secret to her new friend. We have to be careful about who we tell or it could ruin all my chances at getting the promotion.

"Newlyweds, right." Nicky's eyebrows raise as he glances at Quinn. "I better get going, Quinny."

He looks at me and says "Twinin'," and I stand there wondering what the hell he's talking about, but before I can answer, Quinn jumps in and explains how their nicknames sound the same.

"Sure, twinning," I repeat, nodding as if I understand, adding yet another word to my apparently limited vocabulary.

"You don't have to go, Nicky." She props herself up onto her elbows over the pool's edge, her legs swaying behind her under the water.

Nicky's already grabbing at one of the towels on the lounge chair. "I need to stop at the market before I head home, and it closes early. But I had so much fun, girl. Definitely have to do this again." He turns to me. "You have an amazing house."

I nod. "Thank you, and I apologize for the misinterpretation."

"I get it. 'Newlyweds'," he quotes again, this time using his actual fingers to follow through on his meaning. "Quinn is great. You better appreciate her," he tells me with a warning glare.

Quinn is watching our interaction quietly. I can't tell if she's upset with me for assuming she's been unfaithful. We did discuss in earlier days that this wasn't going to be an open marriage.

"I can let myself out," Nicky states as he pulls a shirt over his head and is tapping into his phone.

"Let me see if Henri's nearby, and he can drive you wherever you need to go."

"Really?"

I nod. "Of course, it's the least I can do." I shrug my shoulders and turn back towards the house.

"Girl, text me. And damn, you locked it in with a hottie."

I find myself smiling. I think I'm the one who's lucky and ended up with a hottie.

Sexy too.

"Okay, thanks for coming over, and I'm sorry about Jaxon's accusation. Want me to come with you and wait out front?"

I can hear her lowering her voice, but I don't miss one word.

"Not a worry, Quinny. Jaxon's got me. Bye!"

"Okay, I'll text you, bye!"

I'm waiting for them to finish their goodbyes as I text Henri.

After the black sedan pulls away, I make my way back to Quinn as she pulls herself out of the pool, not bothering to use the ladder. I watch the muscles in her thighs move as she stands up and walks towards me.

Seeing Quinn's skin all wet, her hair slicked back from the water, and the white fabric barely covering her, I'm done for.

I'm fucking done.

"That wasn't very nice of you, Jaxon. The first time I have someone over, and you pull the almighty ass card?"

"I'm sorry," I plead, glancing down at my feet.

"You're lucky Nicky's a good guy and this will roll right off his shoulders. That was embarrassing."

"I know, for both of us. I was an ass for not trusting you, Quinn. Just when I saw your legs all tangled up, I panicked." I place my hand over my chest, my heartbeat simmering down back to its normal rate of speed.

"Maybe you need to remind yourself that I committed to you, too. You might be up for promotion, but I have a lot riding on this marriage as well." She tells me as she pulls at the straps around her neck. I can see a faint tan line when the string settles down in a new place over her collarbone.

"You're right, and I'm sorry. I should have trusted you." I face the pool. "The water looks nice. I think I'll go for a swim myself after dinner."

"You could go right now," Quinn tells me.

"I'd rather wait," I say.

"Or maybe you should go right now," she repeats, "come in with me." Quinn dashes towards the pool and jumps in, water splashing onto my shoes. I shake my feet one at a time and take a step back.

"I don't have a suit down here."

"Strip down to your boxers and come in! The water feels so good."

I watch as she treads water, and I'm enticed to follow suit.

"Jaxon, come in here. Come on," she whines. "You owe me after scaring poor Nicky off."

Embarrassment plagues me.

"I'm not going in my underwear."

She laughs. "Then come in without. Either is fine with me."

I place my hands on my hips. "That's not what I meant, and you know it."

"Jaxon, come on, please?"

Fuck, this woman is pleading with me now. I watch her smile fade, and I find myself not wanting to disappoint her.

I walk back to the lounge chair where Nicky's wet towel is sitting and kick off my shoes, pulling my socks off next.

Quinn whistles, and I can't help but laugh.

This woman. My woman.

When I'm down to my black boxer briefs, I walk towards the deep end of the pool, Quinn's eyes never leaving me, and I dive in. When I come up beside her, she giggles, and I wipe the water from my eyes.

"Pass me that ring, I'm getting tired from treading water." Quinn nods towards the pink floatie beside me.

I grab her hand and pull her back towards me, my hands on her waist under the water, holding her up. "Is this okay?" I ask.

She nods yes and wraps her legs around my waist, her thighs squeezing me like I knew they would.

My legs are kicking under me to keep us afloat, and it feels so good to have Quinn this close.

"About what Nicky was saying...did you tell him?" I ask her.

"I hope that's okay. I just felt like I needed to tell someone, get it off my chest. I mean, I'm married, it's kind of a big deal, and I've made a friend, and I want to be honest with him."

I think about this for a moment. "You're right. You've made a friend here, and I'm happy for you. We just need to be careful who we tell. No one else, okay?"

"I understand, of course." She slithers closer to me, her tits now pressed against my chest.

I move my hands down her sides until they're cupping her ass, holding her steady on me as I move her towards the side of the pool. When we reach the side, I press her back up against the wall, and before I can decide what happens from here, she runs her index finger again over my scar.

Concern reveals itself to me, but only for a second, before she stops suddenly and grabs hold of my hair. A light groan escapes my lips before I can stop myself.

"Can I kiss you?" she asks quietly, tilting her head to the side in that innocent way that she does.

# Chapter Fifteen

## Quinn

Jaxon's breath is hot on my neck, sending shivers up my spine.

I know that I was rejected the first time, and I get it. My ego might have been bruised a bit, because no one likes to be rejected, but I seriously get why he did.

But there's something brewing between us now. There's a connection, a physical one at least, and I know he feels the same way. The way he pulled at me, the way my legs are tightly wrapped around him, holding him close, and the way his fingers dig into my skin is confirmation.

I watched him undress slowly, and I could see him debating whether to come join me in the pool, fighting it in his head, but in the end, he caved, and now my hands are in his hair, and his breath is on my neck.

You'd think I'd be reeling right now at the fact that Jaxon didn't trust me and thought I was two-timing him with Nicky. Not going to lie, I kind of liked that he got jealous. It means he might like me more than *this is just business*.

And why do I want him to like me more than just his fake wife? Because I like him.

Like, *like* him, like him.

I mean, he pisses me off the way he nags me at how I stack the dishwasher, or complains when I reheat dinner a little too hot, or grumbles when I leave wet footprints on the kitchen floor when I come into the house after being in the pool, but there's more to him than this controlling, tough exterior.

When I trace my fingertips over his scar, his eyes tell me a story, one that he has yet to share.

There's pain there, but I'm not going to push it. He'll tell me when he's ready. When he sees me as more than just his fake wife.

But right now, my legs are wrapped around his waist, my back is pressed against the side of the pool, and he's growing hard under me.

"Are you going to play hard to get?" I ask, adding a little distance between us even though my hands are still locked in his hair. His skin is doused with tiny droplets of water, and I've never seen anything sexier.

"I don't play games," Jaxon finally answers me.

The water feels cool, but the way it caresses our skin as we shift lightly is only enhancing this moment.

"No?" I ask, letting go of his hair, trailing my fingers over his damp arms, watching as his muscles flex underneath my touch. I study his expression, and notice the way his hair is clinging slightly to his face from the dive in.

He's closing in on me. You could barely fit a piece of paper between our mouths at this point, and yet we're still not touching, he is still not kissing me.

"I said no," he tells me again, a little more command in his voice this time, the serious, controlling side of him showing, and a part of me wants to hear him tell me that I've been a bad girl, and that I need to learn a lesson.

A hot one.

Holy cheese balls, what is *with* me?

This man is unleashing desires and thoughts that have never once crossed my mind before. I shake my head, trying to rid myself of these dirty thoughts, but since I have yet to get consent to place my lips directly on his, I turn my head and press my lips just below his ear. I can sense goosebumps rising on his skin as I pull away, just to plant another one an inch further down. I taste the subtle hint of chlorine, and I do this a few more times until I reach his shoulder, kissing, licking and nibbling in between, until I feel his chest is rising faster, and falling harder with each breath. When his thumbs press deeper into my waist, I know that these kisses aren't going unappreciated. I trail slowly back up to where I started, landing right below his ear.

Jaxon tilts my chin towards his, and I stare into his eyes, heat shooting through me. I don't know how long we stay in this position, locked in as the world fades to just us.

"Fuck, Quinn, you look so hot in this little white thing. I'm doing everything I can not to tear it right off you. When I saw your legs entangled in his, I was livid. These legs, these legs are *mine*. You're *my* wife." His grasp moves from my waist to my thighs as he says this, and I love the fact that he's claiming me.

A satisfied smile plants itself on my face, knowing that my fake husband wants me as much as I want him. All insecurities from our first night as husband and wife drift away.

My head tilts, ready for his mouth on mine, and I close my eyes, and then—the most annoying sound fires through the air around us.

We both snap our heads back, dazed from the heat that was building between us, and confused, blinking against the sunlight as we search the area, listening at the sound wailing in the air.

"Shit, that's the smoke alarm," Jaxon yelps, lifting himself out of the pool in seconds, and making a run for the house, grabbing a towel from the lounge chair on his way.

And it's in that moment I realize what I've done.

I've burnt dinner.

I run into the house and almost slip in a wet footprint of Jaxon's, but I manage to catch myself before falling onto the hard floor.

Jaxon is waving a dish towel around the room trying to silence the alarm. The burned lasagna is on the counter, smoke still rising from the pan.

I can't believe I forgot about the lasagna. I set an alarm... except I set it on Nicky's phone when I realized my phone was upstairs in my room.

Disappointment washes through me. I've just ruined our almost second kiss.

Shit.

I mutter a string of apologies and explain what happened with the timer on Nicky's phone and how I totally forgot about the lasagna. Trying to avoid Jaxon's eyes, I head towards the small closet to the side of the pantry and grab the mop to wipe up our wet footprints.

I'm just finishing when Jaxon's voice takes over some of the three hundred and fifty-two thoughts rattling in my brain.

"There's something about seeing your fake wife in a tiny white bikini mopping your floor," he says, laughing, and I smile, because I've only gotten to hear his laugh on a few occasions and it's one of my most favorite sounds.

"Oh, yeah?" I ask. "Is this your kink? I should have known when you were so insistent on me doing all the chores and cleaning," I joke back.

"Well, I didn't have a uniform in mind back then, but some ideas are coming to mind."

"I'm sure they are, and I'm well aware to where they're flowing to."

I tilt my head and drop my gaze towards his midline, causing Jaxon to erupt in more laughter, and I snort while trying to hold my own back. I cover my face with my palm as I set the mop to the side, resting it against one of the bar-height chairs.

Jaxon places both hands on the kitchen island in front of him, leaning forward.

"Don't do that," he says.

"Do what?" I pull myself up onto one of the chairs, and I lean my elbows onto the island. A cool chill now replaces the heat that was soaring through me before the damn burned lasagna ruined the moment. I settle onto the cold marble as I wait for Jaxon to continue his thought.

"Don't be embarrassed," he answers.

My cheeks flush knowing that Jaxon is starting to see me, that we're learning each other's quirks.

He comes around the counter, and I turn in my chair to face him. His long fingers tilt my chin up once more to his face, and for a moment, I think he is going to kiss me.

"You are beautiful," he says, and then picks up the mop, leaving me breathless.

Is it okay to like your fake husband like this? Does he like me as much as I like him?

Before I can analyze the compliment he just paid me, Jaxon says, "So, seeing that we're not having lasagna, what should we have for dinner?"

# Chapter Sixteen

*Jaxon*

"Stop fidgeting," I tell Quinn through my smile.

"I'm not," she whispers back.

We're hand in hand as we step away from the curb, Henri and the black sedan driving off.

She fidgets again, fixing her purse on her shoulder, tucking her hair behind her ear, and pulling at the side of her dress. She repeats these three motions our entire walk up towards the restaurant.

When we step inside, I stop and take her other hand in mine so I'm holding both and she can't find something else for her fingertips to play with.

Her expression softens, and I watch her shoulders relax as I rub my thumbs gently over the tops of her hands.

We've grown closer in the last few weeks since the whole pool and lasagna incident. I'm beginning to see Quinn for who she really is, and I'd be lying if I said I wasn't enjoying her company in the house.

She still can't stack a dishwasher for the life of her, and she still leaves the toilet seat up, which just sets off my OCD when I go in to use the washroom on the main floor.

"Close the damned lid to the toilet before you flush," I had said as I stormed out of the washroom one night.

"What does it even matter?" she had asked hotly, hands resting on her hips. She's fucking adorable when she stands her ground like this.

"When you flush the toilet, it sprays everything into the air." I motioned with my hands.

"Stop flinging your arms around, and no, it doesn't."

I stopped. "I don't do that."

She half laughs, but I can see she's still annoyed at my rant. "Yes, you do. And the stuff in the toilet does not fly into the air, you're paranoid," she insisted.

"Look it up," I suggested, tilting my head towards her phone sitting on the island.

"I don't get why you're being this way. Isn't it usually the woman who cares whether the seat is up or not? But you and the freaking lid, I don't get it."

"There's been studies, look it up," I told her once more. "And you don't even have a cap on your toothbrush to protect it, do you?" I said, and she cringed at the thought. "Exactly why you need to close the lid," I tell her more firmly, because germs are legit and it's just common sense.

"Fine, let me see."

I watched as she searched, and within a few minutes she had put her phone down and walked away saying nothing more than "Fine, I'll start closing the lid."

She disappeared for a solid fifteen minutes after the conversation, and I assumed that she had gone to scrub down her entire bathroom and replace her toothbrush with a new

CHAPTER SIXTEEN

one. I can't say if my assumption was completely accurate, but I did see a toothbrush package in the trash the next day.

I push back the memories and focus on Quinn. A few people have stepped around us, so I've tried to huddle us into the corner to have a bit of privacy before we meet Edward and his wife Carole for dinner.

"There's nothing to worry about," I try to soothe her.

Quinn's eyes wrinkle at the corners. "They're going to see right through us."

I lift her hands and notice how soft they feel against mine. This is the first time I've held them since our walk down the aisle after saying our I dos.

We almost kissed that day in the pool, and as much as I'm disappointed and want her wet lips on mine, it's good that we were saved by the burned lasagna.

I can't fuck this up.

With the retreat coming up, I need a clear head, and so does Quinn. We can't let whatever this is brewing between us get in the way, no matter how bad either of us wants it.

"We're fine, we got this," I say. "We've come up with a great, believable story on how we met, and we know the basics about one another. It'll be fine." I nod my head, and a small smile spreads across her face.

"We met while you were away at a conference last summer," she says, repeating our backstory.

"That's right."

"We did the whole long-distance thing, which is why you never mentioned me to anyone, and when it just became too hard to stay away from one another, we took the plunge."

"You got it."

"Okay, we got this. They'll believe it. They have to." She mumbles to herself, but I catch all the words that are slipping from between her lips. "Oh, Jaxon, I don't want to ruin this for you. So much is riding on this."

"Look at me." I squeeze her hands. "You are not going to ruin anything. We are just a loving man and his wife going to dinner, meeting his boss for the first time. We've been having dinner together every night since you arrived, there's nothing to fake. This is just another dinner."

"Just dinner, yeah, right," she says.

"Just dinner," I repeat.

I let go of one of her hands, and we approach the hostess. I nod. "Reservation for Edward Rummens."

"Of course, follow me."

Quinn plasters a smile on her face, the one she probably used when bartending. She appears anything but relaxed, but I have faith. I always win, and we will win at this too. We will have a nice dinner with Edward and his wife. Edward is going to love Quinn, I am going to get the promotion, and Brodie is going to go fuck himself.

That's the plan.

It's in the bag.

"Jaxon." Edward stands as we arrive at the table, and I shake his hand as he clasps me on the back.

I turn towards his wife. "Nice to see you again, Carole." We shake hands, and I tell her, "This is my wife, Quinn." My hand is planted on Quinn's lower back, the soft silk of her black dress smooth under my palm. I smile at her as pleasantries are made, and I realize that this is the first time I've introduced anyone to Quinn as my wife. I like how the sound rolls off my tongue.

Edward makes his way around the table, coming right up to Quinn. "We're not always a big bunch of stiffs, especially not after hours." He refuses her outstretched hand, and he pulls her in for a hug. "Jaxon's like family to us, which makes you family too. It's nice to meet the woman who stole his heart."

Quinn laughs at his jokes while we wait for our meals to arrive, and things are going well, really well. Carole and Quinn are making conversation, and I settle in for dinner when someone catches my attention.

Long, wavy, fiery-red hair, and a set of jade green eyes.

Fucking hell.

It's Casey.

Casey and I dated. No, Casey and I had an *arrangement* at one time last year, after the said conference where Quinn and I supposedly met. This is about to get ugly if Casey comes up to say hi.

I sigh, because of course, Casey is about to come up and say hi.

Now that she's spotted me, she doesn't seem to catch my look that pleads with her to turn and walk away.

Nope, within seconds, she's standing between Quinn and me.

"Jaxon, hi."

I turn to her. "Casey." I nod blandly. "Hi."

"Well, don't I get a hug?" she purrs, leaning onto the back of my chair, arching her back as she bends closer to my ear.

I glance towards Edward and Carole, whose eyebrows are raised.

I stand and hug Casey and turn to Quinn. "Casey, you remember Quinn?" I say, taking a shitload of a chance here.

I mentally beg Casey to wrap her head around what's going on. I turn to Quinn, also pleading for her to go along. Her eyes are wide, but within seconds she gathers herself and stands to greet Casey as if they're long-lost friends.

"Casey, hi. It's so great to see you again," she says with so much excitement. Casey flinches, and Quinn turns towards

Edward and Carole and puts on a show that makes me so proud to call her my wife. "Edward, Carole, this is Jaxon's... third cousin, right?" She turns to us both, waiting for confirmation. Her smile is tight, but her cheeks are swollen and rosy and she looks happy and unbothered.

I watch Casey stiffen under Quinn's embrace. She silently half smiles towards Quinn as they separate.

Edward and Carole both greet her with a smile and a nod.

"Um, hello," Casey replies, sending me quizzical daggers.

"It's so nice to run into you, Casey. Quinn and I are just having dinner with my boss here. Are you meeting someone?"

I turn my head, glancing through the other patrons of the restaurant, trying to find her an out before she says too much.

"Yes, as a matter of fact, I am," she replies, standing straighter, glancing around the room, she takes a step back. When she spots the person she's here to meet, she doesn't hesitate to turn and retreats from our table with nothing more than "Great, see you later."

Edward and Carole exchange glances and then face me.

"Third cousin. We've only met a few times in the last decade. We're not really a close-knit family.

Carole nods. "She seems sweet," she says.

I exhale a sigh of relief.

Our meals arrive shortly after, and the evening couldn't go any better. We're waiting for the bill to arrive when Edward speaks up.

"Now, Jaxon, I couldn't help but notice that beautiful diamond on Quinn's left finger, but her wrist is bare."

I'm trying to think quickly on my feet but find no words to explain why Quinn wouldn't already have an Edward Rummens watch on her wrist.

Shit, why didn't I think of buying Quinn a watch?

Quinn speaks up before I can come up with a response.

"Oh, Edward, Jaxon has been begging to take me to your new store on Kensington Drive, and we actually have plans to go there later this week."

How the hell did she know about Kensington?

"That's great to hear." Edward is beaming. "Kensington was Jaxon's idea."

Quinn turns towards me. "I didn't know that, Edward. Jaxon keeps his wins so close to his heart, doesn't like to brag."

"Jaxon has always kept to himself; I don't doubt that one bit."

I nod my thanks and turn to Quinn. "I was going to tell you about it when I brought you there to pick out your watch." I smile at her and watch her baby blues sparkle back at me. "I will finally get an Edward Rummens on this tiny little wrist of yours," I say, taking her hand in mine and rubbing my thumb over the top of her wrist.

She's beaming back at me. "Can't wait."

The bill arrives, and I finish off my own gin and tonic as Edward hands over his card to the waiter.

When we step into the sedan after Henri has picked us up, Quinn lets out a cackle, the kind that ends with her snorting. I watch her face twist into a wicked smile, and her breathing slows down as she leans into me in the back seat.

I put my arm around her without a second thought, and she snuggles into me.

"I can't believe we just got away with that."

"I told you we had it in the bag."

I sound cocky, arrogant even. I'm not naïve, but like I told Quinn a few weeks ago, I'm here to win. But that didn't stop the panic I felt in my chest when I spotted Casey in the restaurant, and I tell Quinn that.

"I thought Casey was going to out us. You were amazing, jumping in and coming up with that third cousin story."

She sits up straighter so she can turn and face me.

"I think I freaked her out when I hugged her." She laughs. "I kind of felt bad." She turns and fidgets with her dress again.

"What is it?" I ask.

"So, Casey, were you two, um, like dating?"

I knew this question would come up at some point. "No, not dating." I think about how to answer this best. "We just... spent time together here and there," I say, and Quinn nods, understanding.

"Then I guess that really could have gone bad."

"It could have, a hundred percent, but lucky for me, it didn't."

"Lucky for us," she corrects me.

"For us," I repeat. That's right. We're a team. "How the hell did you know about Kensington, though?"

"Come on, Jaxon, do you think I'd fly halfway across the country to marry a man I know nothing about?"

Give a woman the internet and a name, and she'll become a private detective within minutes.

# Chapter Seventeen

## Quinn

I have bags all over the floor of my walk-in closet. Jaxon went on and on about how I needed more clothes, especially with the retreat coming up, so Nicky and I went shopping, and now I think I've got everything I need.

My lingerie is put away in the small drawers, shoes are on display, and my pants are hanging on their respectable hangers.

But these freaking blouses won't stay on the damn hangers. The silk of the light blue blouse I just hung up slides slowly down the sides of the hanger, falling onto the closet floor in a puddle.

Velvet hangers.

I need some of those fancy soft velvet hangers I saw at Urban Goods last week.

The decision is made for me as I watch two other blouses follow suit into a pool of silk on the floor.

Leaving the blouses right where they are, I grab my bag and head towards the kitchen.

I text Henri and get no reply. He must be driving Jaxon somewhere. Jaxon left earlier for work than usual this morning, something about a meeting on location. I'm pacing the kitchen wondering if I should call an Uber when a thought crosses my mind.

Heading towards the small kitchen closet, I open the door and the mop falls out. I push it back into the cabinet and turn to the left where a small box is sitting on the wall, the box that holds the key to the pool house.

I open it up, not sure what I'm looking for. Jaxon has never spoken about a car before, so I don't know why I'm in here searching for a set of car keys when I haven't even been in the three-car garage.

That's when I see it. A key fob with a small picture of an open lock, a closed lock, and a horn in red on a small black ring.

Bingo.

It's like I've just scratched the last number on a lottery ticket revealing a prize. A prize with four wheels and leather seats, no doubt.

Before I can question the decision to take the keys without consent from Jaxon, I head towards the door off the entrance way. I stand and stare at it and wonder why the hell I've never asked to see the garage, or why Jaxon never bothered to show it to me.

Jaxon always has Henri drive him everywhere, so I just assumed the garage was filled with guy stuff. It's not like Jaxon seems like the kind of man with a work bench, tools, or a beer fridge and a ping-pong table, but the thought of what's in the garage never once occurred to me.

A random thought pops up in my head, and suddenly I'm wondering if I should be scared to find out what's behind this door.

What if there's a padded room holding a single mattress and cameras?

A freezer full of dead bodies?

But before I can think of any other horrifying things that might be behind this thick white door, I turn the unlocked handle and swing it open and gasp.

The garage is in pristine shape. A forest-green bicycle with accessories is to the far left. A deep freezer chest is along the wall of the house, and I take a quick peek inside just to make sure there are no frozen bodies. I'm pleasantly surprised when I see it stacked with chocolate-covered popsicles and an insane number of brown bananas.

Someone needs to make some banana bread.

Closing the freezer, I turn to what originally caught my eye.

The shiniest yellow sports car that I have ever come across, and it's gorgeous.

I don't know cars, but I do know that this is one that I want to sit in.

I walk towards the gold chrome rims in the center of clean black tires. I trail my fingers along the yellow metal, the tinted windows revealing nothing. When I get to the driver's side door, I press the unlock button on the fob, and reach for the car door, pressing the small button that's just below the handle when it doesn't open automatically.

The two-tone leather seats have yellow stitching on the side, and I run my hand over the soft material and inhale new car smell. I wonder how long this car has been sitting here, and why Jaxon doesn't ever drive it.

I allow my body to slink into the seat behind the wheel. When I see the manual transmission, I silently thank Mom for teaching me to drive stick when I was sixteen. My old beater was also a stick, so I can drive this car.

I step my new cream-colored four-inch heels back onto the pavement of the garage and walk straight to the garage door opener on the wall beside the door to the house. Without hesitation, the dark garage door in front of the car opens. I make sure that I have my keys and phone and then lock the door to the house behind me.

Jaxon is my husband, so this wouldn't be stealing. Or even borrowing. It'd be nothing more than driving my husband's car to the Urban Goods to get some hangers for my closet.

When I'm seated back in the car, I close the door, buckle up, and then press the start button. I drop the sunglasses I've been wearing on top of my head and shift them over my eyes. I adjust the seat, mirrors, and steering wheel until they're perfect, and I listen to the hum of the car as I let myself out of the garage and into the driveway.

Damn, this is a nice car. Jaxon's been holding out on me.

Ignoring the display screen wanting to connect my phone, I open the windows to let in a breeze as I feather the clutch and turn right onto the street.

Forty minutes later, I'm pulling into a parking spot. My hair is windblown, but I couldn't care less. The smile on my face hasn't faltered since I sat my ass in this bucket seat.

Not only is this car my favorite color but the sounds that came from this car as the engine revved sent a rush of adrenaline through me.

I step out of the car and lock the door, but before I make my way into Urban Goods, I pat at my hair and take a selfie, making sure I've got as much of the car as I can in the photo behind me, and send it to Alysha and Nicky.

## CHAPTER SEVENTEEN

When I've walked through the entire store, and my cart is stacked with hangers along with a few other essentials, I steer towards the checkout area.

I pay for my items and tilt the passenger seat to stuff my belongings in the back before getting in on my side. My phone vibrates in my bag, and I take it out to read the replies from Alysha and Nicky.

> Alysha
> **Girl! Seriously?**
>
> Nicky
> **Quinny, come pick me up!**

I laugh at their messages and respond to Alysha before calling Nicky.

"You working?" I ask when Nicky picks up on the first ring.

"What I'm doing is wondering why you're not in my driveway right now!"

"Ha! I'm on my way."

Nicky lives close to Make Me a Blonde, B, so when it takes me twice as long to get there than anticipated, I finally understand the traffic Jaxon warned me about. But sitting in this little ray of sunshine, my mood can't falter.

When I arrive at Nicky's house, he's standing outside waiting for me. "Get in." I wink and watch his mouth drop open as he opens the door.

"Jaxon bought you a car? Your lasagna must have been like really, really good. That, or have you guys finally forked?"

"Forked, really, Nicky? And oh my God, I can't believe I forgot to tell you about the lasagna," I say as I check my reflection in the mirror. "I burned it."

"No!" Nicky buckles up.

"Yes, the smoke detector went off and everything. The timer was on your phone," I remind him.

"Oh, shit, that's right. It went off while I was at the market, and I silenced it without thinking twice. I figured you were probably already out of the pool."

"Nope, I convinced Jaxon to come in."

"And..."

I pull out onto the street when it's safe and turn left, heading towards the outskirts. I've been meaning to ask Jaxon to take me for a little more sightseeing, but he's always working, and I haven't wanted to bother him.

"We almost kissed, but then the smoke detector went off and that was it."

"That's it? If I had a man as hot as Jaxon, I would have planted my lips on him ages ago. What's taking you so long, Quinn?"

"Wait, it's weird for you to say my name like that."

"Quinn?"

"Yeah, you're saying Quinn instead of Quinny, like I'm in trouble."

He rolls his eyes and smirks. "Come on now, Miss Quinn, tell me why you have not kissed your husband?"

I take a sharp left and roll the windows back down when we get on Highway 972. We're driving adjacent to the ocean, and the beats of my heart speed up thinking about kissing Jaxon.

I don't know why I haven't. I have wanted to. God, have I wanted to. I still think about my body pressed against his, my legs wrapped firmly around his waist in the pool. When we're around each other and close, the thoughts that consume me are wild.

"It just hasn't come up again. I'm not going to force it. I'm here for the long haul, so it'll happen when it's meant to, *if* it's meant to. And by long haul, I mean eighteen months. Well, less now, actually." The thought that time is now ticking leaves me feeling a little sad. But today is not the day to worry about that. I'm with one of my best friends in a gorgeous sports car driving next to the ocean. What more could a woman ask for?

"Well, I've seen you in your white bikini, and you have a fine ass, even if it does nothing for me, but Jaxon? He's probably aching for you, if you know what I mean. He must have blue balls by now."

"Nikolas!"

"Hey, don't full-name me." He shrugs his shoulders and turns on the music. "I mean, I'm just saying. Take that man to bed already."

"Yeah, yeah." I shrug him off.

"So, where are we going?" he asks.

"Wait, look over there." I point to a big sign and a parking lot full of cars. "Let's stop here."

Before we even get out of the car, the sounds of barking dogs, small and large, sound through the ocean air.

"It's a pet adoption festival." Nicky reads the sign overhead. "National Adoption Week."

I squeal with delight. "I've always wanted a cute little puppy."

We head towards small white fences that surround little puppies in the grass.

"Would you like to go in and pet some of the dogs?"

My head turns towards the voice.

"Can I? I would love that," I reply.

We're let into the small area with a litter of Pomeranians.

"My apartment is too small to have a puppy, but I wish I could adopt one." The puppy that Nicky has picked up is licking his cheek, sending him into a fit of laughter. "It tickles."

I wander around the Pomeranians, bending down and caressing their fur with my hand when I spot her. The cutest little ball of fur I have ever laid eyes on. When I pick her up, she yaps lightly and pants. It's as if she's smiling at me, and my heart melts.

"Cuteness overload. Oh, Nicky, I want her." I watch his face crinkle as the puppy he's holding licks his cheek once more.

"You should totally get her. You spend a lot of time at home alone. It's just what you and Jaxon need to bond over. A little fur baby."

"Jaxon and I are bonding just fine. Plus, don't you know that kids aren't the answer to fix relationships? Not that Jaxon and I need fixing," I say in a rush, because we don't, and that's me being completely honest. Our relationship is working fine just as it is. It's business, I try and remind myself.

"I know you don't need fixing, blah, blah, you're happy not boning," he says, and I roll my eyes. "But it wouldn't hurt to have a little something you can both take care of together. That's all I'm saying."

"You're right. I've always wanted one, and now I have the time and space for her to run around outside."

## CHAPTER SEVENTEEN

The worker, whose name tag says Jill, returns.

"So, are you both sold on adopting a Pomeranian? I'd be happy to explain our adoption program to you."

Nicky places his little one back on the soft green grass where we watch her run around with the others, yapping happily.

I stand a bit taller. "I would love to hear more."

"Fantastic. Why don't you follow me and I'll tell you all about our organization and as much as I can tell you about that little one." She nods towards the beautiful dark blonde furball I just set back down.

I bend down and whisper lightly to her.

"I'll be back for you, I promise." We follow Jill out of the enclosed dog area, and I grab Nicky's hand. "Do you think Jaxon will be okay if I adopt a puppy?"

"Quinn, who doesn't love dogs, especially a little one like that?"

"You're right, how could he not love her?" I push any worries out of my mind and sit across from Jill at one of the folding tables where she tells me everything I need to know.

# Chapter Eighteen

*Jaxon*

I'm pacing the driveway in front of the open garage door.

I've called Quinn eight times. Eight fucking times. I've texted her a string of messages with no response since Henri dropped me off precisely one hour and fourteen minutes ago.

When we rolled up the driveway, my first thought was that the garage had been broken into, but with no Quinn in sight, I can only assume she found the keys to my sports car.

I've been a rollercoaster of emotions since, bouncing from anger to fear to worry.

How could she just help herself to the keys to my car without asking?

She had no fucking clue that I had a car, so why would she just take it without asking me?

A part of me was angry. I wondered if this was her plan all along, which had me up in her room, checking to see if her things were still there.

When I saw the chaos of her closet, my heart sank. Had she been packing up her things and then left in a hurry before I got home from work?

I had an early meeting this morning at the Kensington store and left earlier than usual, only sending Quinn a message that I would be home in time for dinner.

But dinnertime has come and gone, and Quinn is nowhere in sight.

I found her bags, among other things that have helped push those thoughts away, but I can't help the tightness in my chest at the thought of losing Quinn.

This house would feel empty if our marriage came to an end. I can't even begin to process how I'll feel in a year's time, but my focus right now is today.

And today, I need Quinn home.

But the minutes are ticking by on my watch, and once I'd convinced myself that Quinn hasn't made me out to be a fool, I started worrying.

Like I said, a roller coaster of fucking emotions.

The car has a manual transmission, and I know Quinn had a car back home, one she said was an old beater, so it has me worried if she can handle a twin-turbocharged V8 engine.

Beads of sweat form at my hairline as the early evening sun still beams down hotly. I have yet to change out of my suit, and my body is starting to warm underneath the expensive fabric.

I walk back into the garage, taking off my suit jacket and rolling up the sleeves to my white button-down. I'm just placing them on the closed freezer when I remember the chocolate popsicles that are in there. I take one out and tear open the wrapper. When I take the first lick of the popsicle, my thoughts are brought back to last year and my wisdom teeth.

My phone vibrates, and I immediately think of Quinn and hope to hell she hasn't been in an accident, but I sigh when I see it's just an email coming through. I walk back outside, popsicle in hand.

Goddamn, this is why I don't get attached.

I hear the roar of the engine as the car comes into view and see blonde curls blowing around her perfect little face, wearing a smile so big it pulls at my heartstrings and my belt. Fuck, she looks hot as hell behind this much horsepower.

When she spots me, I see concern wash over her and wonder what a sight I must be standing here in the middle of my driveway, in my suit, licking a melting chocolate popsicle.

She turns off the ignition, and our eyes lock. Heat plows through me, and it's not just the high temperature the weatherman forecasted.

I walk towards the driver-side door and take my free hand to open it. Her smooth legs are the first to exit the car, and that shiny ankle bracelet sparkles in the sun.

"Have a nice time?" I ask, not revealing the 400-foot roller coaster my heart just stepped off now that she's home safe. When I first noticed the car missing, I was pissed. When I thought Quinn had left, I was terrified. Now that she's home, I'm surprised that I'm able to let things go and want to hear about her day.

What in the actual fuck is happening to me?

"Um, I borrowed your car," she says, as if I wasn't already aware. Quinn appears nervous, and with a train wreck of emotions running through me, I pull her into a hug.

"It's your car now too," I say as I let her go and lick my popsicle. Her eyes follow my mouth as it lands at the top. "But do you have any idea how worried I've been?"

"Worried? Why?" Her head tilts.

## CHAPTER EIGHTEEN

"Quinn, you helped yourself to the keys of a car you knew nothing about. I had no fucking idea that you knew how to drive standard."

"Well, I do," she says with a bit of sass, her wall sliding up a little between us.

"But I didn't know that, and this car is *fast*. I was worried when you weren't here, without even a note telling me where you were, and you weren't answering your phone."

I'm just about done with my popsicle when I hear a bark, and I freeze, panic-stricken.

"What the fuck was that?" I ask.

"I actually have a surprise for you." She smiles, but I can see she's hesitant to tell me what it is now that she sees my body go rigid.

A dog barks again, and I drop the rest of the popsicle I was holding onto the pavement beside me.

My right hand leans onto the hood of the car as Quinn makes her way to the passenger side. Leaning down, peering into the dark space, my heart stops. I'm staring at a *dog*. There's a dog in my car prancing across the leather seat as if it owns the fucking thing.

I stand up straight and peer over the roof of the car at Quinn as she opens the passenger door.

"Tell me, Quinn, why is there a dog walking about inside my goddamn sports car?"

Fear fills me, taking over my emotions as she comes around towards me, the dog wiggling in her arms.

Sweat threatens to drip down my forehead, my heart is beating faster than it should, and I'm just fucking standing here, my eyes blurring. The space around me seems to teeter. I think I'm having a panic attack.

"I haven't given her a name just yet. I thought we could come up with one together."

My breath is short, but I manage to bark out a reply. "Why would we name her, and why is she here?"

"I adopted her."

"You did what?" My tone is harsh, but I can't seem to focus on anything but the fear that's unraveling me. I pinch the skin between my eyebrows.

The smile on her face sizzles as she sees my panic-stricken one. I walk towards the house before she can answer, and I can hear her following close behind.

"Wait, Jaxon, where are you going? What's wrong?"

I spin around as I enter the space where my car used to sit.

"Why would you adopt a dog without telling me, without asking me first?"

"I don't need permission to have a pet," she says. "But I thought you'd be happy. Honestly, Jaxon, why are you acting this way?"

My fingers run over my scar at the memory of that terrifying day when I was attacked by the dog. I haven't been near one since, and I sure as hell don't plan on living with one.

"She's not staying here."

"Yes, she is." Quinn comes closer, and I back towards the freezer. "Give her a chance."

I grab my suit jacket and walk into the house, slamming the door behind me.

## CHAPTER EIGHTEEN

I pace the length of my bedroom until the walls feel like they're closing in on me. I decide to go swim laps, something I've been doing for years when I've needed to let off steam.

What was she thinking adopting a dog without asking me?

Quinn isn't aware of my past, and I was a bit of an ass, more than I should have been, but fuck, who springs a dog on someone like that?

I run my hands through my wet hair, slicking it back before hopping out of the pool. That little fluffy beast is inside my home, prancing around, happy as fuck.

*Our* home, I need to remember that.

Of course Quinn has a right to want a dog, and damn, she deserves to have one. But aren't these the kinds of things a married couple would talk about first?

What the hell do I know? I married Quinn to get a promotion. I am not experienced enough to set a bar for what is right and what isn't.

When I locked eyes with that little monster, I panicked, and then all common sense and emotional maturity flew out the window.

I decide to take a quick shower in the pool house to rinse off the chlorine. I strip out of my striped swim shorts and hang them on the nearby hook, turning the water to a warmer temperature.

I squeeze some of the shampoo from the bottle that sits on the shower rack and lather it in my hands. When it's the perfect consistency, I add it to my hair and scrub at my scalp. Once I've scrubbed, lathered, and rinsed, I stand under the steaming shower and think about Quinn.

This woman has turned my life around, twisted it inside out, and irritated the hell out of me. Her blonde curls and wide smile have pulled me in.

But then this dog.

I shake my head, trying to figure out what to do. Do I try to convince her to get rid of the puppy?

Fuck, I'm not a cold-hearted prick.

Well, that might be debatable, depending on who you ask.

That puppy was one of the cutest ones I've seen, but that could be because I've been intentionally dodging them for years and there's nothing to compare it to.

I turn off the water, and that's when I hear the sound that makes my balls involuntarily contract. Before I can grab for the towel, Quinn is walking by the pool house and the door is wide open.

The enclosed glass shower does nothing to shield my naked ass, not only from Quinn but to the yapping cotton ball of a dog.

I hear her talking to the puppy, but she makes no note of me in here. I stay quiet, not wanting her to witness my shriveled-up prunes.

I grab my towel and wrap it around my waist, and I watch the little four-pawed diva bouncing around at the end of a hot pink leash.

It's a girl. And now I'm outnumbered in my own goddamn house.

Our house.

When I come outside, Quinn is still talking to the puppy, walking her around, giving her a tour.

"I'll just put on some clothes and meet you in the kitchen, say in twenty?" I suggest when she catches my eye.

"Yeah, no problem. Take your time. We'll continue our walk."

I head into the house and up to my room, where I pull on a pair of grey sweatpants, a white T-shirt, and a ball cap.

I'm down in the kitchen in about ten. Quinn isn't here yet, so I drive the car back into the garage. I lean my head

## CHAPTER EIGHTEEN

back against the headrest. My hands run up and down each side of the steering wheel, and I remember what it was like when I first bought this car. I loved taking it on the highway, oceanside, windows down, and music up on the weekends or as the sun was setting. Then work got busy, and it made more sense to get a driver so that I could get some work done while stuck in traffic.

I pull myself out from behind the steering wheel and shove those memories to the back of my brain.

When I walk back to the kitchen, Quinn still isn't there, but then I hear her call me from the rec room, where we've been hanging out and watching movies at night.

We found out we're both into whodunits after I told her all about the book I was reading when we first started talking online. We've been watching every movie we can find.

I stop short when I see Quinn sitting in her spot on the right, because she told me she always has to be on the right at all times, and in her arms is the tiny Pomeranian. I watch as she gives her a peck on top of her head.

The dog is literally smiling, and seeing Quinn smile right back at her has me tripping.

Wincing at the dog, I say, "We need to talk."

# Chapter Nineteen

## Quinn

There is over six feet of man standing before me, and a good 34 inches of that is covered in grey sweatpants. Grey sweatpants.

And not only is Jaxon wearing *grey* sweatpants, but he's also got on a plain white T-shirt that looks to have been melted over his thick shoulders, and a baseball cap. The shirt shows off his muscular shoulders and back from all the laps he swims, and the grey sweatpants, well—you know.

It's like the prim and proper businessman turned gym bro, and I'm here for it.

Good Lord, the man is hot.

And now he wants to have a talk when he's looking like that?

"Talk?" I ask, clearing my throat. I set Puppy on my lap who walks back and forth until she settles on a spot and lies down across my legs. Jaxon is hovering behind the back of the couch. "Come sit." I pat the space beside me.

## CHAPTER NINETEEN

He settles at the other end of the L-shaped sofa, as far from me as he can, and within seconds he stands again and starts pacing behind the couch.

"So, the thing is…" His palm runs down his face as he turns away from me. His shoulders hunch slightly, pulling the damn white shirt tighter.

"What is it?" I press.

"I'm scared of dogs." His arms fold over his chest, his shirt pulling at the width of his biceps, and I'm doing everything I can to keep my eyes focused on what he's just told me.

I suddenly realize how inconsiderate I've been. "I'm sorry, Jaxon, I didn't know." Jaxon's fingertips trace the scar that's mostly hidden by his facial hair, the one that you can't see unless you're close enough to feel his breath on you. "Did something happen?"

He bows his head. I pet the puppy to keep her in place. The last thing I want is for her to pounce off this couch and start yapping at Jaxon's feet and traumatize him further.

"When I was twelve, a dog attacked me."

My hand flies up to my mouth. "Oh my God. I'm so sorry. That must have been really scary for you."

"Yeah, it was." He sits on the armrest at the very end of the couch, as if planning a quick escape, and sneaks a peek at the unnamed puppy in my lap. "This is the closest I've been to a dog since that day. I'm sorry, I lost my cool, I panicked. The last thing I expected you to bring home was a dog."

"Jaxon, don't— no, it's fine. To be honest, I was expecting you to be a bit more pissed that I took your car without telling you."

"I was at first. But then I got scared you had just left entirely, and then that fear turned into worry about your safety."

Jaxon was worried about me, waiting for me to return home, scared that I'd left or been hurt, while I didn't have a care in the world as to how he was going to feel about me getting a puppy.

I feel like I've been a shit wife. A shit fake wife.

"I'm sorry I took your car, and I'm even more sorry that I didn't ask if it was okay to get a dog." I pause and turn my attention to the dog. "Do you want to tell me what happened?"

He tells me how he jumped between his best friend's mom and the dog, how the kids at school wouldn't even look at him when he had that big red scar on his face, too young to grow facial hair to cover it up. I ache thinking about what it must have been like for him growing up after having gone through that. And now I get why Jaxon is the way he is.

"What do you want to do?" I motioned to the dog in my lap.

"I want to... try," he says, wincing slightly.

"Are you sure? She has quite an excitable little personality."

He nods and stands, debating his next step. Puppy is fast asleep, her eyes closed in my lap. Jaxon inches close enough to reach the tip of his fingers in some of the fur that's standing up on her back.

"Okay," he says, stepping back. "That's enough for now."

"One day at a time?" I ask.

"That's a sound idea." He settles back down on the other end of the couch, although I can see he's nervous and not completely at ease. "I found another whodunit movie, wanna watch?" he asks me hesitantly.

"Do you even need to ask? But I've been dying to know: why do you have so many boxes of chocolate popsicles in your freezer, and can I have one?"

Jaxon laughs lightly and turns the TV on, scrolling through the apps until he finds what he was searching for.

"I got my wisdom teeth out last year and went a little overboard."

He stands, careful to not wake the sleeping puppy, and comes back minutes later with two popsicles, the wrappers already removed. I take one from him and notice how Jaxon's eyes don't leave my mouth as I have my first lick.

"So, how was the ride?" He gets comfortable on the couch, but still far enough away that I could spread my legs out across the seat and wouldn't even come close to touching his thigh. He glances warily at the puppy in my lap.

"I loved every single second of it."

"It's yours anytime you want."

"Seriously?" I'm beaming. I got a new little puppy and a yellow sports car all in the same day. I try to contain my excitement so I don't wake this ball of fur.

Jaxon laughs lightly.

"What's mine is yours. Plus, you look good in it."

This new gym bro version in grey sweatpants and a ball cap sends sparks of electricity through me, sparks that I don't think will fizzle out with a cold shower.

"Bitsy."

"No! How about Chloe?"

"We can't call her a *person* name," Jaxon says, shaking his head, laughing.

We've been going back and forth for a solid ten minutes, and we can't come up with a name we both agree on for the puppy.

It's been almost three weeks since I adopted this little bundle of joy that made me a dog mom, and I thought I was being neglectful for calling her Puppy, so I sat Jaxon down and told him we're not getting up until we decide on a name. Puppy is sitting in his lap and he's stroking her fur, while I sit next to them on the navy-blue patio furniture.

If someone had told me I would never see anything hotter than Jaxon in his grey sweatpants and a ball cap, I wouldn't have believed them. But here he is, facing his fears and petting Puppy, and my gosh, it's doing it for me.

The transition wasn't exactly an easy one. Puppy is quite dramatic and always needs to be held or on our laps, and Jaxon doesn't particularly like when his socks go missing after he's laid out his clothes before his morning swim or workout. Each morning he'd come back from his shower to dress for work, and his socks would be gone. We've only just found her secret stash behind the couch cushion.

We went out and bought a few more puppy necessities, including her own bed and pet stairs for the couch and my bed. Jaxon thought it would be best that he close his door at night, as he's not quite at the point where he wants to be startled by her in the middle of the night.

But he's doing amazing. After I got ready for bed that first night, I searched high and low on my phone for the best way to help Jaxon. Exposure therapy seems to be working. After the first few days, I was honestly worried we would have to rehome her. Jaxon was in a constant state of anxiety, but he seems to have gotten used to her, and he makes sure not to make any sudden movements to scare her so as not to scare him too.

He holds her in small doses, and I respect the time he is taking to get comfortable again.

I take in the full moon that is lighting up the backyard, and it comes to me. "Luna?"

Jaxon looks at her. "Luna. I think I like the sound of that. How do you like it?" He's talking to Puppy. "Do you want to be called Luna?"

It's in that moment that Puppy, now Luna, yaps, as if agreeing to the name.

"Luna it is." I take a sip of my tea and smile as Jaxon strokes her fur.

# Chapter Twenty

*Jaxon*

One large suitcase, two duffel bags, and a backpack.

That's what I'm stuffing inside the backseat of the yellow sports car that Quinn insists we take to the retreat.

"Be careful, I have shoes in there," she says over my shoulder, watching me like a hawk. For someone who only had one pair of canvas sneakers when she arrived, Quinn has really taken to shopping. But that was all part of the deal, and I love spoiling her.

"We need to make a stop on Kensington Drive," I say as I straighten and stretch out my back after being bent in half for the last ten minutes trying to make everything fit.

Quinn clasps her hands together. "Is today the day?" she asks.

"Today's the day. Let's get something pretty for that tiny little wrist of yours. I need everyone to know how serious I am about you, and when Edward sees you sporting something from his newest collection, he'll be thrilled." I take her hands in mine. "Plus, you deserve something beautiful."

"I can't wait to see your store."

"It's not mine," I remind her as I open the door for her to slide into the passenger seat.

"Sure it is. It's your concept."

I walk around to the driver's side, and when I'm settled and I start the car, we both wave to Nicky, who's holding Luna like a baby by the front door.

"Are you sure Nicky doesn't mind taking care of Luna for the week?"

"I promise you, Nicky doesn't mind one bit." She buckles herself into the seat and turns towards me. "He hasn't stopped talking about how he can't wait to float in the pool every night after work. Plus, he seems to have his eye on the gardener, so I'm pretty sure he will be soaking up some rays every chance he gets."

I chuckle at that.

"Well, it's great that we have someone to watch her." We've only had her about six weeks, but I have made a complete 180 since the evening Quinn showed up with her. I've fallen in love with that little furball. Luna yaps as we back out of the driveway. "I hope Nicky will be able to handle her. She's got so much energy."

I place my hand on Quinn's knee, and she looks at me with her bright smile and rests her hand on top of mine.

It would appear that I am now dating my wife.

What an odd thing to say, but it does seem to have come to that.

I can't ignore the fondness I have for Quinn. There's been some hand grazing and flirtatious banter. She's been nestling into me as we watch our movies at night, and I enjoy wrapping my arm around her, holding her close enough that I can smell the aromatherapy shampoo she uses and feel her side boob resting against my chest.

Edward Rummens Watches is about forty minutes away, so Quinn connects her phone and turns up the music after she opens the windows.

We sit in a comfortable silence for the rest of the drive, and when we arrive, I pull into one of the reserved parking spaces.

I put the car in park and turn off the engine. I circle back to meet Quinn on the passenger side and open her door. I grab her hand as we walk up to the front entrance and enter the store.

A sales associate beams from behind the counter. "Welcome to Edward Rummens Watches."

I nod in response and take Quinn to the first glass case of watches.

"Have your pick."

"I can choose any watch I want?" Her voice is animated, and she presses her right hand to her chest. She leans over to look at the watches through the glass, grinning from ear to ear.

"I recommend one from the latest collection. They're over there." I point to the lone case standing in the center of the store, with six watches on display.

Her hips sway in the soft yellow linen dress she wore today, landing right above her ankles. She pushes a dainty strap back into place as she stops in front of the watches.

"These are beautiful," she whispers softly.

"They sure are. Would you like to try one on?" the sales associate, wearing the name tag Allie, asks.

I see her eyeing the last one on the left, so I nudge her. "Try it on."

She points. "That one."

## CHAPTER TWENTY

I watch as Allie takes out the watch and slides it over Quinn's wrist.

The watch sparkles with multiple shades of blue sapphires mixed with diamonds along the outer edges of the dial. The modest 34 mm watch has supple, round curves, and the soft leather strap comes complete with a matching gold buckle.

"This phoenix blue watch is part of a set. It's also available in a 40 mm watch with features that are a little more on the masculine side." She points to the one that Edward had recommended a few weeks ago.

"We should get matching watches," Quinn suggests, and my mouth pulls into a grin.

Matching watches with my wife, the woman I'm trying to date, the one that I flew here from the other side of the country to help get me a promotion. I fucking love it.

"Is this the one that you like the best? Do you want to browse through the rest of the store?"

"No, I like this one. What do you think?"

"It looks beautiful on you."

"Would you like to try on the matching one?" Allie asks, turning to me.

I shake my head. "Not necessary. I'll take both, please."

Allie hands the watch over to me, and Quinn says, "Twinning," as she lifts her forearm next to mine. Her giggle is soft and light.

A chuckle escapes me, this time fully aware of exactly what she means.

She holds her wrist up under the light and admires it, and I stand here, admiring her, like she's the only one on this goddamn planet.

I hear Allie locking up the case behind the counter and snap back to reality. I hand her my credit card, along with the Edward Rummens employee card.

Quinn stands on her tiptoes and plants a soft kiss on my cheek. "Thank you, Jaxon. I love it."

"You're welcome, Mrs. Baker," I say, catching her off guard. "You'd better get used to my name following yours." I wink.

We leave the store, *twinning*, and I stop at a drive-thru just as we're about to head out of town to get one of those caramel-colored coffee drinks for Quinn. "You should try one," she tells me.

"Why not?" I place an order for two, and when I bring the straw up to my lips, I'm hit with the cool liquid and a mix of whipped cream.

I never in my goddamn life thought I would drink whipped cream on top of my coffee, nor would I have tried an iced one at that, but just as I'm learning to navigate marriage, I'm also learning to relax a little and try new things, with Quinn's help.

"We should be there in three hours."

Quinn's been swaying to the music for the last hour, singing to herself, and I've been quietly navigating through the twists and turns of the road.

"We should play a game," she says.

"What kind of game can you play while driving?" I glance at her, taking my eyes off the road for only a second, as we come up to another bend in the road.

"Hmm, let's play Yes or No."

"How do you play?"

She turns down the music. "We each make a statement, and the other person guesses whether we've done the specific thing."

I can't believe I'm about to play a fucking car game. The oddest part about it is that I want to, with Quinn.

"I'll go first." She pauses, trying to come up with her statement. "I have three tattoos."

The thought of Quinn having tattoos that I have yet to see, even when she was in that tiny white bikini, has me hot. I replay the collage of images from that day in my head, tits and ass are swirling through my vision. I don't see how she could possibly have any tattoos that weren't exposed while wearing that string bikini.

"No," I tell her.

"Wrong." I see her cheeks blush faintly.

"You have three tattoos? Where?" How do I not know this, and where the fuck are they?

"That's for you to find out," she teases, and I throb at the thought.

"Your turn."

I think for a minute and try to come up with something she wouldn't already know.

"My first job was at Edward Rummens Watches."

"Yes."

"Nope, my very first job was at a yacht club."

"Okay, I can see that. Young Jaxon dressed in white pleated pants and a blue polo?"

I laugh. "You're not wrong. Your turn."

"I've never been to a concert."

"No. Surely you've been to a concert before."

She shakes her head. "Nope, never. My mom was supposed to take me to one when I was ten, a group that sang pop music, but I got sick the day before and couldn't go. I cried for hours that night."

"That's sad."

"So, you've been, I'm assuming?"

"Yeah, I went to a couple of rock concerts in my twenties, but it's been over a decade since."

She grabs hold of my hand that's resting on her knee once more. "Maybe it's something we can do together one day."

There are so many things that I want to do with this woman.

And *to* this woman.

The thought of her having those tattoos I have yet to see still gnaws at my brain.

We play another few rounds before Quinn texts Nicky to see how Luna's doing. While she does this, she asks, "What type of activities are we going to be doing at the retreat?"

I sigh. I wish I could tell her they won't be awkward shit that I don't want to do. I settle on, "I'm not sure. Every year's different."

She takes a selfie, sending it to Nicky, who apparently is sending pictures of him and Luna by the pool.

We drive the next few hours talking about random stuff and singing along to music when I see the sign for the retreat.

"Looks like we're here," I say, wishing we were anywhere else.

# Chapter Twenty-One

*Quinn*

When Jaxon placed his hand on the small of my back, leading me into Edward Rummens Watches, shivers spread through me.

Having his hand on my knee for the length of the car ride kept the butterflies in my belly fluttering.

But this, right now, the butterflies have turned from those of excitement to ones of fear.

"Are we really doing this?" I ask Jaxon.

"No turning back now."

We drive up another winding road, and when we arrive at the top, I can't help myself. "Holy shit."

"Quinn." He laughs. "You okay?"

"No, no, I'm not okay. Check this out."

Jaxon pulls into the parking lot, off to the left of the main doors. This place is huge. It's tucked away far from the road, and it seems to be an estate. The sign above the main door reads Villa Bella.

The top of the villa peaks out from the trees above.

Jaxon squeezes my thigh. "Ready?"

"No."

Jaxon opens the car door for me and takes my hand, leading me out of the leather seat I've spent the last four hours in. When I stand, I realize how stiff I am, and notice Jaxon stretching his arms overhead, revealing a tight stomach.

So. Many. Feelings.

I am suddenly overwhelmed by everything happening around me.

First, all the butterflies from Jaxon. The fear of getting caught pretending to be a loving married couple. And being in this place, which looks like it belongs somewhere far away from here on a remote island somewhere tropical.

And abs. So many abs.

Jaxon tilts my seat forward as he grabs our bags from the backseat. I check out his ass as he bends over the seat. It's a really nice one.

I fan myself in the heat because it's hot, and not because Jaxon's doing a number on me when he looks up at me, bags in hand. "You sure you're okay?" I nod and close the car door. "Can you grab the keys from my pocket and lock up?"

He wants me to put my hand in the front pocket of his shorts and take his keys?

Yes, please.

He moves his arm out to the side, showing me which pocket his keys are in by protruding his hip forward, and I'm careful to touch the keys and nothing more.

When I turn back to him to see if he wants me to hold on to the keys, I notice his shorts are a little tighter across the front, and I abandon the words I was about to say, shoving the keys in my pocket.

"Let's go," he says, leading the way.

I reach for him and take one of my bags. "Do you want me to take my backpack? You're sort of overloaded."

"Nah, I'm good." I watch as he nods at someone who's just pulled up. "Lester, my assistant," he explains. "You'll meet him after. He knows about us, by the way." He says the last part in more of a whisper.

"Okay, good to know."

We walk up a small hill until we reach a cobblestone pathway that takes us to the main entrance. I run up ahead of Jaxon and hit the button for the automatic door. When it swings open, we both make our way inside, and I gasp.

Warm yellow light fills the space. There are a few large brown oversized leather sofas and chairs spread throughout the space, matching the art that is tastefully displayed on the walls.

"Your company really goes all out on these retreats, don't they?"

"No expense is spared when it comes to Edward taking care of his staff and company."

I drop my bags on the floor near the main desk where we're to check in, and I leave Jaxon to deal with getting our room. My dress sways around me as the warm summer breeze blows in from the back of the room. The large glass doors have been pushed to the sides, making this room half indoor and half outdoor, a larger scale of Jaxon's home.

The same cobblestone that's out front is found at the back. Wooden furniture with thick cream-colored cushions are throughout the outdoor space, and I count two gas fire pits.

"Look! We can have s'mores," I say, pointing towards the sign telling me so by a water station. I'm taken aback when Jaxon's arms sweep around me from behind. A breath catches in my chest, and I lean back into him as we look out at the view. We're on the main level, but the villa continues ten stories high. I can only imagine the view that we'll have from our room.

"Well, if it isn't the newlyweds."

Jaxon releases me, and I shiver without his arms holding me tight, despite the high temperature today. We both turn towards Edward's voice.

Edward looks much different from the man I met at dinner. Instead of a dark business suit, he's wearing a white shirt, khaki green shorts, and flip-flops. I never would have recognized him if we had been walking past one another on the street.

I smile and greet him and Carole, Jaxon's hand reassuringly firm at the small of my back.

"Good to see you, Edward, Carole." He nods to them both. "Did you have a nice drive up?"

"Sure did. We arrived this morning, beat the traffic." He settles in on one of the sofas next to Carole. "Would you look at you, both wearing the phoenix blue watches. See that, Carole?"

Carole turns to Quinn. "That watch looks darling on you, Quinn."

"Thank you." I turn to Edward. "Your watches really are beautiful. Thank you for having me here. I can't wait to see what you have in store for us."

We're already six months into our arrangement, and I can't even fathom not being around Jaxon one day, so I push these thoughts out of my head and focus on Edward.

"Take tonight to enjoy the grounds. Tomorrow we'll all meet for breakfast, and everything will be explained to you then."

We head back to where I dropped my bags, and Jaxon explains that we're on the ninth floor.

## CHAPTER TWENTY-ONE

The bank of elevators is down a long corridor. The button lights up when I press it, and the doors open immediately.

When the elevator stops at our floor, we head out in search of room 913, and with a swipe of a card, Jaxon opens the door, and I shriek. My hands fly over my mouth, and I make a string of apologies to Jaxon when I see that I've startled him.

"I'm still not used to these high-pitched sounds coming from such a tiny woman."

I laugh and nudge him with my shoulder playfully. "I'm sorry, it's just this place... wow."

A white duvet covers the king-size bed along the far wall. Two small side tables sit on each side, and a soft green throw blanket is folded and sitting on the bench at the foot of the bed.

I drop the bag and my purse that I've been carrying onto the floor and throw myself onto the king bed with a giggle. I turn my head to the side, taking in the fresh linen scent.

"You should really take off your shoes, Quinn."

I roll my eyes at Jaxon as I turn onto my back. I use my toes to kick off my sandals. Jaxon bends down and picks them up, taking them to the door of the room.

"Why don't you join me over here, hubby?" I say, rolling to the side, making room for Jaxon. I pat down the bed next to me. "Lay back and feel this mattress. It might almost be as good as the one back home."

He removes his own shoes and comes towards the bed, sitting on the very edge, his back rigid. When he doesn't move, I sit up on my knees facing him. "Everything okay?"

He turns towards me. "I hadn't thought about the fact that there'd be only one bed. I'm sorry, Quinn." He lets his head drop.

"Jaxon, I'm okay with it, really. Are you?" I ask, not wanting the answer to be no.

It feels like we have a real relationship forming. One that hasn't just been for show, one meant just for us.

"Yeah, I just don't want to make you uncomfortable."

"You won't."

I stand on the bed and I'm jumping as if it's my first time away from home. And if I'm being completely honest, this is only the second time I have stayed at any type of hotel or resort. The first time was when I stayed at The Cartier, the eve of our wedding.

"Quinn, get down from there," Jaxon says, rising from the bed, his hands landing on his hips.

I'm in a fit of laughter, unable to stop myself, and I ignore Jaxon's command.

"Get up here, Jaxon. Come, jump with me."

I continue to bounce, sending Jaxon into a stressful state. When I see his body stiffen. I take one last jump and land on my butt, giggling.

"You're such a party pooper."

"I am not a party pooper. This isn't how you behave in a place like this. Or in any place, for that matter." With this last comment, I see his mind wandering. "Do you jump on the bed back at home?" His eyebrow rises, waiting for my reply.

"How should I behave, Jaxon? Tell me." I'm a little annoyed. We've been getting along so well. "You need to let go a little, relax, have fun." I hop off the bed and stand next to Jaxon. "And no, for your information, I have not jumped on my bed back home." I walk away towards the balcony. "Don't worry, I won't dare be so free-spirited when we're out around your coworkers and Edward. I won't cost you the promotion."

Just like at Jaxon's home, the wall with the view has floor-to-ceiling windows. I open the door and step out into the humid air. Leaning on the railing, I take a deep breath and let it out slowly. My eyes close, and I listen to the birds and the sounds of nature.

Jaxon joins me a minute later and spins me around until our eyes lock. He tucks a strand of hair behind my ear. "I'm sorry. I'm not telling you how to behave. I won't. It's just... I guess I have a lot riding on this week, and I'm a little stressed out now that we're here."

I don't blame him. I'm stressed too.

This is his career—and our marriage, for that matter. I've been wondering what happens to me if he fails to get that promotion. I know what the contract says, but when you have money, rules can be broken.

Will he want a divorce sooner than later?

Will he send me back to where I came from?

"Yes, you're here to get that promotion, and to bond with your coworkers, but you can let yourself have a little fun while you're at it too."

I close my eyes, and neither of us says a word. I'm thinking he's about to kiss me, his fingertips still propping my chin up towards him, when he says, "We should probably get some dinner. I'm starving." Disappointment runs down through my belly, and my stomach growls in reply, taking his side over mine. "Seems like your stomach would agree with me."

Damn stomach.

# Chapter Twenty-two

*Jaxon*

When I open my eyes, Quinn's arm is draped over me, her breath hot on my face, and her soft curls blanketing my chest.

Fuck, she smells great, even with morning breath.

I blink my eyes several times to adjust to the morning light. This room has everything except for room-darkening shades.

I woke up a few times last night to find us cuddling every time, but right now I have to take a piss before Quinn wakes up and sees my involuntary morning tent.

"Mm-mm."

Too late.

"Morning, handsome," Quinn murmurs, stirring. "How did you sleep?"

I'm trying not to move under her, staying as still as I can, hoping that her eyes are still closed, and that she's not gazing down towards my morning erection.

"Great," I mutter.

# CHAPTER TWENTY-TWO

As Quinn rolls onto her back, I sit up in one swift movement, taking the first chance I get. "Be right back," I say, peeling back the soft green bamboo sheets and dashing for the washroom.

When I come back into the room a few minutes later, Quinn is out on the balcony in nothing but tiny shorts and a tank top.

I place my hands on the railing beside her. "Breakfast is at nine a.m. Want to hop in the shower first?"

She ignores my question and sends me a shy smile. "It was nice cuddling last night, waking up in your arms." She blushes and turns away.

"Hey." I nudge her arm. "I liked it too." I'm grinning. "So, shower?"

"Yeah, I better get ready. We have a promotion to get you."

She turns, my eyes following her and her ass as she walks away.

If she had asked me to join her, I don't think I would have had enough strength to say no.

There are three long tables that seat sixty, and only a few chairs are empty. The corporate retreat is comprised of all upper-level employees, their administrative staff, and significant others who wish to join. Anyone without a partner may bring a family member or a friend, so no one's left out. I've never bothered to bring anyone before.

There's a hot buffet set up on the side wall filled with pancakes, eggs of all kinds, waffles, bacon, hash browns, pastries, and fruit. There's a large gluten-free and vegan section at the end, with just as many options. And there's so much noise, people talking and laughing around me, that I've just dropped my fork on the floor for the second goddamn time.

"Let me go get you another one," Quinn offers. She's wearing a light blue summer dress that sways with each movement, and her hair is pulled up into a messy bun on top of her head. I can hear the clack of her heels returning to our table, with two forks in hand.

"Got an extra one just in case." She winks at me, and I take both from her, setting them down beside my plate on the linen napkin.

"Thank you."

My knee is bouncing, and my breath is shallow, anxiety running through me.

I hate corporate retreats.

I smile when smiled at, respond to questions asked of me, and hide out in my room when I can. Having Quinn with me and the promotion on the line makes this year's retreat different. Participation is mandatory, and having Quinn on my arm is key.

I introduce Quinn to those who pass by us and smile a big toothy grin when it matters.

We're seated next to Lester and his cousin Vinny, and beside them is Brodie and his wife Julie. We were here early enough that we managed to get seats at the end of the table, my go-to strategy so I don't have to converse with as many people and I have an easy exit.

When everyone finishes eating, the staff clears our plates, and Edward stands at the end of the room. He places two fingers in his mouth and whistles loudly, seeking everyone's attention.

"I wasn't sure I could still pull that off." He chuckles, and some people clap and holler in response. "I want to welcome everyone to this year's Edward Rummens Watches corporate retreat!" he exclaims with a fist pump in the air.

As much as I want the CEO job, work won't be the same without Edward around. These retreats have always been his favorite part of the year, but I can only assume he will keep coming to them even when he steps down.

Edward continues, "We are here to spend time with one another, to build trust and communication between team-building exercises. But I also want you to think of this as a little vacation. As I'm sure most of you toured the Villa Bella yourself yesterday, there are a lot of amenities, so take advantage during your free time. We have the entire villa to ourselves for the duration of the week, so venture out, and try something new while you're here." He walks towards the long table on the right. "I hear there's a beach buggy that can take you to the private beach. Check out the times at the front desk and book your spots. There's also a beachside bar. But there's one important rule everyone needs to follow, same as years before, everyone will receive a card." He holds one up to show us as he walks towards the other end of the dining hall. "You will find it in your welcome package. Every time you have an alcoholic drink, you get a stamp. There is a two-drink maximum per day, per person."

Some of the group boo at this, and Edward frowns.

"This is a corporate retreat, not spring break. We're here to have fun responsibly, and respect one another, on company time and dime. If you choose not to have your two drinks one day, you lose them. You cannot double up the following day. Understood?" He glances around the room, and we all turn and look at one another, nodding in agreement with a low murmur of replies.

A man in linen pants and a button-down shirt walks up to where Edward is standing and pats him on the back.

"This here is Manuel. Anything you need, he's your man." Edward shakes his hand. "He'll be providing each set of partners with an itinerary for the week and the welcome package. Look it over. You need to know when and where to be. Since we're such a large group, we have been divided into smaller groups for the activities. So, the seats you have chosen are your seats for the rest of the week, and your coworkers and their plus-ones will be your group for the scheduled activities.

Motherfucker.

I glare at Brodie, and the prick is smiling back at me. Quinn elbows me, so I return Brodie's smile with my own bullshit one.

I told Quinn all about Brodie late one night a few weeks ago. Apparently, she thinks I need to get over it.

Get over Brodie, the boss's pet.

Fuck no.

Edward begins speaking again. "We'll all be meeting here for breakfast, lunch, and dinner, every day."

Everyone is eagerly awaiting their schedule, and I watch as Manuel stops behind Quinn.

"Your package includes the villa map, and you're going to want to keep this on you the first few days so you don't get lost," Manuel tells the room.

Quinn smiles at me, shimmying her shoulders in excitement. Brodie and Julie are laughing about something.

Everyone is buzzing, and when Manuel places ours between us, I lean closer to Quinn, smelling her sweet fragrance to read over her shoulder.

# CHAPTER TWENTY-TWO

"What the fuck is hot yoga?"

A laugh erupts from Brodie, and Edward sends a stern look my way.

*Shit, did I say that out loud?*

Quinn elbows me again, and I make a note to internalize all negative thoughts for the duration of this retreat.

I've somehow bent over to where I'm upside down, my head facing my legs. Apparently, this is a down dog. We're scattered around the room, and right in front of me is Brodie looking back at me.

Quinn is in bike shorts herself and a sports bra, and she is sexy as fuck bending over this way and that way. Sweat is slick on her arms, chest, and stomach, and it makes me want to rip off those damn clothes and take advantage of this down dog.

Sweat is dripping down the back of my neck. Although I work out and swim laps often, different muscles are being worked as we move through all the postures. And in this forty-degree room, I can safely say, I'm sweating out this morning's bacon.

We move into warrior pose, and I can confidently say that I nail this one.

The class passes in a blur, Quinn distracting me with every twist and turn.

We pick up our towels and walk back up to our room to shower and put on our swimsuits. I'm surprised when

Quinn comes out in a modest lavender two-piece. The top, though strapless, hides more than that little triangle one she has, and her bottoms cover more of her ass, leaving me to once again wonder where those three tattoos lie on her ivory skin.

The beach buggy is an orange van from the '70s and has been painted with a mural. Six of us pile into the back seats to make the ten-minute drive through dense trees on a gravel road. We're told there is also a walking path and trails if we want to venture out ourselves at some point.

We unpack the van, carrying tote bags, books, and hats. Quinn slips off her sandals onto the golden sand as soon as she steps out of the beach buggy.

"The sand is hot," she says, bouncing from right to left. She doesn't put her sandals back on, though, but runs, giggling in delight, to the closest set of lounge chairs that face the ocean. Brodie, Julie, Lester, Vinny, and I all follow behind her.

I've taken Quinn's advice and let the whole nemesis thing go, at least for the length of the retreat, so as not to make things more awkward, seeing that we're in the same group all week.

But that doesn't change a thing. The promotion is mine.

We unpack our belongings and see another van arrive with more from our group, and within twenty minutes, a game of volleyball is orchestrated.

We choose our teams. Brodie named himself captain and for whatever reason has chosen me to be on his team. Quinn is playing opposite to me, which is great because I get to watch her jump and giggle. It's nice to see this side of her, laughing and having fun with everyone. Her laugh is contagious, and she's making friends quickly.

## CHAPTER TWENTY-TWO

We're midway through the game when Brodie calls us in for a huddle.

"Okay, so the game is tied, and it's our turn to serve. Jaxon, I think you should take this one."

What?

"Um, sure, yeah," I reply, nodding.

I was into sports when I was younger, but I'm more into solo-type sports as an adult, so the fact that Brodie is asking me to take the lead on this next round has taken me aback. "You've got a great overhand float serve. Let's get this!"

We take our places, and suddenly this isn't just a random beach volleyball game, not to Brodie and me. Our business shark personalities want to win.

I transfer my weight forward and rotate my shoulder, swinging my arm quickly to send the ball flying over the net. It goes back and forth until Brodie hits a cut shot over a blocker, and our team wins the game.

We're cheering and laughing at the win, and Quinn comes back around to our side of the net. I wrap my arm around her shoulder and plant a kiss on her lips in greeting. She pulls away, a wicked grin at the surprise kiss, but her eyes are sparkling. I feel my heart growing in size, as if I were a big furry, green thing who hates Christmas.

I smile back at her, and she wraps her own arm around my waist, and we stay like that until we reach our lounge chairs.

"Can you put sunscreen on my back?" she asks and passes me one of the bottles from her tote bag.

"It would be my pleasure."

I slide my hands so no skin is left untouched, and by the time I'm done, she's blushing just as much as I am.

# Chapter Twenty-Three

## Quinn

We spent the rest of the afternoon with sandy toes and sun-kissed skin. I pull my bottoms up a notch to catch a glimpse at the tan line that's forming on my hip.

Today has been amazing, and I'm so proud of Jaxon. I caught him talking to Brodie twice. It seemed like he was enjoying the conversation and not just faking it.

He's softening in all the right ways, and it looks good on him.

First, he faced his fear of dogs, and now he and Brodie are connecting. There's nothing more attractive than a man who is upping his game and growing emotionally.

We're sitting outside the main lounge, having one of our allowed drinks for the day. Dinner was great, and now that our bellies are full of delicious food, we're hanging out with a few of the others. I pull my feet under me and rest my head on Jaxon's shoulder.

Even though we both showered after the beach, I can still smell the sunscreen that was smothered across his skin, and it reminds me of the kiss he planted on my lips.

I think it surprised him as much as it did me.

"Do you guys want s'mores?" Lester's holding two sticks and a bag of marshmallows. Vinny's hands are full too, holding a container of graham crackers and chocolate.

Nodding, I sit up. "I do."

Lester told me he loves working for Jaxon. He thinks so highly of him and wants to be like him when he's older. Jaxon chuckled when I told him that, saying he was only a decade older than Lester. I don't know, I think it's sweet. I know Jaxon can be a jerk, but I think those of us who have been fortunate enough to see what's hidden under the brooding businessman know the soft heart Jaxon holds.

I reach into the bag of marshmallows, taking one and sliding the squishy white marshmallow onto my stick. I lean closer to the fire, hovering the marshmallow over the flame.

"Jaxon told me you got a dog," Lester says as I'm blowing out my flame-lit marshmallow.

"Luna, yes. She's a sweetheart." I lean back to see if Jaxon is listening. When I see that he isn't, I continue. "Jaxon has really fallen for her."

Lester pushes up his glasses as he laughs. "That's hard to imagine."

"I know, right? But believe me, he is." I lean closer to him and whisper, "I know you know."

Lester nods. "Is it going well?" he asks quietly.

"Yeah, it really is. I like him," I admit. There's something about Lester that makes him approachable.

"Like him? So, this is more than just the..." He lowers his voice another level. "This is more than just an arrangement for you?"

"That's what it was in the beginning, of course, but Jaxon is growing on me."

"Interesting." Lester nods, fixing his own s'more. "I've seen a different side of him lately. He seems happier, a little less uptight than usual. I think you're good for him."

Hearing this information from the guy who spends seventy-five percent of his time with Jaxon has me feeling some type of way. I lick some of the leftover marshmallow from my fingertips after I've placed the sticky white goo on my waiting graham cracker with a sliver of chocolate. I decide to change the subject before anyone gets wind that we're not legit.

"Did you guys have fun at the beach today?" I ask Lester and lean over to include Vinny in the conversation. Lester talks about the day while I continue to eat my s'more.

"What a game that was," Vinny speaks up. "You've got a wicked serve." He nudges Jaxon with his elbow.

Jaxon faces him with a tight smile. "Thank you, Vinny. You boys played a good game," he says awkwardly, accepting the compliment. I catch his eye, sending him a flirtatious grin.

"I'm not really one for sports," Lester reveals. "I hope not all of the activities will be sporty."

I nod in agreement. "Same. I liked the yoga, though."

"That was my first time trying a class," Lester tells me.

"It felt good, but I'm going to be sore tomorrow morning after a day of yoga and volleyball."

I watch Jaxon lick some of the marshmallow that's squeezing out from his s'more. I can't help but wonder what it'd be like if that peck on the beach had turned into more.

Or if we had been somewhere private.

Jaxon catches me gawking, and my cheeks heat.

His eyes darken, like that day in the pool before the smoke detector went off. The longer I stare at him, the more heat builds inside of me, sending a pulse between my thighs.

I cross my legs, willing the anticipation to die down—for now.

We finish up with Lester and Vinny, and they tell us they're going to walk around the villa and explore. I shift closer to Jaxon on the seat and take his hand in mine.

"What did you and Brodie talk about today?"

He swats at a bug, and leans back, crossing his foot over his knee. "Turns out Brodie played volleyball during college. He was telling me about tournaments and shit he used to do." Jaxon stops, and I wait for him to continue. "He said I was pretty decent."

"Yeah, I didn't know you could serve like that. I'm not so good," I respond, uncrossing and recrossing my opposite leg.

He turns to me. "You looked sexy as hell, and you sure looked like you knew how to spike." His eyes trail over me, and I like when they land ten inches from my mouth.

For dinner, I chose the same dress I wore to breakfast, a blue sundress that flares below the waist with tiny spaghetti straps that tie up on the shoulders in little bows and a deep V that ends an inch lower than where my bra would be, if I were wearing one.

"I think that was more me being afraid of the ball. I was trying to whack it away from me."

A deep laugh escapes his throat. "Fair. What do you think, you want to head up to the room?"

"Yeah, let's head up."

We make our rounds, wishing everyone a good evening, ending with Edward and Carole. I smile like the doting wife that I am and laugh when Edward tells us a joke, even though I really didn't understand it.

We stay hand in hand until Jaxon lets go to swipe our way into the room.

I kick off my sandals and walk to the bed, but this time instead of jumping on the bed, I let my body drop into the center and close my eyes. The mattress dips next to me with Jaxon's weight. I'm thinking about the kiss on the beach and holding his hand when he interrupts my thoughts.

"Can we talk?"

My eyes spring open, and I see Jaxon lying on his side watching me. I turn my body to face him and place my right arm under my head, propping myself up with my elbow dipping further into the pillowtop. "What do you want to talk about?"

Jaxon reaches for one of the decorative pillows and places it between his arm and his tousled chestnut-colored hair.

I try to control my thoughts, but all I want to do is run my hands through his hair and pull his face into mine.

"I was just thinking that even though we're putting on a show for the retreat... I'm sorry if I went too far with that kiss."

My stomach plummets.

Does he regret it?

"You didn't go too far." Maybe now's the time to tell Jaxon how I feel about him, but I quickly change my mind, unwilling to be completely vulnerable. What if he doesn't want me that way? It could ruin this retreat, our whole arrangement, everything.

I decide to vanish the insecure thoughts and be the confident-as-fuck woman that I know I am.

# CHAPTER TWENTY-THREE

There's no doubt about it that Jaxon wants me and I want him, but neither of us seems to be brave enough to make the first big move.

This marriage is already beneficial to both of us. A promotion for Jaxon and a lavish lifestyle for me.

But this new idea that's floating around in my head involves sweaty skin, salty kisses, and lustful cries.

We can be emotionally vulnerable later, when the time's right. Right now, I want to have some fun.

Project Benefits Included in full force.

Which of us is going to fold first?

"I want to take a shower before bed," I say, as I sit up on the edge of the bed. "Do you mind unzipping my dress for me?" I stand, peering over my shoulder, pouting my lips and gazing at him from under my eyelashes.

A classic move.

"Um, yeah, of course."

Jaxon comes to the edge of the bed, so I move slightly until I'm standing between his legs, my back to him.

His fingers dance up my sides, and I close my eyes, goosebumps fluttering across my skin. I grab hold of my long, loose curls in one hand and pile my hair up on top of my head to reveal my neck and the zipper.

This dress can easily slide down if I were to just untie the spaghetti strap bows on my shoulders, but this will be more fun.

I hear Jaxon inhale, and he takes his time slithering the zipper down its track. This whole idea of trying to get Jaxon to cave first has me weak in the knees. The light graze of Jaxon's soft fingertips trailing my spine has me thinking I might be the one to fold.

I hear him swallow before he speaks again.

"There you go."

His hands trail down the rest of my dress until they're resting on my bare legs, thumbs circling the skin on the side of my thighs. I stand still, a moment longer before replying.

"Thank you."

And with that, I take one step forward and release the straps down my shoulders until my dress has nothing left to hold on to. The blue cotton falls into a puddle at my feet. I peer over my shoulder one last time, meeting his darkened stare.

It takes about twelve steps to get to the washroom, and I take those steps slowly, giving him a sneak peek at one of the three tattoos before closing the door behind me and starting the shower.

I let the cool water drip through my hair and down my skin. This was a good idea, I tell myself. Jaxon won't be able to keep his hands off me.

But until then, what am I supposed to do with all this pent-up energy?

# Chapter Twenty-Four

*Jaxon*

I run my hands through my hair.

Fuck me, Quinn's body is out of this world.

The curve of her ass is etched into my brain. The point of her hips, sleek, lean thighs, tanned skin, and her smooth back, all bare except for the tiniest of tattoos, a small outline of a butterfly on the top left of her cherry-shaped backend.

One down, two to go.

Tattoos, I mean.

Did Quinn want me to follow her into the shower?

I glance at the dress lying in the middle of the floor.

Quinn closed the door to the bathroom. If she had wanted me to follow her, she would have left it open. Right?

Fuck.

I stand and pace the room. The shower is on, and I can envision the water dripping down Quinn's pebbled nipples, running down her smooth stomach, cascading off her bottom.

My body heats, and I can feel myself growing thick.

I groan in frustration thinking about Quinn gripping me in her hand, and I push open the balcony door.

Since a cold shower is out of question right now, fresh air will have to do.

I pick up the novel I left on the side table this morning. That will distract me from the ink on Quinn's body, her supple shape, her silhouette.

It takes a while to focus on the book in front of me, especially when I hear Quinn come out of the bathroom.

To my relief, and also brutal disappointment, Quinn comes out dressed. But she's wearing a pair of jogging shorts that barely cover her ass and a loose-fitting T-shirt with nothing underneath. Dear Lord, this woman. The shirt is slightly damp, sticking to her perky tits, and I will my eyes to meet her gaze.

"What are you reading?" she asks casually.

*So, we're just going to pretend that I didn't just see you in nothing but your birthday suit?* Okay, this isn't the first time.

I shift the book so that the cover faces Quinn.

"You like 'em dark?" Quinn asks seductively, sitting down across from me, propping her feet up on the nearby ottoman and crossing her arms.

"What gave it away?"

She eyes me playfully. "What's it about?"

"These two hikers find an abandoned cottage, and one gets hurt in a trap that was set up for trespassers. They take cover in the empty space for the night, since obviously they have no cell phone signal."

She nods. "Obviously."

"I brought a couple of books with me, if you're in the mood to read.

# CHAPTER TWENTY-FOUR

"I know what I'm in the mood for, but it isn't reading." She bats her eyelashes in the playful way that she does and then turns away, peering through the glass wall of the balcony that separates us from a steep drop. The scenery is unbelievable.

I hesitate, not responding.

Is she trying to tease me or torture me?

I said no sex, but things are different now, aren't they?

The whole point of Quinn being here was for this retreat. Her job was to help me get this promotion.

We need to keep our heads out of the clouds, and our feet firmly pressed on the ground.

Yet now I'm consumed with thoughts of Quinn on her back, her feet firmly pressed into my shoulders, hands grasping at the duvet beneath her, screaming my name.

Can I have both?

Will it fuck up my chances at the promotion if we start something physical, if I succumb to this desire, this sexual tension between us?

I watch as loose strands flutter around Quinn's face in the breeze. Her eyes crease at the corners as she peers through the trees, watching the sunset. Her shoulders are relaxed, and I can't tell what she's thinking.

When she's angry at me, that's another story. I can see it all on that pretty little face of hers.

Quinn didn't just start teasing when she dropped that dress, she took it to a whole other level.

A level I don't know how to play on. This is unfamiliar territory for me.

I know what a woman wants, and I know what she would like—but her teasing just to tease and walking away? I don't know where to begin.

Quinn started this, though, and I'm going to make her regret the fact that she thought she could play with me and win. I'm going to have her begging me to touch her.

I *always* win.

I lean my arms on the ledge of the balcony. "What a beautiful sunset."

I smile when Quinn does what I expected her to, joining me at my side.

"It's so pretty, the red tones mixed with pink. It's like the sky is blushing," she says.

"Just as you will be when I finally get the chance to hear you scream my name."

I turn on my heel, avoiding any eye contact, knowing Quinn is watching me walk away, her mouth open in surprise. I head straight to the bathroom where I close the door, turn on the shower, and count to ten as the ice-cold water beats at my skin.

"I'm too short! I can't unclasp the latch."

Quinn is yelling at me from the other end of one of the shorter ziplines.

I cup my hands around my mouth and shout back to her.

"I'm coming, stay put."

"Like I can go anywhere, even if I wanted to," I hear her holler back to me.

Our bullshit schedule had us waking up at dawn for treetop zip lining. Our group gathered in the villa lobby for coffee and pastries before Manuel shuffled us into the beach buggy. Turns out the buggy is also the mode of transportation to take us up 175 feet above the forest floor.

The drive up was rough, especially when the buggy puttered and slowed down and a few of us thought we'd be stranded midway. But here I am, ball-sack deep in a harness.

Our group of fifteen has been cut in two for this event. Brodie, Lester, Vinny, Quinn, and I are starting with the ziplines, while the others are strolling sky bridges. Julie's a bit under the weather this morning, so she's sitting this event out.

I adjust my helmet and make sure my hook is locked before I let myself go. As I'm speeding through the trees, I take in the view. I've never seen anything like it. When I see that I'm getting close to Quinn, I watch her eyes bulge, and I can tell that she's worried I won't stop on time. I follow the instructions that were previously taught to us, wrapping my leather-gloved hands over the cable.

I come to a complete stop just inches from Quinn.

"Well, look who's all tied up waiting for me." I say, winking.

"Jaxon, come on. Help me."

I can see that she's about half an inch too short to unclasp herself. That's a lawsuit waiting to happen.

I purposely lean my left hand over her so that she's pressed against the tree underneath me. The sound of Quinn gasping sends an electrifying shock through my skin, landing in my harness. I put pressure on the zipline, allowing enough give for me to unclasp her hook and clasp it onto the next line.

"There you go," I say in a low tone while she's still under me. I laugh as she blinks a few times, steadying herself on the small platform, my fingers digging into her waist.

"Thanks."

She scans our surroundings and across to the next zip line, and we can see the four others waiting for us. We're the last two in our group.

"You guys coming or what?" Brodie is yelling back to us.

"Coming!" I shout back loud enough for the breeze to carry my words to the group. I turn to Quinn. "You ready to keep going?"

"I didn't think I had a fear of heights. I mean, I'm fine on the balcony, and I don't have a problem flying." Her gaze lowers to the ground. "But this…"

I lift her chin with my fingertips until those ocean-blue eyes meet mine. Small gold flecks sparkle in the sea of blue.

"Hanging by a cable over 100 feet across treetops is a lot different from sitting on a balcony or being in first class with a glass or two of wine in the system."

"Hey, I only had one glass." She crosses her arms.

"You've got this. Only five more ziplines, two sky bridges, and treehouses to visit."

"Oh, well, if that's all that's left, then what am I worrying for?" Her laugh is a mix of sarcasm and nerves.

"Want me to go first?" I ask.

"God, no, don't leave me here on my own."

"Alright, then you're up. I'll see you soon."

She exhales a heavy breath. "I'm coming," she yells to the group, and then sets off on her zipline.

I watch as she soars effortlessly through the tops of the trees.

When we first read that we'd be zip lining, Quinn was her adorable self, bouncing around the room like a goddamn child on Christmas morning. But when the buggy made its way to the top, Quinn stood there frozen in fear as the twentysomething's instructor explained how high we were.

## CHAPTER TWENTY-FOUR

She calls out to me, telling me the coast is clear.

This zipline is longer and faster than the first, and after I take off, I reach just over thirty miles an hour, or so I remember reading on the brochure.

I make my way around the tree to join the others. I'm just in time to see Lester take off from the next line. When he gains traction and reaches his fastest speed, we all hear a high-pitched scream come from somewhere deep within his chest.

The group is laughing in good fun, and we all do the same as we take on the fastest line of them all, noted by the instructor at forty miles an hour.

By the end of the last zipline, Quinn turns to me, eyes wide and hyped up on adrenaline. "I want to go again!"

"Take it easy, tiger, there's still bridges and ladders to walk through." I point to my right. "Check out the treehouses."

Everyone takes in the small bridge made of planks with rope handles. It wobbles as Vinny steps one foot on. We're all clasped to the steel cable above us, and one by one we make our way to the first treehouse.

When we've huddled into the small cabin, we see a note with our names on it.

Brodie slides his gloves off and picks up the note.

"Describe the person to your left in three words." Brodie tells the group and then turns to me, the lucky fucker on his left.

I inwardly groan, and Quinn eyes me from across the circle, sending me encouragement. These types of activities stress the shit out of me, and although she's a few feet away, somehow her being here makes this activity easier. Or it will once I let Brodie's hits pass in one ear and out the next.

"Assertive, unfazed, tenacious."

Brodie's words stun me. I thought the man would take this opportunity to dig a little, but he's smiling at me as his left hand clasps my right shoulder, and he gives me a little shake like we're old buds.

I don't know what's happening here, but they say keep your enemies closer.

That must be Brodie's plan: Kill me with kindness, then steal my promotion when I show weakness.

I nod my head at him in thanks and then turn to Lester, who's on my left.

"Reliable, trustworthy, organized." Lester pushes his glasses up the bridge of his nose, smiling at me. I take a step back, a little uneasy at sharing, but Lester is a great fucking assistant. I wouldn't survive the workday without him, and I probably should tell him that more often.

"Thank you, Jaxon."

He's still beaming as we go around the rest of the circle. Compliments are made, and bonds are formed within the five of us.

"We should get going if we're done here," I tell the group as Brodie places the card back down on the table.

We head down a circular staircase matching the plank bridges we just walked across until we reach the next tree house.

Of course, once we enter, there's a card with instructions waiting for us on the table. Lester takes off his gloves and picks up the card this time.

"What's your go-to karaoke song?"

The fuck?

I don't do karaoke. Singing in front of a group of people? I'd rather show up to work buck-ass naked.

Quinn answers first, then Vinny, and we make our way around the circle until I'm the last to go. When I say I don't have one, Brodie gets on my case about how there's got to be a song. I tell them I've never done karaoke before. There are gasps from the group.

Quinn speaks up. "That song you sang on the way up here, what was that called?" she asks.

I'm bad with names, but I don't worry about it for more than a few seconds when Quinn remembers the name of the song. When I nod and agree, the team leaves me be, and we head to the next treehouse.

The third treehouse is similar to the other two, and we finish the activity and head down the last rope bridge until we're back on land.

The other group is waiting there for us, and laughter and chatter fill the air. The instructor leads us to a small building for snacks before continuing the second half of the activity.

When we've all been fed, we divide up again, and my group trudges towards the first sky bridge.

An hour later, we're back at the main clubhouse and gift shop. Quinn is browsing the T-shirts and postcards while I find myself next to Brodie. I'm handling the love locks, and an idea forms. I choose a gold heart lock, and I know exactly what I'm going to do with it.

"That was pretty epic." Brodie is playing with the magnets, some with pictures of the bridge we just walked, others with quotes saying shit like, "I did it." Brodie picks up one of the square black ones from the magnetic tower that reads, "Nothing scares me, I have kids."

And I pray to the fucking gods this marriage is enough for Edward.

# Chapter Twenty-Five

## Quinn

Every muscle that I have is aching, and every inch of me is lusting after Jaxon.

I let my body mold into the soft cushions of the lobby couch while Jaxon is off getting us a drink and snacks.

It all started when I saw him in the harness. Not the most attractive attire for a man, or anyone to wear, for that matter, but good Lord, I could see every inch of him. My heart speeds up at the thought, and I twiddle my thumbs, suddenly feeling disoriented.

If that wasn't bad enough, I got myself caught on a rope, like a damsel in distress, and needed saving. Of course Jaxon would be up for the job. Ever since I pulled the stunt of dropping my dress, the innuendos and smoldering eyes have been growing heavier on my heart and sending flutters to my nether regions.

When Jaxon placed his hand above me, pressing me back into the tree, I wanted him to take me, devour me with his mouth, be in control like the boss man that he is—or will

## CHAPTER TWENTY-FIVE

soon be. I can still feel the tingle of his breath on my neck as he helped unclasp my hook.

So now I'm sitting here, rolling my tired shoulders, and trying hard to hide my flushed face from the thoughts that have taken over my mind.

"Hey, you sore?"

Jaxon's voice startles me from behind.

"Yeah, I am." I rub at my shoulder, trying to loosen up the tense muscles.

"Let me help you with that." He places two glasses of juice and a plate of cookies on the nearby table and walks back around until he's directly behind me and the couch. "Sit up straight." I do as I'm told, my back erect against the pillow behind me.

His hands come down hard on my shoulders, and a sound escapes my mouth.

My eyes close as his fingertips dig into my muscles, releasing some of the soreness. My head tilts back, leaning into the edge of the sofa, and my body sinks heavier into the cushion. The melting of the knots that formed themselves under my skin sends me floating on a cloud into oblivion, and I'm startled when I feel Jaxon's lips come down on mine. An upside-down kiss from behind.

My lips move against his in a passionate kiss that unravels me.

"Get a room," I hear someone joke nearby, and my lips are suddenly cold as Jaxon peels his off mine.

"Original," Jaxon mutters.

My eyes are heavy when the sunlight hits them, and I lift my head back up.

I rub my shoulder where Jaxon's hands were only moments ago.

"Thank you. That felt great."

He walks around and hands me a glass of juice. "Cookie?" He's holding the plate in front of me, and I could get used to this. Shoulder rubs, upside-down kisses, and cookies? Yes, please.

"Thanks." I take a bite and savor the chunks of chocolate that swirl around my tongue.

"If you're still sore later on, I can finish you off upstairs." I cough, choking slightly on my cookie. Jaxon's expression turns to one of embarrassment once he realizes what he said. Although he's been suggestive in his comments to me, I don't think he meant that the way it sounded, but I take the opportunity to get him back.

"I think I'd like that," I respond with an eyebrow raised, and Jaxon's eyes grow dark.

I watch as he shifts in his seat, and the tension in my muscles settle.

Edward is standing at the head of the center table. "So, we're wrapping up day two. How is everyone feeling?"

There are hands clapping, a few hollers, and some low chatter throughout the room.

We've just sat down for dinner, and my stomach is grumbling after all the action from today. Jaxon and I ended up spending the late afternoon with our group hanging about in the lobby and by the pool. We've been making sure to talk to everyone, especially Edward, showing off our marital bliss. Jaxon's been proving his capabilities by being more involved than in previous years. Conversations flowed, and connections were made.

Edward continues his speech about how this is great for company morale and that he's happy everyone is taking part in all the activities.

My phone vibrates, and I peek under the table. I have a message from Nicky with a picture of him and Luna. I type a quick reply, telling him I will respond after, but not before tilting the phone towards Jaxon so that he can see Luna.

Jaxon smiles, and warmth spreads through me as I think about my little found family.

We all stand and head to the buffet on the side of the room. Tonight's menu is prime rib with a selection of three different kinds of potatoes, salads, and vegetables.

I pile my plate high, and I watch Jaxon do the same. Our meals at home are usually portion controlled, but after today, I think we need the fuel.

"So, what's on the schedule for tonight?" I ask Jaxon.

Julie, Brodie's wife, overhears our conversation and jumps in as she picks up a whole wheat bun, placing it on her plate next to her mashed potatoes. "We're doing a sound bath meditation."

"What the hell is that?" Jaxon asks me.

"You just lie on a yoga mat and listen to different sounds. I've gone to a few of these classes back home. I love it. It calms your nervous system," Julie tells me and Jaxon.

"That sounds nice," I say. But not as nice as Jaxon's earlier offer to finish me— my shoulder rub up in our room.

We eat in silence, listening to Lester and Vinny talk. Brodie and Julie are at the other end of the table tonight. Silverware clatters against dishes and conversations flutter through the air.

I'm spearing some broccoli with my fork when Jaxon turns to me.

"Are you enjoying yourself here?" he asks with genuine concern.

I notice that the stubble on his face is a little longer than usual, with a few white hairs peeking out. His green T-shirt from the zip lining gift shop is tight on his arms, showing off his shoulders, chest, and the roses and thorn tattoos across his forearms. I convinced him to get matching shirts with me, and I was surprised when he didn't argue or complain. I'm wearing my own matching green shirt and jean shorts.

"I'm having a lot of fun." I'm meeting so many new people and trying things I never would have back home. It's really getting me out of my shell, and the happy go-lucky, quirky girl I used to be is coming back. Plus, I'm getting to torture Jaxon, even if it's at my own cost.

"Today was a little scary at first," I say and Jaxon nods. "That feeling, though, soaring through the treetops like a bird was wonderful." I close my eyes a second, remembering the feeling of zip lining through the sky, hair wisping dramatically around my face, and the helmet head Jaxon had when we finished for the day. The last part has me giggling.

"What's so funny?"

"I was just thinking of your helmet head."

"You're one to talk. You had helmet head with a mix of bird's nest."

I watch as Edward makes the rounds, talking to everyone. He seems like an amazing boss. He couldn't be more different from sleazeball Rick.

It's been a while since I've thought about the bar and my hometown. Alysha and I still text constantly, but she's it. If only she would pick up and move to this sunny state, my circle would be full. We'll never lose touch, but she's my only connection back home. I still haven't decided what I'm going to do when this whole thing ends, but I'm not ready to think about the end yet.

When we've finished dinner and conversed with Edward and some of Jaxon's coworkers, we decide to head upstairs and get ready for our last activity of the day. Everyone at the retreat will be at this one.

I pull on my lilac bike shorts and matching sports bra. I haven't bothered going into the washroom to change since last night. Jaxon's already seen everything, and Project Benefits Included is still underway, even if it's slow headway. That upside-down kiss this afternoon was fire, and I can't wait for our next one.

I think I'm becoming obsessed with Jaxon's mouth.

As I'm changing, I notice Jaxon being polite and not watching me. He grabs his own change of clothes and heads to the washroom.

I settled into my usual balcony chair, the one on the right, and wait for Jaxon to join me.

When he sits down next to me, I turn to him.

"So, that kiss..." I say, a little excitement in my voice.

He leans back further in his chair, arms draped over the armrests, hands clasped at the edges, and I watch his eyes follow me from head to toe, sending jolts through me after each point that he passes.

Jaxon's wearing a pair of black shorts with a small white logo on the thigh and a simple grey T-shirt from the same brand, plus his ball cap. He's been playing my game, and the anticipation of what's coming next has me breathing a little shallow.

"Yeah, well, there's more where that came from," Jaxon tells me.

"Is that an invitation?"

He's canvasing me with a smoldering look. His eyes narrow, so I decide to call his bluff.

I watch him swallow when I stand. My bare feet are cool on the balcony floor, the sun no longer beaming on the balcony, and the only light is coming from the one small bulb on the side of the patio door. I make my way the few steps to his chair, where I kick his feet open enough for me to fit in between his legs.

"Can I taste?" I ask sweetly and innocently, as if I am asking nothing other than for a French fry from his plate.

He nods, his lips parting, waiting for mine.

I bend over, placing my hands on the sides of the arm rests next to him, and lower until our mouths collide in a fast, hard kiss.

Within seconds, Jaxon is sitting up in his chair, meeting me halfway. We're kissing like the night is short and tomorrow isn't promised. His hands grab at my sides as he tilts his head up towards me. I take hold of the visor of his cap and swivel it until it's facing backwards on his head. My hands take hold of his neck as I straddle him, my shins firmly against the wood. He groans into our kiss.

His mouth pulls away, and before I can miss his taste, he distracts me by nibbling, licking, and sucking a line from below my ear to my shoulder.

And then he stops.

"How do your shoulders feel?"

I look at him, shocked.

*How do my shoulders feel? Really, Jaxon?*

I ignore his question and plant my lips back on his. The heat is building between us again when he pulls away.

"We need to stop." He shakes his head, and I watch him in a tormented state. "I won't be able to stop myself from pulling down these shorts and bending you over the balcony." He's playing with the waist of my shorts, his fingers dipping past the waistband, and I wiggle, moving to accommodate them.

He presses his lips together and rubs his palm down his face. I lean back, admiring the beauty of this man.

"Promise?"

He chokes on a laugh.

A loud knock on the door distracts us both, and we immediately look into the room.

I peel myself off of Jaxon and watch as he adjusts himself. "Let me."

My eyes trail down to the bulge in his shorts. "I think I better go."

He looks down and grins. "That might be a good idea."

I run my hands through my hair and straighten the waist of my shorts. When I open the door and peer out, no one is there but Brodie's voice can be heard throughout the corridor.

"Time to meditate!" he calls, and I can hear Julie laughing by his side.

I close the door. "We'd better get..."

Jaxon's mouth cuts my sentence short. This time, our lips linger. His hands cup my face, locking me in. We move slowly this time, his tongue circling mine. When we finally pull away, I'm caught a little off balance.

"Ready?" Jaxon takes my hand.

I know what he's referring to, but my mind flutters to thoughts of diving deep with Jaxon.

I think I am, but ready or not, my heart isn't giving me a choice.

# Chapter Twenty-Six

*Jaxon*

The balcony door closes with a thud.

My back is to Quinn. I peer out through the glass door to where we were just a few minutes ago, before Brodie had to fuck everything up.

The taste of Quinn's watermelon lip gloss is fresh on my lips.

Turning around, I watch her bend down to tie her shoes by the door. There's not a hint of a panty line, and I wonder what she's wearing underneath the tight spandex. I want to take her on or up against every square inch of this room and the balcony.

Quinn is slowly stepping through a door that has magically appeared in the walls I built around myself.

My heart belongs to her. We're only on day two of this retreat, but people say you'll know when you know, and I don't know who the fuck those people are, but I believe them.

# CHAPTER TWENTY-SIX

Because I know.

I know everything I need to.

I know the shit she does that pisses me off.

I know the way her lips curve into a smile.

I know the pouting face she'll make when she doesn't get her way.

And I know that Luna and I are her family.

"Did you hear me?" Quinn is watching me with a confused expression.

"Huh?"

"I asked if you had your key."

"Oh, yeah."

*Get your shit together, Jaxon.*

We walk hand in hand to the yoga studio where this sound meditation is happening, and the whole way down, I come up with a plan.

First, get the promotion.

Second, tell Quinn I'm falling for her.

Third, fuck her till the end of time.

And in the meantime, I'm going to kiss her every chance I get.

"You seem lost in thought," Quinn states as we turn a corner into another long corridor. She waves to Edward and a few others standing outside of the yoga room.

"I'm sorry. I guess I'm nervous about this whole laying down on the floor in front of everyone and doing nothing shit."

The last part is true. Quinn's taking up a whole lot of space in my head, but still not enough to distract me from the anxiety I get before each activity.

"It's called relaxing, Jaxon." She smiles up at me. "It'll be good for your uptight ass." I chuckle. "And I will be right beside you. You'll be safe."

She squeezes my hand. And this is why she has my heart.

I don't remember a time where I've felt this much comfort.

The dim room has a soft yellow glow, and there are yoga mats, towels and blankets spread out over the length of the room.

"Come in, come in." The instructor motions for us to find a spot. "There's enough room for everyone. Find a spot on the floor, take off your shoes, and get comfortable." She's walking between some of the bodies that are already lying still.

We find two spots side by side, and I pull off my runners and watch Quinn do the same. When she lies down, she worms her body over the mat, settling in.

She catches me watching her. "What?" she whispers, her forehead creasing.

I smile and follow suit just to make her laugh. I'm not disappointed when that familiar sound finds its way to my ears.

The instructor tells us to close our eyes and just relax.

She starts off with a short reading, something about life and challenges, and I struggle to focus. I don't know how the fuck this sound bath is supposed to work, but my promotion is on the line, so I will lie down wherever Edward tells me to.

My eyes just jolt open at the first sound, but Quinn intertwines her fingers in mine, and I allow myself to settle in.

I spend the next hour in and out of sleep, dreaming, waking, and rubbing the back of Quinn's hand with my thumb on repeat.

This shit is magical. Like if there was a far-off place where fairies lived, this would be the sounds you'd hear instead of car horns, sirens, and protests.

What the hell happened the last hour, and why the fuck am I thinking about fairies?

I've fallen back to sleep when a loud sound awakens me, and my body jerks, sending me upright.

Everyone else is still lying down, eyes closed, and I turn to where the sound came from. The instructor is holding some kind of wooden stick, and I watch as she strikes a large gong, sending the sound throughout the space once more.

I face Quinn. Her eyes are open, and she's staring at me. I don't look away until the gong has turned silent.

Twenty minutes later, we're on our way back to the room.

"That was amazing, wasn't it, Jaxon?"

I'm going to sleep like the dead tonight, and the best part about it is that Quinn will be with me, in our shared bed.

We brush our teeth, and then I listen to Quinn lecture me on how I need to wash my face with special soap. Once I'm scrubbed and moisturized to her satisfaction, I wait in bed for her to come join me.

My jaw drops when she finally comes out of the bathroom.

Good Lord, how am I going to keep my hands off of her?

Quinn is wearing light pink shorts and a matching pink tank top, the bottom edge landing just above her bellybutton.

Promotion. First comes the promotion. I remind myself of the plan I came up with only a few hours ago.

She gets in beside me, moving the covers around, and nestles in the crook of my arm.

I'm lying there still, afraid to move, when her fingernails trail across my chest.

Fuck me.

# Chapter Twenty-Seven

## Quinn

"Lying in your arms is one of my new favorite things to do," I say, letting my body get comfortable next to his.

Jaxon stiffens under me, but the lump in the blanket just below his waist tells me he's not *not* enjoying this.

My fingernails play in the small amount of chest hair that he has, and he lets out a heavy breath. I let my eyes fall closed and relax into him. He trails his fingers at the base of my tank top, the soft fabric tickling my midsection.

"It's nice," he tells me. I move my hand towards the side of his torso, scratching up and down lightly, scattering tiny little goosebumps across his skin.

We stay this way for a long time. I'm fighting to stay awake after that meditation class, but being in bed with Jaxon, where there's the possibility of something more has me holding out.

I don't have to wonder if Jaxon feels the same. I felt it this afternoon on the balcony when I was straddling him.

## CHAPTER TWENTY-SEVEN

Jaxon groans lightly, barely a whisper, so I tilt my head towards him. My movement stirs his eyes open, and he grins down sleepily at me.

"That feels so good." His voice cracks as if he hasn't spoken in hours.

"It could feel better," I offer sensually.

I move my hand down and across his abdominal muscles and let my fingers trace them. As I do this, Jaxon takes it upon himself to move his own fingers down to the waist of my shorts, caressing me, back and forth, until he suddenly rolls me onto my back.

He lays down on top of me, steadying himself on his left elbow, and holds my gaze as he pushes back pieces of my hair.

"You are so beautiful, Quinn."

His lips meet mine, and I let him take control of our kiss, sliding his tongue around mine. I cross my legs behind his back, lifting my hips to meet his, and I gasp when I feel him moving in rhythm with me.

I push all my worries aside. Worries about whether Jaxon will get the promotion, or what will happen if he doesn't. What will happen to me, to us?

Promotion or not, I want Jaxon as my husband. My *real* husband with benefits, with love and everything in between.

"Is this okay?" Jaxon asks in a whisper.

"Mm, yes."

I let my legs fall to his sides. My hands trail over his shoulders, and over each muscle of his arms, and back up again, until one of my hands runs through his hair and the other reaches for his ass, which is just out of reach. He exhales my name into the crook of my neck, like I am his and his alone. I adjust my body under him so he's right where I need him to be, and when a moan escapes me, he responds by deepening our kiss.

"Jaxon." I shift, pulling at his shorts. "More," I demand between kisses.

He takes hold of my hands and pulls me up so that I'm sitting, and he lifts my tank top over my head, my breasts tightening at the cool air of the room. I let my body fall back down onto the mattress, and he shifts to the side and hooks his index fingers in the waist of my shorts. He pulls them down around my ankles and slides my feet through, releasing them into his hands before he folds them neatly and places them on the bed beside us.

His fingers slide up my body over the curve of my hip, sending flutters through me. He's taking his time with me, and I'm throbbing with need. His hand comes to my breast where he cups it lightly, palming me, until his fingers graze my nipple and gently twist it back and forth.

"Jaxon, please," I tell him again, and his eyes darken. He replaces his fingers with his mouth and starts toying with me all the same. His hand cups my other breast, and he moves his body over me as my hips move trying to find his to relieve some of the pressure building between my legs.

He trails down my stomach, kissing and licking at my skin until he settles himself between my thighs. His hungry eyes meet mine. "Quinn, I've wanted you in my bed since the first night you showed up in that blue lace bodysuit."

This information shocks me, but I watch him wet his lips before lowering himself down onto me. My lips part as a soft moan escapes, and I watch him tease a little before diving in for a taste. When I can't take it any longer, I let my head fall back onto the pillow in bliss.

"Jaxon." I call out his name. "Fuck, Jaxon."

He reaches for my breasts as his tongue flicks and circles, sending my body into tiny convulsions. I run my hands through his thick hair and take hold while I unravel beneath him.

He comes up beside me and our mouths collide, and his hands take hold of my face, kissing me harder than before. I dive inside his boxer-briefs, wanting to feel him raw in my hand. He groans into my mouth at the first touch, and with little room for motion, I tell him to take his boxers off.

His hand clasps a fistful of my hair as he breathes into my neck. I grip him firmly, sliding up and down, my thumb caressing his tip. Jaxon quickly becomes breathless, and I feel his body stiffen next to mine, his muscles clenching as he nears breaking point, as I whisper into his ear.

"You like that?" I ask.

"Yes, fuck," he groans again into my neck.

When his body jerks, I press my lips to his, and I catch his raspy moans with my tongue as he shudders beside me.

# Chapter Twenty-Eight

*Jaxon*

We fell asleep twisted between the sheets, Quinn's head on my chest.

Last night was incredible, and it's safe to say my rules may be out the fucking window.

Quinn stirs beside me, and her eyes flutter open.

"Good morning, handsome," she says, licking her lips. I respond with my own throaty version of the same.

I glance over at the bedside clock, blinking a few times so that the time comes into focus.

"Fuck, we're late." I jump out of bed quickly, forgetting that I'm stark naked until I see Quinn's eyes scanning over me, a satisfied smile on her face. "Like what you see?" I tease.

"Do I ever." She's not even trying to hide the fact that she's checking me out.

She sits up, her hair tousled into a bird's nest of sexual satisfaction, and it's fucking hot.

"Not that I want to rush this morning waking up next to you, especially after last night, but if we don't get going soon, Edward might send a search party."

"Got it, boss." She winks at me, and fuck, does it not soften me.

By the time we got down to the dining hall for breakfast, everyone was already taking their last bites. We each grabbed a pastry and a glass of orange juice and finished up just in time for Edward to divide us up into our three groups.

Our schedule today told us that we would be going on a scavenger hunt.

I've never in my life done a scavenger hunt. Not even at Easter. My friends used to brag about their hunt for chocolate eggs left behind by the Easter Bunny, but my parents never bothered hiding anything. I'd wake up Easter morning to a basket of eggs sitting on the kitchen table. It was the same every year as far as I can remember into the past, until my parents decided I was old enough to know that the Easter Bunny wasn't real.

So, here I am, a thirty-six-year-old man about to take part in his very first scavenger hunt. Quinn, on the other hand, has been gabbing with Lester and Vinny for the last five minutes about what the theme might be.

I wasn't aware that scavenger hunts needed a theme, but apparently it makes them more fun, or so Lester said and Vinny agreed.

There are three tables divided up in different corners of the room. Each table is empty except for a colored tablecloth and matching cotton scarves.

Manuel faces us by the entrance door. "The scavenger hunt will be begin shortly, if everyone can gather close." The fifteen of us nestle elbow to elbow as we wait for the instructions. When the crowd quiets, he continues. "Today you will all get to take part in building your very own watch."

There's a whistle from the group and a few excited claps and hollers. Building a watch makes total sense to me, but I can't for the life of me understand how this game is going to roll out.

"You will be three groups of five. This activity will have you working together as a team, and I have the teams already picked."

There are a few exchanged glances within the group, and Manuel continues by calling out names.

My group is Brodie, Ashley, Edward, Lester, and me. Quinn is with Vinny, Carole, Julie, and Ashley's husband, Shawn. It's probably for the best that they've separated me and Quinn, because after last night, I'm not sure I'd be able to concentrate on the task at hand with her so close.

"There are three team colors, go pick your color."

There's a mad dash from Lester and Quinn. Quinn heads to purple, and Lester to blue.

"We're purple!" she says to her teammates. She picks up the purple scarf and wraps it around her head like a bandana, and the others follow suit, wrapping the scarf around their arm, head, or thigh.

I place my blue scarf around my bicep because there's no fucking way that I'm tying that shit around my head. But when I glance over at Quinn, she's laughing with Shawn and Vinny and coming up with a team handshake.

We're definitely sugar and spice, but fuck if we aren't everything nice together.

"You will find your clue cards in the envelopes that are sitting on your respective tables. Each card will have a clue to get you where you need to go to find your items. Do you want to know how this ties into building a watch?" he asks.

## CHAPTER TWENTY-EIGHT

"Yes!" a few people shout at the same time.

"Your clues are going to lead you to items that will help you build a watch. But this won't be your average watch. This will be a five-foot watch by the time you are done assembling it as a team."

The teams are talking among themselves, and some of them have picked up their envelopes from the table.

"Do not open your clues just yet," Manuel warns as he walks around us, trying to create tension and suspense. "After each clue, you will locate a piece that you will need to build your watch. Between each card, you will need to bring your item back down here and set them on the table. All three teams have the same clues, but they will be given to you in different orders so there's no clustering in areas or cheating by following another team. So, go in order of the clues in your envelopes. No mixing them up because you're stuck."

Quinn's nodding, taking it all in.

I'm only half listening to Manuel explain the rest of the details. I'm still thinking about Quinn, the balcony kiss, her perfect nipples, and how she jerked me off last night. She got dressed while I was in the shower this morning, and now I'm wondering what she has on under those tiny jean shorts and tank top.

Manuel clears his throat, snapping me out of my daydream.

"When you've completed all the clues, you will return here where you will assemble the watch as a team. The first team to build their watch correctly wins!"

Okay, so find watch parts, bring them back here, and build a watch. How difficult could that be?

"There will be no time limit, first ones done win. It's that simple. Maps have been provided to you in the envelope; use them as staff is not to answer any questions during this game. We are not an escape room; there will be no walkie-talkies, and no additional clues provided. Are you ready?"

The group responds loudly.

"I said, are you ready?" Manuel repeats louder with more excitement in his voice.

A mix of animated answers are shouted around me, and I clap in response.

"Ready, set, go!"

Edward has our envelope. He's slowly pulling out the map and unfolding it as if it's an old newspaper and it's Sunday morning. At this rate, we're going to lose. I love the man, but Christ, he is thoroughly inspecting the map.

I peer over my shoulder at Quinn's group, where they're already reading the card with their heads together and looking at the map.

"With all due respect, sir," Ashley speaks up, her hand is outstretched, "may I?" Edward stares at her a second before handing over the clues.

"I won't slow you down. I may be getting old, but I still play tennis," he tells us. Lester chuckles in response, but the rest of us have our game faces on.

Ashley reads out the first clue:

> I'm filled with words and stories about great love affairs.
> You will find what you're looking for near a set of stairs.

She's practically jumping out of her shoes. With her competitiveness, we might just have a shot at winning this thing.

"The map, Edward, the map. Where are there stairs?" she asks.

## CHAPTER TWENTY-EIGHT

Edward places the map on the table, and we all hover over it. Behind us, I hear Quinn giggle, and her group scuttles out of the room on the way to retrieve their first object.

Fuck.

Lester chimes in. "There are stairs near the back here, just around the corner from us. But there are stairs up here, near the game room and library. Read the clue again, Ashley."

Ashley reads out the clue again.

"The library," Brodie calls out. "Words, stories—the library!"

"Shh," Ashley warns. "We don't want the other teams to hear us."

I scan the room. Both teams are already gone.

I grab the map off the table, and we hurry towards the door, racing through the resort until we reach a dark mahogany door with the word "Library" engraved in gold.

All five of us enter the medium-sized room. There are bookshelves from floor to ceiling on two of the walls, books lining every shelf. They vary in height and color, and I flinch at the lack of symmetry. We separate, all looking around, not sure for what but assuming that we will know it when we see it.

Edward calls out from his spot near the leather couch, "I found it! It's the crystal." He's tossing a blanket out of a basket that sits on the floor beside the couch.

We all head over to where he's standing, and I bend to pick up the plastic crystal that's to be placed on top of the dial. It was strategically placed in a basket covered with blankets.

"Brodie, want to cover up the other two?" I nod at the blanket Edward discarded on the floor. "We don't want to make it any easier for the other two teams."

"Yeah, I got it." He covers the two remaining crystals with the soft beige blanket, and we all head to the door.

We make our way back to the room just as Quinn's team is leaving, most likely on the search for their second clue. The third team is nowhere in sight.

I place the crystal on top of the blue tablecloth, where Ashley pulls out another clue.

> You come here to relax and unwind,
> and leave all your tension and troubles behind.

We're looking at one another, considering what the clue means.

Brodie takes the card from Ashley and reads it out loud again. I look over the map that we've spread back down on the table, and my fingers trail different areas of the resort. Edward peers over my shoulder. "Outside near the hot tub?"

"Hmm, maybe." My eyes scan the map.

Ashley repeats the last line. "Is there a spa?"

Brodie leans in to look at the map. His fingers trail the right side as mine trail the left.

"Right here." I point to a spot on the map. "Breathe, it says. There's a picture of a robe." My fingers trail to the bottom left corner of the map where the symbols are decoded. The robe image means massage. "Massage room."

We take about ten minutes to get to the spa, and we approach quietly. We're the only ones here, but it somehow feels wrong to be loud in this space.

The spa has numerous small rooms, so it takes us longer to find the hidden object, which are the straps for the watch. Brodie is carrying two large blue straps with a buckle, meant to be pieced together after we find the rest of the watch.

We head back once again to the conference room, with Edward in the lead. He wasn't wrong. He might have been slow when he first pulled out that map, but he's quick on his feet when push comes to shove.

I have no idea what place our team is in, but when we get back to the room, we're the only ones here. I take a second to check out the other two tables, and it's difficult to tell who is in the lead since each table now has two objects. Looks like we could be coming in last.

Time to pick up the pace.

# Chapter Twenty-Nine

*Quinn*

> I am usually made of metal and known for my sound.
> If you tap me with your index finger, someone will come around.

I read our newest clue while I stand by the table next to Vinny. Julie's full of fire; I can only imagine the type of team she and Brodie make back home with their kids.

We're standing around whispering ideas of random metal objects we think the clue could hint at but have yet to figure it out. This is the first clue we seem to be stuck on.

I read the clue again, seeing that we're getting nowhere.

"'If you tap me with your index finger.' What does this even mean?" I ask the group.

"Someone will come around," Carole repeats. "It's a bell. The front lobby." Carole is speed-walking to the door of the conference room, and we follow behind her. I'm the last one out when Jaxon's group is arriving with one of their objects.

As I pass by him, our hands touch briefly and our eyes meet, sending shivers up my arm and throughout my body, stopping me in my tracks. Flashes from last night come to mind.

"You coming, Quinn?" Julie calls out ahead of me.

I run to catch up. "You betcha," I say, shaking the thoughts away.

When we get to the front lobby, we see a bright gold bell sitting next to Manuel.

Carole turns back to us, smiling widely. "It's the bell, I knew it."

"Good one, Carole," Julie replies, patting her on the back.

Vinny pipes up when he gets to the small desk printer nestled in the corner of the counter behind the desk. "Found it."

He pulls out the purple case. The watch we're building matches our team color and will be a five-foot purple watch when we're done. After we pulled out our first clue and the map, we looked over the pieces that make up a watch in the instructions, so we had some type of idea what we would be looking for since none of us actually work for Edward Rummens Watches.

We head back down with our purple case that will hold all the contents of the watch, and when we get back to our table downstairs, we look at everything we've accumulated so far.

It's been about an hour, and I'm thirsty. We decide that since we're in the lead, we can take a quick break. When we're hydrated, we're set to go again.

Vinny looks over the next clue and reads it out loud to us.

> You can reach me by foot, but you may want to drive. If you're feeling adventurous, you can come and scuba dive.

"The beach!" I exclaim out loud as I push a piece of hair out of my face.

"What are we waiting for?" Carole is at the top of our train again, leading us to where the beach buggy is parked.

We pile in and wait for the driver to get behind the wheel.

"To the beach," Julie hollers from the back seat, and we all laugh.

The beach buggy takes us through the bumpy road to the ocean, and we all pile out of the van and onto the warm, soft sand. We head straight for the cabin that houses the life jackets and supplies.

When we finally arrive at the small wooden hut, there are a few paddleboards leaning against the back wall and canoes tipped upside down, but the back door is unlocked, so we walk right in. The five of us search high and low. It doesn't take us long before Shawn grabs a purple bag hanging on a hook on the back of the door. He opens the bag, revealing three hands for the watch.

"To the villa," Julie shouts, taking the lead next to Carole. They're both speed-walking through the sand.

We all pile back in the buggy and make our way to the villa, where we set the hands of our watch with the rest of the items.

After I've pulled and read out the last clue, we review all the items we have and figure out the one we're missing, the thing that you turn to adjust the time. Carole informs us that the correct word for it is a crown.

## CHAPTER TWENTY-NINE

The other two teams pile into the room and pull out their own cards. It looks like we're still in the lead, second is Jaxon's team, and the green team is behind with two clues left.

We move quickly, and in less than fifteen minutes, we're back and ready to build our watch.

Before we can even get started, I hear Brodie's voice, loud behind me. We're all huddled over our purple table, looking at our items.

I guess we're tied for the win.

Time to rally.

# Chapter Thirty

## *Jaxon*

I'm just attaching the straps of this giant-ass watch to the case when we hear Quinn's team shout, "Done!"

Brodie lets the other strap fall onto the table, giving up across from me. He shrugs his shoulders towards me and mouths, *Next time*.

Brodie and I actually work well together. It's something that I've always considered a nuisance, because if I liked the guy, it'd be hard to hate him for going after my job.

But I'm allowed to hate the guy for going after my promotion.

Manuel looks over the purple watch and holds it up when he's done inspecting.

"Purple team wins!" he exclaims. "Everyone did such a great job with the clues. You should all be proud."

I'm not proud unless I fucking win. Losing's not an option. But I'm trying to be more of a team player so I clap for the winning team. It's Quinn's team that won, so I can't be mad at that.

## CHAPTER THIRTY

Quinn comes to my side, and I give her a quick kiss on the cheek. "Great job."

She's smiling ear to ear. "That was so much fun."

"Everyone from the purple team will be entered in a draw to win a watch from Edward Rummens Watches." After a couple of minutes, Manuel declares Vinny the winner.

Vinny is jumping up and down excitedly, and Edward takes his hand in his when he's settled. "Your prize can be picked up at Edward Rummens Watches on Kensington," he tells him.

We all clap, and some pat him on the back.

Edward comes up between me and Brodie, placing a hand on each of our shoulders. "What a team we were."

The end of this week can't come soon enough. I need to know that promotion is mine.

Quite a few of us came down to the beach during free time before dinner, but the sky has recently clouded over, and most have already left. Quinn and I are just deciding if we should try our luck on the paddleboards.

"Do you think it's going to rain?" Quinn asks, looking up at the sky. "It might be better to wait."

"I think we'll be fine."

We walk hand in hand to the cabin where we were this morning looking for scavenger hunt items. We each take a life jacket, and I help snap Quinn's tight across her chest, tugging on it to make sure it fits her properly. After I've zipped my own, we head around back to the paddleboards pressed up against the wall.

"I want that one," she says, pointing to one that is a mix of pink and purple.

I grab hold of the eleven-foot board and carry it to the edge of the water. I head back and grab my own board, and I'm placing it next to Quinn's when raindrops begin to splatter on my shoulder.

I look around and see the last few people packing up to head back to the villa. "We're going to get wet anyway. A little rain won't hurt us."

Quinn nods, and we continue into the water.

It takes me a minute to get on my knees and slowly stand. Quinn is still on her knees when I look over at her.

"How did you get up?" she shouts at me, as she's drifting away.

"Place your feet hip width apart, in the center, at the widest part of the board. Scoot up a bit until you're in the middle." I paddle until I'm right next to her. Quinn stands in a quick swoop, and I see her wobbling. "The more relaxed you are, the less you're going to wobble."

"Have you done this before?" she asks, and I tell her no. She pouts. "Then how the hell are you looking all pro paddleboarder?"

I let out a chuckle. "I don't look pro."

She purses her lips and lets out a slow, even breath. "I'm doing it," she exclaims.

I watch her glide her paddle through the water on her right. Within a few minutes she's paddling in front of me, and I get a nice view of her ass in a hot-pink bikini bottom.

The rain has begun to come down in a light drizzle. We stay close to shore and paddle for a short time. Then the

## CHAPTER THIRTY

sky kicks it up a notch, and the rain starts falling faster and harder.

"I think it's probably time we call it," I say through the raindrops splattering on my face.

By the time we've pulled the boards out of the water, the rain is coming down hard and thunder cracks overhead. We make a dash for the storage cabin, and just as I'm closing the door behind us, another thunderbolt cracks loudly outside. Quinn jumps, startled.

We both start laughing as we take off our life jackets and hang them on a hook to dry.

I take two towels from the pile sitting on the counter and toss one over to Quinn. I watch as she towel-dries her hair. When she catches me staring, I take my towel and ruffle my own hair, trying to look away.

But my eyes dart back to her and land on her tits, her hard nipples pressing against the wet pink fabric. Her bottoms come high on her hips, revealing tattoo number two at her bikini line.

I wonder if she can tell I'm hard under these blue swim trunks.

"What are you looking at?" she asks me.

"Your tattoo. It's sexy."

She looks down at the rose. "Roses always reminded me of Granny, so I got this after she passed."

"And your butterfly?"

"The butterfly was for my mom. She used to always tell me as a child that I would one day come out of my cocoon and flutter about like a butterfly." She's lost in her thoughts, her spark dwindling. "I don't think I ever lived up to that butterfly part my mom talked about."

"What do you mean?"

"I never flew away." She looks sad, and I watch her take a seat on the high stool next to the counter. "I stayed in that cocoon. Stayed in a dead-end job and even more dead-end town."

"Hey." I walk towards her, tilting her chin up towards me until I see that her blue eyes are glassy. "Look where you are right now."

"Stuck in a beach cabin during a thunderstorm?"

Thunder cracks again and we both laugh.

"Quinn, you moved across the country to marry a man you barely knew and are now making friends with his coworkers, running around doing scavenger hunts and propelling off trees. You are not in a cocoon anymore."

I take her hair in my hands and set the wet length of the thick blonde down her back, revealing her slender shoulders. I skim my fingertips over her collarbone, watching as her skin prickles with goosebumps.

"I guess you're right, I am more butterfly than cocoon now. A lot has changed since moving here."

"It took a lot of guts to do what you did. To answer my message and fly across the country to help me."

"You've helped me too. You're helping me come out of my shell and find out who I really am."

"You're doing that all on your own, Quinn."

She lets out a soft sigh and tilts her head to the left as my fingers trail down her right side. I see it as an open invitation to plant a soft kiss right in the center. Her skin is still wet and salty from the ocean. I continue my kisses until they reach right below her ear. I grab hold of her wet hair with my left hand and take my right one to graze over her hard nipple, my lips crashing down on hers.

My thumb rubs back and forth over the fabric until I feel her nipple peak, and I roll it in between my forefinger and thumb. "Mm, I like the way you touch me," she purrs. I pull her hair back gently, and a moan escapes her this time. My hand cups her full breast, palming it, teasing her, making her say my name. "Jaxon."

She wraps her arms around my waist, her nails digging into my back as our kiss deepens. I'm hovering over her on the stool, groaning into her mouth, and I move my body closer to hers, until she wraps those legs around me, holding me tight. When she feels me hard against her, her breath catches in her throat, and she dips her head back.

I lift her up in one swift motion and set her down on top of the counter. She lifts her arms over her head, and I take that as an order, dutifully lifting the wet material over her head and dropping it lightly on the counter beside her.

My dick twitches at the sight of her. And there's tattoo number three, a small heart at the base of her left breast, filled black, so small it could easily be missed if you weren't paying attention. This woman, my wife, and her fucking sexy body, slick, tasting like salt and ocean. My tongue flicks fast at her nipple, and I place my hand over the naked one that's waiting for its turn. Her body is arching for more, and I give it to her.

She's leaning back into her hands, and I stop to admire her.

"Do you like it when I do this?" Both my hands come up to her breasts, and my fingers twist her nipples.

Her breath shallows, her eyes never leaving mine. "Yes."

I do it a few more times, which has her hips moving back and forth on the counter.

"Do you like it when I do this?"

I place the pad of my thumb on top of her bikini bottoms, just over where her clit would be. Her hips immediately move faster as I circle her.

"Yes, Jaxon."

I bring my mouth down on her perky tits, one at a time, giving them both the attention I know she wants.

"Oh, Jaxon."

Her hips move faster against my pressure. I stop, and I place a flat palm between her breasts to gently press her down on her back. Her feet come up to find the edge of the counter. When she shudders at the cold countertop, I take another towel from the pile and place it under her.

She lifts her hips as I hook my fingers into the high-waisted swimsuit bottoms and drag them over her ass and down her legs. I spread her legs, looking at the folds of her body, licking my lips, wanting to taste more of her.

I bend down, and the whimper that escapes her is primal. She meets every lick and suck, her legs shaking on either side of me. I wrap my arms around her legs and hold her tight.

"Jaxon, I'm so close."

I unhook one arm and slide two fingers deep inside her to feel how wet she is for me.

"Fuck, Quinn, you're so wet."

Within a few seconds, she comes undone under the pressure of my tongue with my fingers still deep inside her.

"She sits up at the edge of the counter, taking me in her hand. "You're so big." The rain is coming down loud; her words drowned out by the sound.

I lift her off the counter and turn her around until her back is to me, and she presses the palms of her hands into the wooden stool.

"Is this okay?" I ask her, nibbling at the back of her neck.

"Yes, Jaxon, I need you."

When she feels me against her ass, she pushes back against me, telling me with her hips what she wants. Thunder cracks again overhead, and I feel the energy of the storm take over us.

# CHAPTER THIRTY

My hands run down her back, squeezing her ass as she arches just enough to let me in.

I fill her slowly, not wanting to hurt her. She's so tight around my hard dick, but I feel her ready for me. I kiss her neck, one hand tugging her hair, as I slide into her further. I groan, my voice raspy, whispering her name. She arches further, and with my free hand, I grab hold of her hip and fuck her harder.

Her needy little ass bounces off me with each thrust as she gives me short, broken pleas for more.

I groan, leaning back, spreading her cheeks, watching as I slide in and out of her.

"Fuck, Quinn."

Her legs are trembling, and my own shaky over the hardwood flooring.

"Jaxon, yes. Faster."

I choke back a grunt as I let go of her hair and grab at her tit, my mouth landing on her neck as she cries out.

When I've shuddered and finished, I stand up, weak in the knees. She stands and turns around, her breath shallow, matching my own.

I pull her in for a hug. "That was fucking amazing." I dip my head until I'm in the crook of her neck. "Are you okay?"

"I am more than okay, Jaxon. Oh my God."

She nuzzles into my chest, and we stand there catching our breaths.

I will never be able to go another goddamn day without Quinn in my life.

# Chapter Thirty-One

## *Quinn*

I'm tugging at my bikini bottoms, trying to pull the wet spandex over the thicker part my thighs.

My heart is still beating hard. Jaxon placing me on the counter, lying me on my back, pulling my wet hair, and bending me over will be flashing through my mind for the rest of the week.

"Do you think they're looking for us?" I ask Jaxon. "The rain sounds like it's starting to let up."

Just as I am finishing my sentence, we hear a horn honk. Jaxon stands, and I hop off the counter. We make our way outside to where the beach buggy is sitting, windshield wipers on.

Jaxon runs up to the van and tells him something I can't hear. When he comes back to me, he says, "I'm just going to prop the boards back up against the wall. Grab your stuff, and I'll meet you at the van?"

## CHAPTER THIRTY-ONE

I nod, heading back into the cabin where our bags are. I toss the wet towels in the hamper marked *used* and run through the sprinkles of rain to the van.

Jaxon meets us a few seconds later.

"That storm came out of nowhere. A few from your group mentioned that you were still down here. Figured you'd taken shelter in the cabin." The driver pulls around and starts back up the road to the villa. "Happens here quite often with the hot temperatures."

We sit side by side still in a post-fuck state, smirks being shared between us when he intertwines his fingers in mine.

When we reach the villa, we thank the driver for coming to get us, and head up to our room, nodding at some of his co-workers as we pass.

"I could really use a shower." I set our bags on the floor next to the door and slip off my wet cover up.

"Mind if I join you?" Jaxon asks me, pulling off his own shirt.

"I think there might be room for the two." I wink.

We're sitting with Brodie and Julie by the fire pit when Lester and Vinny join us. Brodie asks how the paddleboarding was, and Jaxon answers him, smiling, and I know that he's thinking of the hot cabin sex.

This week was supposed to be about him getting the promotion, but it's also been helping us build our connection.

I couldn't imagine life without Jaxon and Luna now. I can't go back to how I used to be.

Jaxon's right, I've turned into the butterfly Mom always said I would be. Maybe I did do this on my own, by making the choice to come marry this man, but this sense of freedom wouldn't have happened without him.

If I were still back at home, maybe one day I'd eventually have pulled myself out of debt and found a man and a life. But Jaxon helped speed up that process, and I couldn't be more grateful that he showed up when he did.

It feels like it was meant to be.

"The games are all set up in the dining hall," Manuel mentions this to a group sitting at one of the other couches in the lobby.

Tonight's activity is just good old board game fun.

I'm carrying my tropical drink in my right hand, Jaxon's hand intertwined in my left, when we walk back into the dining hall.

There are games that involve memory skills, others that involve murder mystery, but we settle at a table with Brodie, Julie, Vinny, and Lester and a deck of cards.

Brodie and Jaxon teach us a game they both know how to play, and an hour later, I place my hand on the table. "I'm done. I keep losing," I huff, pouting at my lack of luck.

After another round, Julie and Lester call out too.

It's not long before Brodie wins the game, and Jaxon takes the last sip of his drink.

"Good game." He bumps Jaxon's fist as if they're old buddies, and Jaxon gives him an agreeable smile.

"Good game," he repeats. Jaxon turns to me. "What's next?"

## CHAPTER THIRTY-ONE

I shrug my shoulders, tired from the active day. I wouldn't mind bowing out and lounging in our room, I tell Jaxon when we're out of earshot.

Jaxon tells me to wait where I am, and he heads towards Edward. I watch them exchange a few words before Jaxon returns and Edward is waving a hand at me. I return it with a smile.

"Want to get out of here?"

I nod. "Yes."

He leads me around the exterior of the property by the pool. We take our time, walking back to our room. After we swipe our way back in, I watch in astonishment as Jaxon leaps up onto the bed and starts jumping.

"No. Fucking. Way."

"Are you going to join me or what?"

I let out a giggle and run to the bed where Jaxon takes my hands, helping me up.

"You're going to hit your head on the ceiling." I laugh, noting how close he comes to the ceiling with each bounce.

When we're both in a fit of laughter, we fall onto the bed and lay back. His arm is around me, nestling me close to his chest.

"So was it everything you thought it would be?" I ask him.

"It was so much more," Jaxon tells me, and I know he's not just talking about jumping on the bed.

# Chapter Thirty-Two

*Jaxon*

I was today-year-old when I jumped on a bed for the first time in my goddamn life.

Thirty-six and jumping on the bed like a child.

"When's your birthday?" I ask Quinn. She told me when we first started chatting, after we matched, but suddenly I don't remember.

"September twelfth," she says as she outlines the sea goat tattoo on my thigh. "You're a Capricorn."

"January third." I want to make a mental note of things Quinn likes, because, well, she fucking deserves it. "What's your favorite kind of cake?"

"I don't know. I eat whatever is made for me."

"Well, if you could choose any cake, what would you choose?"

She doesn't answer me right away, and I start to wonder if she's falling asleep in my arms when she speaks again.

"I think I like lemon."

"Lemon?"

"Yeah, it's such a light flavor." She wiggles, moving around to get comfortable.

"Lemon it is."

"What about you?"

"Chocolate."

We're both quiet, secretly storing this information for later. "You must miss your parents," she says out of the blue.

I sigh. I do, but it's something I've gotten used to. She asks what they're like, and I answer her truthfully.

Life growing up was good, decent. My parents took care of me, and they provided me with what they had. I didn't go without much, except for affection and attention. Which some would argue is more important than the material things.

Her nails start tickling my skin again, running up and down my arm, and it's something I've come to realize I want, her affection. Something I've missed out on my entire life.

"I don't think I said it, but thank you for coming here and being such a good sport about everything."

Quinn props herself up on her elbows to look at me.

"Jaxon, I'm having the time of my life. Plus, it was kind of the whole deal, right?"

"Yeah, I guess you're right."

"Are you getting nervous about the promotion?"

"A little. I've worked hard to get here. It'd be a disappointment to not receive it, especially to Brodie, who's only been in the business a short time, and with Edward Rummens even shorter."

"I think it's more your idea of someone taking the job from you than it actually being Brodie, am I right?"

I hesitate to think about her question.

"You might be on to something." I stall, not wanting to be vulnerable and tell her all my secrets, but at the same time,

I want to tell her everything. Quinn is the closest thing I've ever had to a best friend since Matty. "Ever since that dog attack, I don't trust people." I look away, not wanting to meet her eyes while I divulge my greatest fear. "And with my parents taking off, traveling the country, it's obvious that people will always leave you behind."

"How old were you when your parents left?"

"I was in college, and I recognize that it was time for them to live their lives. But I think they've always been a little out of reach ever since I can remember."

"Not everyone will disappoint you in life." She takes my hand when I don't look convinced and leans over, kissing me lightly on the cheek.

"Let's brush our teeth and get ready for bed."

We head to the bathroom, and I'm brushing my teeth while Quinn pulls her hair on top of her head into a messy bun. I'm admiring her in the vanity mirror, brushing my teeth for longer than the two minutes I was always told to do, because I don't want to miss another minute with Quinn.

"Are you going to spit anytime soon? I need the sink."

I nod at her and rinse my mouth. When I'm done, I give her space to get ready for bed.

I'm on the balcony looking over the schedule for the rest of the week when Quinn finishes up.

My finger circles Saturday's event, when Edward will most likely announce the new CEO. There are no other activities planned that day; it's a free day for all. You're even allowed to leave the villa and venture out to the nearby town.

Three more days, that's all I have. I fold my hands over and crack my knuckles, and notice the tension forming in my neck.

"What are you doing?" Quinn comes up behind me.

"Just thinking about the gala and the promotion."

## CHAPTER THIRTY-TWO

"What gala?" Her eyebrows knit together, and I can smell the mint on her breath.

"The promotion, Quinn. The night Edward is going to announce it." I remind her.

"There's a gala?" She places her hands on her hips. "Jaxon, you never told me there will be some fancy event at the end of this. I didn't bring any formal dresses!"

She's shooting me daggers with her eyes.

I'm well aware that it's wrong to think this way, but she's so fucking sexy when she's angry. I want to lift her up and have my way with her.

And I do just that.

My lips are on Quinn's in seconds, and she softens as her lips part, meeting mine.

Without breaking our connection, my fingers grab her midsection as I lift her up. The oversized T-shirt that Quinn is wearing hikes up around her waist as she clenches her thighs around me. My left arm is holding her up as I carry her towards the wall, my palm squeezing her ass cheek, and my right hand slips under her shirt, cupping her perky breast. Her arms are wrapped around me, and her lips dash from mine to my neck, and I groan in response.

This isn't the first time I dreamed of fucking Quinn out here. With the villa above the trees and the modern design, no one has a view of our balcony. I made sure of that.

Anyone out on their balcony may unwillingly hear something, and I tell Quinn this, so we're not the talk of the dining room hall tomorrow morning at breakfast.

But the thought of having to stay quiet has me pulsing harder against Quinn.

I slip my fingers from her breast down her abdomen until I find her panties. I curl my fingers around the soft material and slide them in to see if she's ready for me.

Groaning, I pull the waistband of my boxers down and push her panties to the side once more, sliding in with one thrust. She gasps as I fill her, and my mouth immediately lands on hers again, smothering her moans.

My thrusts quicken, and this only makes our kisses harder. My groans muffled by her own. We're gasping for air between each kiss, taking what we need.

Her hips thrust forward, meeting mine.

"Fuck, Quinn." My voice is muffled against her.

I can feel her tightening around me. I pull my mouth from hers and bury myself between her soft hair and the even softer skin of her neck. And after a few more thrusts, and my heart pounding, my body begins to shudder.

My knees are weak, but knowing that Quinn hasn't finished, I set her gently on the balcony chair and get on my knees. I don't stand until she's sopping wet and her body is shaking under the pressure of my tongue.

"Nice way to distract me from the fact that I don't have anything to wear to the gala," she tells me, breathing heavy, her words barely coherent after we make our way to bed.

"There's some free time on Saturday. We will get you any dress you want." I hear her breath steady, and within minutes we're fast asleep.

"I get to design a watch! How fun is that going to be?" Quinn is sitting on the balcony, knees up to her chin and arms wrapped around her legs as she looks over the schedule for the last few days. "I can't believe our time here is already almost half over."

"I can't draw worth shit, so I don't know how I'm going to design a watch."

"Hmm, I hadn't thought about that."

We only have two activities today. One is to design a watch, where Edward, Carole and Manuel will be the judges. And tonight is trivia night.

I wish Quinn and I could sneak out and spend the day at the beach, have a repeat of yesterday, but that wouldn't exactly show team spirit or CEO behavior. I push the thought out as quickly as it came in, leaving behind only memories of the beach cabin and the balcony quickie.

I'm just finishing my hotel room coffee when Quinn tells me we need to head down for breakfast.

"Come here," I tell her and pull her onto my lap when she's within reach. Quinn wiggles around on top of me, laughing as she settles in, and the movement has me stirring beneath her.

Her arms drape themselves around my neck, and she kisses me before I have a chance to make my move.

She pulls away first, her eyes glimmering with excitement, gold speckles sparkling against the blue.

"I'm going to miss going to bed and waking up with you every morning," I tell her and regret it as soon as the words slip out of my mouth. Not wanting to come on too strong, I try to remedy the fact. "I mean, it's been nice cuddling and shit."

Quinn giggles. "Yeah, cuddling and shit has been nice." She's mocking me, so I stand and drape her over my shoulder like she weighs nothing. "Hey, put me down." Hiccups begin to interrupt her laughter, and she's smacking my ass as

I walk. When I get to the bed, I throw her down gently into the soft duvet.

"You were making fun of me."

"No, I wasn't." But she's still laughing.

My smile widens, and I decide to come clean. "What I was saying is that I like going to bed with you."

"If you want, when we get back, I could move into your room with you." Her eyes are filled with mischief and seduction, and I wish to fuck we weren't on a schedule.

"In all seriousness, would you want to?"

"Yeah, of course, Jaxon. You're my husband."

"That's right, wifey."

"Wifey. I like the sound of that. You should totally make that my nickname."

Her stomach rumbles in response.

"I think your stomach feels otherwise about that suggestion."

"Pull me up, I want food." Her arms stretch out in front of her, and I pull her up off the bed and into one final embrace.

I kiss her hard, and when I pull away this time, I tell her that I'd love for her to move into my bedroom.

A small seed of doubt shivers through me. We just started dating, and now she's moving into my bedroom?

I hope to hell coupling up with my wife doesn't end in disaster.

# Chapter Thirty-Three

*Quinn*

We're at trivia night, and Jaxon is talking with Lester and Vinny, so I take this opportunity to have some one-on-one time with Brodie. I see Julie is busy with Edward and Carole, so I stand from my seat and make my way over.

If working at a bar has taught me anything, it's that I can handle uncomfortable situations. And if Brodie really is the prick that Jaxon says he is, I can handle him. But I have a feeling Jaxon's been shielding himself from potential disappointment, therefore keeping Brodie at a distance.

"Hey," I say, sitting next to him. I'm hoping that Jaxon catches me here and comes join us so he can see for himself.

"Hey, Quinn. I know you guys are in the lead, but next round, we've got it." His laugh is confident as he sits back in his chair.

Our team is ahead by ten points, and only because I spent so much time by Mom's bedside watching reruns on TV while she was sick. Hand me any early 2000s sitcom trivia, and I got it in the bag. Quiz me on anything geographical or scientific, and you will hear the buzzer go off as the time runs out.

"I don't doubt it. You've got a good team."

He folds his arms on the table in front of his empty glass. "How are you enjoying the retreat? Julie found the first year or two awkward, not knowing anyone, but look at her now."

We both turn to where Julie is dancing with Carole on a makeshift dance floor.

I watch them for a beat before replying.

"Honestly, I'm having a lot of fun. The activities are great, the food is great, and the company too. What else can I say?"

"It came as a surprise to a lot of us at the office when news spread that Jaxon got married. No one knew he was seeing anyone."

"I guess I was his little secret," I joke, and Brodie laughs with me. "So, how about you, how long have you and Julie been married?" I take this opportunity to turn it on him. The last thing I want to do is make a mess of things for Jaxon and his promotion if I'm wrong.

"We've been married for six years." He puts his left hand on display, showing me his wedding band as if he's Beyoncé. I'm starting to get the feeling that part of what Jaxon says about Brodie is true. He might come across as a little arrogant, but I don't think he means any harm. My gut feeling is that Brodie is only a competitor in Jaxon's imagination.

"And I hear you're also in the line for a big promotion?" I'm about to fish for information when I hear Jaxon behind me, clearing his throat.

I turn and glance at him. "Jaxon, sit with us."

Brodie kicks out a chair for Jaxon beside him, and the energy at the table turns heavy with awkward silence. I can't exactly dig into Brodie with Jaxon here, so I change the subject when Julie approaches.

## CHAPTER THIRTY-THREE

"What are you two up to on Saturday during our free day?" I ask, glancing from Julie to Brodie.

I feel Jaxon nudge me under the table.

Julie glances at Brodie, shrugging her shoulders. "We'll probably just go to the beach or hang out by the pool."

"We're heading into town. You guys should come," I offer.

Jaxon interrupts before they can respond. "I'm sure they want to spend some time together, since they've got some free time without the kids and everything." He turns to them with an emotionless smile.

I ignore Jaxon. "I'm going dress shopping, do you want to come, Julie? Give the boys a chance to hang out?"

"That sounds great," Brodie replies, and I can feel Jaxon's disappointment next to me. I know I shouldn't meddle, but this will be good for him. He should spend some real time getting to know Brodie on another level. Bond, do what bros do. Go to a pub or have coffee or something.

"Great, we'll leave right after breakfast."

Before Jaxon or I can say another word, Manuel stands on the small stage in front of the projector screen, letting us know it's time for round two. We head back to Lester and Vinny, but not before grabbing our second allotted drink for the day.

"What were you thinking, Quinn?"

Jaxon's seething through clenched teeth. A familiar yet annoying trait of his.

I roll my eyes. "It'll be fine, Jaxon. He's not your enemy."

"We'll see about that."

I squeeze his hand, and a flash of worry crosses his brow. This will be good for him. I know it.

The game is tied between Brodie's team and ours, and we have one round left to go.

Jaxon's spirits have lifted since Brodie agreed to come with us on Saturday. He's sitting a bit taller, and he's even participating, calling out some answers during the second round of trivia. His sleeves are pushed up, showing off the tattoos on his forearms, and the material crinkles at his shoulders, pulling it tight across his chest.

He turns to me with a smirk, catching me watching him, and I don't bother to turn away. He's mine, and our marriage has been consummated since being here, and I'm moving into his bedroom when we get back.

What more could I ask for?

I got the marriage, the benefits, and now we're developing the love.

We may have done this a bit backwards, but isn't it the journey that matters?

Manuel's question interrupts my thoughts.

"Where are a grasshopper's ears located?"

The buzzer on our table sounds. Lester pulls his hand back and pushes his glasses up the bridge of his nose. "On their abdomen."

Jaxon and I both turn to him.

"How do you know that?" I ask Lester.

"I was in Boy Scouts."

"Great job." I tell him, and he's beaming.

"They're actually called tympanal organs, and they're right under their wings."

## CHAPTER THIRTY-THREE

Impressed, I clap with everyone else, and Manuel marks us with another point on the board.

Our last category is called Anything and Everything. We have no idea what kind of questions will be asked.

The four of us turn back to Manuel and wait for the next question.

"What is a single strand of spaghetti called?" Manuel reads from his deck of cards.

A buzz comes from Brodie's table.

"Spaghetto!" Julie calls out.

I lean into the center of our table, on my forearms. "I didn't know that," I say, and everyone nods.

"What is acrophobia a fear of?" The next question is asked, and Jaxon hits the buzzer.

"The fear of heights," he calls out, and Manuel marks us another point. Jaxon looks at us, and he shrugs his shoulders.

I set my palm on his thigh next to me and squeeze it gently as he shifts under my hand, and I smile at him.

He gives me a little kiss on the cheek, and we both turn back as the next question is read.

"What color of flame is the hottest?"

Someone buzzes from a table across the room, and they call out orange. Manuel sounds his own buzzer indicating that the answer is incorrect. This gives us another chance, but Vinny taps ours a second after Brodie.

"Blue."

"Correct." Manuel adds a mark on the board.

We go through another ten questions when we're told there's going to be a lightning round. We're tied with Brodie's table. Three questions between the two tables.

"What is a group of flamingos called?"

Vinny sounds our buzzer.

"A flamboyance." Lester pats him on the back, and we clap and smile at him as Manuel marks us down for another point. "I spent some time in Africa after college," he tells us.

Jaxon rests his arm on the back of my chair, his hand on my shoulder. I lean back and wait with the others for the next question.

"This might be a tricky one, but those of you working for Edward should probably know this," Manuel tells us, and I see Jaxon and Lester exchange glances and then across to the other table. "What was the tiny pocket in a pair of jeans originally designed for?"

Brodie buzzes a split second before Jaxon.

"I had that one," Jaxon tells us.

I turn to Brodie, waiting to hear the answer.

"To hold a pocket watch."

We hear Brodie's table cheer in excitement at winning the second last question.

We're still tied.

"Are you ready for the last question?" Manuels engages the crowd, walking back and forth on the stage, clapping his hands over his head. People are cheering, and fists are being pumped into the air around the dimly lit room. He stops and stands in the middle of the stage, and the group grows quiet. "How do you perform a plié in ballet?"

I hit the buzzer, squealing in excitement of finally knowing an answer only seconds before someone at the other table does. Manuel points to me.

"You stand with your toes pointing outward and bend at the knees with your back straight." I grew up wanting to be a ballerina after watching *The Nutcracker* on TV one Christmas. I used to watch it repeatedly, mimicking their movements, teaching myself because Mom couldn't afford

# CHAPTER THIRTY-THREE

classes. Granny used to watch me dance about the room and clap after my final bow.

"We won!" Vinny yells out.

Manuel calls us to the stage, and I see Jaxon trail slowly behind, not wanting the attention on him. He explains how our names will go into a hat, and one of us will win a prize from Edward Rummens Watches.

I glance down at my own and watch it sparkle under the stage lights. I secretly hope that Lester wins this round, since Vinny won the first one and Jaxon and I already have new watches. My wish is granted when Manuel shouts into the microphone that Lester is the winner.

Once the crowd quiets down, and everyone is talking amongst themselves, we head back to our table where we congratulate Lester and finish up our second drinks.

Vinny and Lester tell us they're going to go mingle, and I nod to Jaxon, raising my eyebrows in question.

"Lead the way," Jaxon hesitantly agrees.

# Chapter Thirty-Four

*Jaxon*

It's Saturday morning, and we're just finishing up breakfast.

Quinn wouldn't quit talking about how it'll be fun to spend the day with Brodie and Julie, but after the trivia game, I was exhausted.

Loud voices, constant movement, over-stimulated senses, but I pushed through, determined to show that I have what it takes to be CEO.

My day-to-day job is great. I have meetings with a few individuals at a time, sometimes a boardroom full of people, but everyone is professional, tame, reserved, and that I can handle.

My personality thrives in that position. I'm always early, the projector is always ready and working, and there are jugs of water and coffee waiting. Well, that last one is thanks to Lester. But put me in a room with fifty other people and force me to be social, and it's goddamn torture.

## CHAPTER THIRTY-FOUR

This is the first year that I don't retreat to my room right after an activity, and that's because I want to be CEO, and if Brodie is going to show up, then I will too.

Yesterday's event did me in.

We started the day in groups as per usual, and I ended up with co-workers I rarely see and barely know. I guess it was the universe trying to prepare me. If I'm going to be CEO, I need to get used to learning more about the staff and face some of these uncomfortable situations.

But we had to create art, painting a giant canvas as a team.

And I don't fucking do art.

I will buy art, read art, listen to art, and watch art happen.

But to create art, fuck no.

It all started when we were told to wear something we wouldn't mind getting dirty. I should have known. I showed up in a pair of casual sports shorts, a plain T-shirt, and a ball cap.

A four by six-foot canvas stood waiting for us with bottles of paint and brushes.

Our group—me excluded because I didn't know how to even contribute an idea—came up with the idea of painting a ship on the sea during a sunset.

We each had a section of the mural to paint, and our colors had to combine with one another's, and I kept fucking up.

It was embarrassing.

I would add too much yellow to the sunset, or I made bold splotches of blue in the sea and it never looked right. The group would tell me it looked great, and then I'd watch as they would add more color on top of mine, blending it in with the others, fixing my shit.

Needless to say, we did not come in first, second, or third.

I shake the thoughts out of my head.

The only thing that made that day better was yoga later in the day with Quinn.

Yes, yoga. Hot yoga where I dripped sweat and struggled, but every time Quinn bent over in her tight spandex shorts, I would dream about my hands squeezing that tight ass.

But today is a new day.

*The* day.

The day I find out that the promotion is mine. And tomorrow I can drive back with Quinn, hand on her knee, windows down, music up, and kiss that pretty little mouth of hers before we drift off to sleep in my bed. Our bed.

We haven't talked about the promotion. But here I am sitting in silence, trying not to be the awkward person who I am in social settings, sweating as Brodie shows pictures of his little blonde kids to our coworkers.

Anxiety, check.

Intrusive thoughts, check.

I feel Quinn's hand on my leg, and I turn to her.

"Almost ready?" I ask, and she nods.

I glance at Brodie, who pockets his phone, and Edward stands to speak.

"Today is your last day here. I want everyone to enjoy themselves whether it's here at the villa or venturing out beyond the gates. The pool, beach, game room, and all amenities are available to you." He pauses, adjusting the collar on his polo. "Everyone is to be back in time for cocktails at six, followed by another lovely meal prepared by the very talented kitchen staff, who have been spoiling our palates all week." A few claps and cheers fill the air. "There will be music and a dance following dinner. You will not need to use your drink card today, but I expect everyone to be on their best behavior so that everyone can enjoy the end of a fantastic week."

## CHAPTER THIRTY-FOUR

We all clap as Edward finishes his morning speech. Chairs scrape against the floor as people rise.

"We'll meet you in the lobby, say fifteen?" I ask Brodie.

"Sounds good."

"Okay if I drive?"

"Sure, buddy."

I wince at the term buddy.

I turn towards Quinn. "Let's go grab our stuff."

I follow Quinn to our room, and thirteen minutes later we're back in the lobby, where Brodie and Julie are waiting for us. If there's one thing I appreciate about Brodie is that the man is always early.

We walk out into the sunlight, the day already warming quickly despite the morning hour. There's a soft breeze whistling through the leaves that surround us. We get to my car, which stands out like a peacock among crows.

"I don't think I've ever seen your car at the office," Brodie is quick to tell me.

"I like to work on the commute," I tell him.

"You boys are always working, can't even enjoy a nice ride to the office," Julie says.

"The traffic is shit in the mornings. I get it," Brodie pipes in.

We each tilt the front seats so that Quinn and Julie can slip into the back. When I finally get to the open road at the end of the long driveway to the villa, I make a right, heading to the closest town based on my memory from the drive up.

Quinn's mouth is moving a mile a minute in the rearview mirror, but I don't hear her over the roar of the car. Brodie tells me about a car show he went to last year.

I respond and enjoy the easy conversation as I parallel-park on Main Street. The street is lightly buzzing with shoppers going in and out of the small boutiques.

We let the women out of the car, and I check for a parking meter, confused when I can't find one.

"We're in a small town, it's probably free," says Quinn.

I guess one of the benefits of being out of the city.

Quinn and Julie walk ahead of us, and I'm staring at my wife's ass when she turns around and motions to a shop. "I want to go in here."

Julie is already on her way to the door, and I nod.

"Let's leave them shop, and we'll check out what else this town has to offer," Brodie says.

"Is that okay with you?" I eye Quinn, asking more for myself than her. I know she will be fine with Julie and will probably have a lot of fun, but it's me I'm worried about, hanging out with Brodie one-on-one.

Quinn nods and I give her a quick kiss on the cheek before she makes her way to join Julie at the doorway.

The door chimes as they step inside, and we turn to continue down the sidewalk.

The entire Main Street is only two blocks long and filled with small shops, a pub, and more trinket shit in the large window displays. We both stop walking when we see a large arrow advertising axe-throwing behind the last building on the right.

"Let's throw some axes," Brodie suggests. "A bunch of us went for a bachelor party, it was a good time."

Of course he did. I didn't even know people still had bachelor parties these days. How would I know when I don't get close enough to anyone to be invited? I didn't exactly have one myself. As if reading my mind on the latter thought, Brodie turns to me.

"What did you do for your bachelor party?"

"I didn't have one."

"What, why?"

## CHAPTER THIRTY-FOUR

I hate fucking prying.

"We decided to get married pretty quickly, just no time." I shrug his question off, and I feel relieved when there's no follow-up to it.

The axe-throwing is done outdoors under wooden pergolas. We walk up to a counter made of tree logs and a man in a red plaid shirt.

He leads us through to the back and explains the game and how to throw. We settle into a spot facing a large wooden wall with a colored circle inside.

I watch Brodie throw two first before I give it a go.

My toes are at the edge of the blue line painted on the floor at twelve feet from the board. I raise my right arm and throw it. I feel a satisfied spark when I watch it stick to the board, and Brodie whoops. The second one embeds itself into the target, and another rush spreads through me.

"Feels good, eh?"

"Fuck yeah," I respond, and we both laugh. We pick up our two axes at the same time and return to the starting point. The hour is almost up when Julie and Quinn shout from the sidewalk. I wave to Quinn, and Brodie and I gather our stuff and head out to meet them.

I notice Julie has three bags and Quinn only has one.

"Did you find a dress you liked?" I ask, leaning in and kissing her on the lips.

"Hmm, I did. I think you'll like it."

"Can't wait."

I take the bag from her, and our hands clasp together at our side, her thumb rubbing the top of my hand.

We cross the street and step into a shop with trinkets and kitchen gadgets and shit we don't need. Quinn oohs and ahhs, picking up candles, sniffing them, and setting them back down. She leaves with a pair of blue novelty socks that say My Dog is Cool AF.

When lunchtime rolls around, we head to a pub and decide on sharing a party platter, and Brodie and I grab a beer.

I find myself feeling relaxed by the time we get back into my car and are heading towards the villa.

When we enter the villa, we say our goodbyes, and head up to the room.

"What do you want to do until it's time to get ready?" Quinn asks as I close the door behind us.

"Take you in my arms, for starters." I kick off my shoes.

Quinn is backing up slowly away from me towards the bed, her hands behind her back, shimmying her shoulders playfully and giggling.

"And what do you plan on doing with me once I'm in your arms?"

"Let me show you."

# Chapter Thirty-Five

*Quinn*

"Can you zip me?" I ask Jaxon, looking over my shoulder up at him.

"You look stunning," he tells me, so I spin around after I'm zipped in.

I went with a simple backless cocktail dress in black. The dress lands mid-shin, and the material hugs my body tightly. I paired it with black high-heeled sandals that tie around my ankles. My hair is curly, and I'm wearing earrings that dangle to my shoulders.

"You, my husband, look great." Jaxon is wearing a black suit and a light blue dress shirt that lights up his face. I get to see him dressed up five days a week, but tonight he looks even more handsome. "Excited about the promotion reveal?"

"Does it show?"

I laugh. "Yes, it does." I pick off a small piece of lint. "I'm happy for you."

"I have you to thank for this." He pulls me into his arms.

"I have nothing to do with this promotion, Jaxon. It's your hard work and dedication."

"I might not have had a chance without you, if the rumors were true."

I shake my head. "Edward obviously loves you like a son. It shows in the way he speaks so highly of you. This promotion was always yours."

He places a gentle kiss on my forehead, and I pull away. I've never been this happy in my entire life.

We walk hand in hand down to the dining room. High tables are along the edges, the long dining tables moved about so that a dance floor is in the center of the room, and people are gathered, talking amongst each other.

The bright lights have been dimmed, and there are fairy lights streaming overhead. I saw the pamphlet in the lobby with all the different accommodation packages. The villa is home to weddings, corporate retreats, mindful and health-conscious vacations, and more. It would be so pretty for a wedding ceremony. I don't regret our city hall wedding, not one bit, because I have Jaxon. I don't really need all this big fancy stuff. I know money brought me to him, but if it were all gone in a heartbeat, I'd still be happily by his side.

We each have a cocktail and sit down for dinner. Tonight, we're seated with Edward, Carole, Brodie, and Julie.

Brodie talks about the axe-throwing the men did, and Julie about our shopping. The conversation is sailing along, but I can't help but notice the rigidity in Jaxon.

When everyone gets up to mingle as the plates are being cleared, I lean in and whisper, "Are you okay?"

"Just nervous," he tells me, looking around the room.

He's acting like a small-time thief getting ready for a big heist. His eyes roam over his coworkers, looking for Brodie and Edward, keeping an eye out for anything suspicious.

"When do you think Edward will make the announcement?"

"I'm assuming towards the end of the evening." He plays with his tie, so I take his hand to distract him. "There's always a speech on the last day after dinner."

I nod. A few people come up to us, so we chat, and I sway a bit to the music once the volume level is turned up and the dancing begins.

"Come dance with me." I urge Jaxon onto the dance floor when a slow song fills the room.

I wrap my arms around his neck, and his hands are firm on my lower back. He leads me through the song, his gaze fixed on mine. His eyes crinkle at the corners with each smile. We stay that way for a second song, couples coming and going around us. When the music turns to a faster pace, Jaxon releases me.

"I'm not dancing to that," he tells me, and I laugh.

"Why not?"

"I can't dance for shit."

"But you just did, and you were great."

"That's different. I'll watch you from here." He stands at the closest bar-height table to the dance floor, and I move to the rhythm of the song. A few of the other women and men are dancing around me, and I fall into the crowd. After a couple of songs, I lose track of Jaxon. I decide to go find him when a tap to the microphone interrupts the music.

Edward is standing on a small stage. My eyes seek out Jaxon, standing against the wall on his own. I move my way through the crowd until I'm next to him.

He's holding a new drink, and I watch him take a sip and then press his lips together. I can feel the anticipation rolling off him. We listen to Edward thank the staff of the villa and Manuel and all his employees for the week. He talks about a few of the departments and the work they contribute to the company, and about how sales are up from last year. Edward continues on about teamwork, and his belief about how these retreats benefit everyone, not only the company. He goes on to say that he feels they really set them apart from others in the business.

Manuel comes up and joins Edward and speaks about the villa itself and thanks Edward and all of us for coming and being such great participants throughout all the activities.

"It sounds like he's wrapping it up." Jaxon lowers his voice so only I can hear him.

It does sound like Edward is almost done with his speech, and a few seconds later, the applause around the room confirms that his speech is over.

Jaxon stiffens next to me.

Not a word is said about the promotion or CEO.

"It's not me," he tells me. "I didn't get it."

Edward is shaking hands with Brodie now, and we both watch silently. He pats him on the back and leads him up to the bar, where we watch as the two accept another drink from the bartender. "I can't fucking believe this."

"You don't know that Brodie got it," I try to reassure him, but I only half believe what I'm telling him, because once they raise their drinks in cheer, I look away, my heart sinking for Jaxon.

"I gave that man everything," he starts but then stops just as quickly as the space around us fills. "Come on, let's go."

He pulls me with him towards Edward and Brodie, and my heart rate speeds up. My palm starts to sweat in Jaxon's, and I find myself feeling sorry for him. I worry he's about to cause a scene, but when we stop at the bar, Jaxon clears his throat.

"Edward, Brodie." He nods to them both. "We're going to head up and call it a night." Edward returns my polite smile, but my insides are churning.

How could he do this to Jaxon?

"Jaxon, Quinn, we'll see you both at breakfast in the morning?" Edward asks, taking another sip from the brown liquid over ice in his thick glass.

"Yes, sir," Jaxon replies. I have my customer service smile plastered on my face when I look from Brodie to Edward. I stay quiet, Jaxon's obedient wife, and follow him when he turns and takes us up to our room.

The door closes loudly as Jaxon releases it, coming into the room behind me.

"Fuck" is all he says as he paces the length of the room.

I sit down on the edge of the bed, unsure how to comfort him as he walks back and forth.

"I can't believe Brodie fucking got the promotion. The prick probably knew it all day and had the audacity to play goddamn axe-throwing with me. Chat me up like we're fucking best friends."

"We don't know that," I offer. "And you don't know for sure. I mean, he didn't make a statement or any mention of it."

Jaxon stops in his tracks. "You saw them clinking their glasses and whispering."

I stand and take both his hands in mine, pulling him to the bed. I press my hands into his firm chest and push him down onto the bed until he's sitting.

When he sits like this, and I stand, I'm not much taller than him. I pull him in for an embrace, comforting him, his head against my chest.

"It's going to be okay," I tell him, and I feel him shake his head, his shoulders slumping against me, his arms holding me close.

I close my eyes, and we stay like this for a few minutes, neither of us talking.

His hands lower down to my ass, and he squeezes, sending warmth through my body. I open my eyes, and he pulls his head from my chest just far enough to peer up at me.

"I really thought the job was mine."

"I know."

"I don't know where to go from here."

"You're going to go in to work on Monday and hold your head high and be the fucking amazing man that you are," I order him.

"You're fucking hot when you're mad."

"Stop." My eyes pierce through his. "I'm mad for you." I take his face in my hands, and his sullen eyes look up at me, and it tears at my heart. "Your pain is my pain."

He squeezes my ass again, and I bring my lips down to his.

I run my hands through his hair and down to his neck, kissing him gently. His mouth opens in response, his tempo matching my own.

Pulling away, my eyes never leaving his, I loosen his tie and remove it from around his neck. When I've untied it, I take it and place it over his eyes, securing it behind his head.

"Quinn..." Jaxon starts but I place my lips back on his, silencing him. Our kiss deepens, and I hastily take off his jacket. My fingers fumble at the buttons on his shirt, our lips parting for no more than a few seconds. I let my hands roam over him, after his shirt falls open, and I only pull away to get down on my knees.

I look up at him, his covered eyes, tousled hair, and parted lips, waiting for what comes next.

## CHAPTER THIRTY-FIVE

My hands slide up and down his thighs, the muscles in his legs hard against my palms. His hands find my hair and tangle up in my curls as I unbuckle his belt and unbutton his pants. I stop to tilt my head up and kiss him when his lips find me. "Fuck, Quinn."

One of his hands finds my neck, and I kiss him firmly, trying to melt the pain and anger away. He lets go of my neck and leans back on the bed, moving his hips so I can shimmy his pants and boxers down just enough to release him from the material that was separating him from my mouth. I lower down, taking as much of him in as I can fit. His right hand supports him on the bed, while his left clumps my hair together at the back of my head. I move swiftly, stopping only to lick the slippery beads of pre-cum at his tip. I place my hand at his base, and I move back and forth to the sounds of him groaning, my mouth and hand sliding together in rhythm.

He's growing thicker against the inside of my cheeks when he stops me. "I need you, Quinn."

I swirl my tongue around him one more time and then release my mouth and stand up. His hands come up to his head, removing the tie. His eyes are full of hunger. "I need to see you." I step back and bend to take off my sandals. "Leave those on."

I smirk at him. "Okay." I stand and reach for the strap of my dress, sliding it off my shoulder and then switching to the other while his gaze holds mine. I turn for him to unzip my dress, and after he does, I feel his lips on my back, his hand sliding the dress down my body. I turn around, careful not to trip on the material now pooled at my feet.

"I want to watch you take that off slowly."

I do as I'm told and hook my fingers into the thin waistband of my thong, sliding it down my legs and stepping out of it. I'm only inches from him when he pulls me close and his mouth finds my breasts.

Moaning at how his tongue swirls and flicks my pebbled nipples, I let my head fall back in pleasure. His hands roam down my body, and I gasp when his fingers find my wetness. He groans louder this time.

"Fuck, Quinn, you're so wet. I want to feel you drip all over me."

He grabs my ass, and I kneel on the bed with him between my thighs. I waste no time lowering myself onto him in one quick motion.

I move at a quicker tempo, my lips stealing kisses from him in between moans, but when his thumb presses down on my center and starts circling, I cry out and ride him with determination until I'm unraveling over him.

I don't stop until I hear the final groan of his release.

He falls back onto the bed, taking me down with him and pulling me close. My hair spills over and around him, and I nestle myself in the crook of his neck, him still inside of me.

"You're amazing."

"You're not so bad yourself," I say in a mix of bliss and fatigue.

He rolls me over until I'm on my back and kisses me gently. In a state of pure satisfaction, I sigh into his mouth.

We stay like this, intertwined, naked, and vulnerable until our eyes feel heavy.

"I need to go brush my teeth," I tell him, sitting up.

"Wait."

I stay seated as Jaxon gets up and comes around to the foot of the bed.

He nods at the heels that I'm still wearing, so I stretch out my legs. He lifts one at a time, undoing each strap and slipping the shoes off gently, kissing around my gold anklet.

# CHAPTER THIRTY-FIVE

I take in every inch of him. The tattoo on his thigh, the indentations from his abdominal muscles, and the way his chest flexes when he moves.

When he's done, he pulls me down to the edge of the bed and, in one fast swoop, his mouth is between my thighs.

"Jaxon, I..." My eyes close. "I already..." I let my sentence fall short as he devours me. My hips move, inviting him in further. My breath shallows as I come close to peaking, letting myself feel the intoxicating pleasure. My pulse is quickening, and my ears are ringing when I clutch at the duvet under me and cry out his name.

Jaxon is still disheveled, and we're both glistening with sweat when I let my head rest on his chest as I snuggle up against him.

I'm falling in and out of sleep, and in a state of utter exposed, raw feelings, I whisper, "I love you."

# Chapter Thirty-Six

*Jaxon*

My eyes flutter open.

I peer down at Quinn on my chest, but she's fallen asleep. Her hair is spread over my bare chest, and I think about the words she just said.

Did she mean it?

I wonder if she's saying it out of sympathy for not getting the promotion. Or if she's in some sort of delusion from the effect of two orgasms. She couldn't possibly love a man who couldn't even land a damn promotion above someone younger with way less experience.

My mind spirals with thoughts of Quinn wanting to leave, to go back home.

Technically, she's supposed to stay another year under our contract, but maybe she'll just up and leave, thinking she already got enough out of this deal.

I drift in and out of sleep over the next seven hours, and when I feel Quinn stir beside me, I turn over to look at her.

## CHAPTER THIRTY-SIX

Her eyes are still closed, and her mouth is parted slightly. Without her makeup on, I can see a few freckles sprinkled over her nose and cheeks. Waking up to Quinn at my side is a feeling I will always cherish, even if she decides to leave.

When I signed up on the matchmaking site and offered her the position of my wife, I wasn't sure what would come of it. I never expected to fall in love, and yet here I am.

A man and a husband who has fallen head over fucking heels in love with this woman.

A woman who drove me crazy over the first few weeks. One who took my car and adopted a dog without asking. A ray of fucking sunshine on my cloudy days, who chose to participate in this crazy scheme of mine to help me get a promotion that was probably never mine to begin with.

I'm pretty sure I've been in love with her since the first time I laid eyes on her at city hall, that very first day.

My heart sinks again at the thought of losing both her and the promotion. I know it's going to sting for a while, but I don't see myself anywhere else other than working for Edward Rummens Watches. It's my second home. Hell, it's my first home. I spend more hours at the office than anywhere else.

But how do I move past the fact that I will be reporting to Brodie Fucking Mullen?

You could say we became friends over the past few days. Well, friends is pushing it, maybe better acquainted coworkers to say the least—but was it all an act? Had he already known the promotion was his and befriended me, knowing full well he was going to blindside me?

Quinn lets out a sigh, and her eyelashes begin to flutter as her eyes strain to open.

A smile spreads across her face when she sees me looking at her.

"Well, good morning, husband."

My chest tightens at those words, and I wonder if this is the last time I will hear them. We head home after breakfast, and I think I should probably have a talk with her when we do.

"Good morning."

"Hmm, I dreamed of last night."

My dick twitches under the duvet at the thought of her down on her knees. Her covering my eyes was fucking thrilling, and without seeing it firsthand, my mind is making up the most beautifully seductive scene in my head.

She kisses me on the lips.

"You sleep okay?"

"Better than okay." She sits up, covering herself with the sheet. "How are you feeling?"

I turn onto my back and cover my eyes with my forearm. "Not bad," I tell her. I don't want sympathy or pity, not from her. Not from the woman who's going to walk away.

She gets up and heads to the bathroom, and I watch her backside sway with each step, and the feeling in my stomach sinks further. She doesn't even remember telling me that she loves me. Maybe it was her way of soothing me after she fucking distracted me this entire week when she knew I had the promotion on the line.

I can't blame her. It's just as much my fault for any distractions I've had. Plus, I participated in every activity, smiled, and acted exactly as a CEO should. This isn't either of our faults.

It's fucking Brodie's.

I get up and pull on my swim trunks and a T-shirt. We have an hour and a half before we have to be down at breakfast. I shout through the bathroom door, "I'm just going to swim a few laps in the pool."

# CHAPTER THIRTY-SIX

Swimming laps always calm my racing mind, but this morning proved that they won't always solve all my problems. My head is still a fucking basket case.

I shower quickly when I get back up to the room after planting a quick kiss on Quinn's cheek.

When we're both ready for breakfast, we head down in silence. Quinn's oddly quiet, but I'm not speaking much either.

We walk into the dining hall, which has no evidence of the party that took place last night. The tables are all back in their spots, and the buffet breakfast is in full swing, lights on overhead, fairy lights gone and put away until the next event.

I feel Quinn's hand pull me back. "You sure you're okay, Jaxon? You've been quiet."

"I'm good. Just still trying to process the whole thing." It's only half the story, but now's not the time to ask Quinn if she'll be staying or what my lack of promotion means for her.

We sit and greet Lester and Vinny next to us. It takes everything in me to return the same greeting to Brodie and Julie.

Every part of me is raging, and disappointment is running its course right alongside that anger.

I shove a forkful of pancakes into my mouth, and only half listen as everyone around me talks.

When everyone has finished eating, we all gather around to say our goodbyes to Manuel, the staff, and each other. Hands are shaken and hugs are exchanged.

I overhear Vinny, Lester, and Quinn exchanging phone numbers and talking about getting together sometime. Lester tells Quinn that he wants to meet Luna, and I wonder if Quinn and Luna will be around to follow through.

I roll our suitcases out and shove them in the back of the car. When we're settled in our seats and buckled, I wonder what the fuck I'm going to do come tomorrow morning.

# Chapter Thirty-Seven

## Quinn

I'm singing softly to the music playing in the car, pulling my hair into a bun on top of my head to stop it from wisping into my face. The windows are open, and the saltwater air tickles my nose.

Jaxon's been quiet all morning, and I'm letting him have the space he needs to process everything that happened, but it makes the car ride home long, and the silence is feeding my own doubts.

What if Jaxon decides it was all my fault? What if I didn't live up to his or Edward's standards, and I cost him the promotion?

I refuse to think the worst and console myself with the fact that we had an amazing time together. I just need to be patient and wait it out, let him process his disappointment.

"Do you want me to drive?" I ask during our third hour of the drive.

He turns his head for a split second, not wanting to keep his eyes off the winding road for too long.

"I'm okay, thank you."

The remainder of the car is brutally quiet, and I end up falling in and out of sleep, while the sun kisses my face through the front windshield, and I dream of the intimate moments I had with Jaxon last night.

The car is pulling up to the garage, and I hear Luna barking before I see her.

"Oh. My. God. I missed Luna so freaking much," I exclaim to Jaxon before hopping out of the car once it's parked.

"Don't worry, I'll take care of your luggage," he calls after me.

"Thanks, Jaxon," I say, sprinting through the house.

I find Nicky in hot pink swim trunks sprawled on a lounge chair in front of the pool, a margarita in hand. Luna is yapping at a couple of birds in a tree.

"Luna," I call to her, and she comes running at the sound of my voice. I bend down and take her in my arms, nuzzling my nose into her soft fur. "Look at you," I say to Nicky as I sit down on the chair next to him. "Living the life, are we?"

"Girl, I'm moving in." His mouth pouts. "Seriously, please don't kick me out. I can't go back to a stuffy studio apartment." I laugh, and he sighs. "You look good." He sits up and peers over his sunglasses. "Wait, Quinny, are we in love?"

I nod. "I may have fallen for my husband."

"Wait, then why do you look sexually satisfied with a hint of sadness?" He sits up in his chair and turns his body to face me, eyeing me like he's an investigator in a true-crime documentary. "Tell me everything."

"Well, everything was amazing, actually, until last night."

"What did he do? Do I need to kick his ass? And by kick, I mean spank?" He wiggles his eyebrows at me.

# CHAPTER THIRTY-SEVEN

"Nicky!" I sigh. "Ugh, I missed you," I tell him. "And I missed you too," I say to Luna in a high-pitched voice, squeezing her close to me until she yaps.

"So, tell me everything," Nicky says, and before I can respond, he continues, "Wait, I'm burning up. Go put on one of your itty-bitty bathing suits and come in the pool so we can catch up."

"Let me go find Jaxon and see if he minds. It's been a day."

When I find Jaxon's bedroom door half closed, I push it open.

"I'm just about to take a shower," he tells me.

"Okay. Hey, do you mind if I hang out with Nicky a bit, catch up?"

"Of course not. I think I'm just going to read for a bit."

I nod. His face is sullen, and he looks like he hasn't slept despite the night we had last night. But I know he's got a lot on his plate, mentally. "Yeah, sure. I'll let you know when dinner is ready." I walk up to him and place my hand gently on his arm. "You okay?"

I'm startled when he pulls away and walks into the washroom. "Yeah, I'm good," he says, right before he closes the door.

I stand there in shock. I know Jaxon's going through shit, but after the week we've had, to be dismissed this way leaves a bad taste in my mouth.

Time, he just needs time.

I turn out of the room, and head to my own to get changed to join Nicky out back in the pool.

It's now Tuesday, and I haven't seen Jaxon since we got back on Sunday afternoon, where he turned on his heel and left me standing in his bedroom.

By the time Nicky left, and I came in to check on Jaxon to let him know dinner was ready, his bedroom lights were off and the door was closed. Not wanting to wake him, I ate dinner and went to bed early myself after unpacking from the retreat.

So much for moving into his bedroom when we got back.

Monday was much of the same.

Jaxon didn't come out for breakfast or lunch while I was home, but when I came back from running some errands in the afternoon, I noticed a plate and mug in the dishwasher. At least he was eating.

But is he just going to avoid me forever?

I shook away those thoughts, but when he didn't come down for dinner again on Monday night, I began to worry.

The week of the retreat was one of the best weeks in my entire life, but the moment we came home, everything changed. I honestly thought we were in love, but I'm beginning to doubt the feelings and attention Jaxon showed me.

It's Tuesday morning now, and there's still no sign of Jaxon. When I knock on his door and ask him if he wants breakfast, he tells me he's not hungry.

I'm trying to be patient, but my patience is wearing thin. I know Jaxon is going through shit, but he can't just disappear for days without talking to me. My anxiety has me teetering on the edge of a full-on meltdown, not knowing what's going on, waiting for him to come tell me the whole reason he didn't get the promotion was because of me and kick me out for good. Contract null and void.

"I'll get something later," I hear from the other side of the door.

My head rests on the closed door, and I feel tears forming at the edges of my eyes.

"I can't do this," I whisper.

I retreat from his door and make the decision that I need a night away. I pack a bag and text Nicky.

> Quinn
>
> I'm coming over for the day with Luna and bringing an overnight bag. That okay?

When I've entered the garage and thrown my belongings into the backseat of the car, I hear my phone sound.

> Nicky
>
> Aww, girl. Come on over.

I've been updating Nicky, so it isn't brand-new information that my husband is acting all sad boy and holed up in his room. I've given Jaxon time and space, and offered comfort and kind words, but I don't respond well to being ignored.

Things were going amazing. I fell in love with my fake husband, and I know he fell for me too. But this whole avoiding thing he's doing has got to stop.

I huff and start the car. He can have the house to himself for the night. Maybe he needs to be reminded of what life was like without me so he can appreciate what we have and realize that I am only trying to be there for him. But I need to take care of myself too.

I send a quick text to Jaxon, telling him that I'm going to Nicky's. I don't wait for a response before shutting off my phone and turning to Luna.

"We're going to Uncle Nicky's," I tell her, and she yaps in response.

# Chapter Thirty-Eight

## *Jaxon*

I open my door a crack and run my palm down my untrimmed beard. The house is silent, so I walk out to investigate. My feet are cool against the flooring. A lump forms in my throat as I head towards Quinn's room. It lands in my chest when I don't find her or Luna in their room or anywhere in the house.

It's Tuesday evening, dinner time has come and gone, and Quinn failed to make her usual appearance at my door, begging me to come out and talk.

My horrible mood continues to irritate me as I search by the pool and still find no sign of Quinn.

She's gone.

I knew it. I fucking knew it.

I grab two slices of bread and place them in the toaster. When I've made my sandwich, I sit at the island and only manage to finish half before I push the plate away from me, swallowing my bite and dignity with it.

The last forty-eight hours have been a roller coaster of emotions. I'm pissed at Brodie, Edward, Quinn, and my goddamn self, which is the reason that I've taken additional time off work. It wasn't difficult to ask Edward to approve the time off considering I have weeks of leave built up, according to HR.

So how have I been dealing? Like a fucking pussy-ass sad boy brooding to no one, waiting for Quinn to pack her bags and leave.

I've been playing out all the scenarios in my head.

Is she going to ask for partial payment considering she wants to end the contract early?

Or is she just going to fuck off and leave me like everyone else, and screw the money?

It's my own goddamn fault. I refused every single one of her attempts at comforting me while I hid out in my room full of self-loathing.

A thought occurs to me. I walk to the garage, and just as I expected, the car is gone. And that's all the confirmation I need to know that Quinn was only ever in this for the money. Maybe she considers that to be her payout.

I'll let her have it, I think.

It only makes sense that she wouldn't want a sad, pathetic, grown-ass man who can't land a promotion he was sure was his.

A sinking feeling floods my chest, and I turn back towards the kitchen after closing the garage door and let my head fall into my hands as I sit on the edge of the stool at the island.

I fucking fell for her. I should have listened to my own goddamn rules, that this was business and only business.

I put my plate in the dishwasher and head down to the rec room. I slump on the couch and prop the pillows up behind my head, where Quinn usually sits.

## CHAPTER THIRTY-EIGHT

Who am I fucking kidding? It was love at first sight for me, and now I've lost her.

And this house is as quiet as the day I moved in, and I fucking hate it.

My eyes are heavy and my neck is sore. I fell asleep on the goddamn couch watching reruns of '90s sitcoms. My palm rubs the stiff side of my neck as I sit up and reach for the watch that I abandoned last night on the coffee table.

A thought occurs to me, sending a jolt through me.

Did Quinn come home while I was asleep? I'm suddenly hopeful, wishing.

Is she in her room?

I pause listening, and no sound can be heard from the rec room.

I woke over and over throughout the night, wanting to hold Quinn, my body shivering in the mix of disappointment and grief, full of self-pity and heartache.

This isn't me.

The fucking lightbulb turns on inside my thick head, and I know Quinn is too good to let go of.

She's fucking amazing. Those lips, that spark, her determination and strength to put me in my place, not to mention the caring side she had been trying to show me the last few days while I nursed my ego alone in my room.

I need to get out of this fucking slump, find her, and make this right.

She couldn't have gone very far yet. I have to at least try.

I get up, and walk through the house once more before I commit to this new pursuit.

Her bedroom looks exactly as it did the night before, not a wrinkle in sight across her duvet, which is odd on most days. I can't let this be true. I can't believe that she would just disappear into thin air after how close we became at the retreat.

I just need to pull myself together and win her back. She deserves so much more than the neglectful husband I've been the last few days.

I can only imagine how she feels right now. I want to kiss each and every part of her while I'm down on my knees begging for her forgiveness.

This isn't over yet.

I need to find my wife.

# Chapter Thirty-Nine

## *Quinn*

I turn off the ignition and close my eyes.

The last twenty-four hours with Nicky were exactly what I needed. I never heard from Jaxon, and I'm not surprised. Guilt washed over me for leaving him after such an upsetting event. Nicky reassured me he would be fine, and that I just had to let him pout it out.

But it's Wednesday now, and not that I'm rushing Jaxon's healing, but the silent treatment needs to end.

I have every intention of walking into that house, climbing those stairs straight to Jaxon's room, and letting him have it.

My love, that is.

I love Jaxon, and I need to tell him.

He can mope, brood, pout, whatever he needs to do, but he needs to know that I am right there with him, every step of the way. What we have is special. I was meant to quit my job that night, log on to that website that lured me in with its fluttery hearts and elevator music, and meet Jaxon.

End. Of. Story.

This is it. This is my new life, for now and always. It's Jaxon's too, even if he won't let himself see it through the thick haze of disappointment.

I step out of the car, and scoop Luna up into my arms. With my bag slung over my shoulder, I head to the front door.

The key slips easily into the lock, but before I can turn it, the door opens.

"Quinn," Jaxon says my name sighing, relief crossing over his gorgeous face. His beard looks freshly trimmed, his hair coiffed in its place, and he's wearing a pair of dark jeans and a fitted light grey T-shirt.

I almost forgot how amazingly attractive my husband is. I'm standing there, silent, staring, when Jaxon says my name a second time.

"Wait, let me get my key out." I step into the house and wiggle the key out of the lock and fold my palm around it. I close the door and let Luna out of my arms, and she shuffles her tiny little legs, speeding off like lightning. "Are you going somewhere?" I ask him, noticing his own keys in hand. "I didn't see Henri out there."

"I was just about to call him," he says, lifting his phone. "Doesn't matter now. I was coming to find you."

"Find me?"

"Yeah." He takes my hand in his and leads me into the kitchen where we both sit, each on a stool.

I squirm on the stool until I'm placed just right, and then I cross my right leg over my left. Jaxon leans towards me and places his right hand on my thigh. "What is it, Jaxon?"

"I fucked up, Quinn." He releases my thigh and sits up straight, twisting his Edward Rummens watch on his wrist. "I'm sorry."

"What are you sorry for, exactly?" I ask, hoping he will tell me everything that I need to hear.

"For being a neglectful husband." His eyes are somber, and I see the regret in the slouch of his shoulders. "I've been a selfish ass, so caught up in my own misery. Even though you were trying to be there for me, I just cast you aside. You didn't deserve that."

His words chip away at the insecurities that made me doubt his love the last few days. I take his hand and squeeze.

"Oh, Jaxon."

"I was just so caught up in losing the promotion, and I honestly thought you'd leave me. I just sat up in my room waiting for you to pack up your shit and go." He looks away. "So, when I saw that the car was gone, I figured that was that." He pauses, and I wait for him to continue. "But when I woke up this morning on the couch with a stiff fucking neck after having dreamed of you all night, I knew I had to try and find you." He squeezes my hand this time. "I can't let you leave."

"Jaxon, I'm not going anywhere."

"You're not?" He peers at me, unsure whether to believe me.

I shake my head.

"Quinn, I am head over heels in love with you. I can't go back to a life without you. Job or no job, I want you here. If you want to stay, of course."

"Of course I want to, Jaxon! I don't want to be anywhere else. That's what I was coming home to tell you."

He smiles, and his shoulders relax.

"Oh! And I love you too," I exclaim, laughing.

His hands cup my face, and they bring me towards him until our lips meet.

"Okay, so I love you, and you love me, and we're going to live happily ever after with our fur baby," Jaxon says with a deep chuckle.

"And we need to figure out a game plan for you."

"What do you mean?"

"I've been thinking about it. You can't take this whole loss of promotion lying down. You worked your ass off to get where you are. Edward knows that, and so does Brodie. You need to walk into that office tomorrow morning and remind them who the fuck you are." I cross my arms over my chest to show I mean business. "Respectfully, of course."

"Respectfully, of course." His smile grows wide as he takes me in his arms again. "Fuck, Quinn, you are one amazing woman."

# Chapter Forty

*Jaxon*

"I don't think your closet is big enough," Quinn tells me, her arms full, trekking down the hallway towards *our* room.

"There is more than enough space."

"I don't know, you have like an unnecessary number of suits." She drops her items on an ottoman, then pulls out one of the drawers on the island, revealing my ties.

"Oh, well, now that we know you like to be blindfolded, you'll definitely be getting more use out of some of these." Quinn's finger trails over the neatly folded silk ties. "Do you color-coordinate everything?" She turns around and looks at the clothes that are hanging on hangers. "Never mind, I can see that you do."

"There is nothing wrong with being organized."

"You're right."

She's hanging up her clothes on the opposite side, mixing her jeans with skirts and blouses, and I cringe on the inside.

"I can feel you wincing behind me." Her back is turned to me. "Don't go messing with my clothes."

"I promise nothing," I tell her, even though we both know the first chance I get, I will be organizing her clothes by style and color.

"Well, just keep your hands out of my panty drawers. They do not need to be organized by color."

"I would disagree." I open my own drawer of boxers and show her the sections of greys, blues, and blacks.

Quinn insists on carrying all her stuff from her room and setting it up. I told her we could have housekeeping do it, but she said she'd rather do it together.

I still can't believe that Quinn is mine—and because she *wants* to be, not because of a business deal or a debt to be paid off, but because she loves me.

She fucking loves me, and I'm on cloud nine.

I'm still going back and forth in my head, wondering what I'm going to do tomorrow when I walk into work.

Do I talk to Brodie first?

Do I approach Edward?

I thought Brodie and I were becoming better acquainted, something that would one day lead to a friendship in the office, but to fucking pull the wool over my eyes and not have the goddamn courage to tell me is fucking bullshit. And for Edward to not tell me to my face why he's not giving me the promotion? That's not the man I know.

We spend the rest of the day organizing my bedroom closet and Quinn's side of the bathroom. The primary bathroom has double sinks and a separate area for all her creams and shit. I look around at what used to be a bachelor's bathroom and bedroom, which went from boring and mediocre to one full of life and love.

A little sprinkle of Quinn everywhere.

# CHAPTER FORTY

My palms are clammy on the handle of my briefcase as I walk through the building and ride the elevator up the fourteenth floor.

Everyone seems happy and relaxed after a week away, and here I am a fucking mess.

I need to straighten things out with Edward and Brodie.

I settle into my office chair, after I've closed the door behind me. I look out at the boats anchored in the water and wonder how to approach the day.

I don't need to prove my worth. Edward knows I'm a hard worker, but I want answers. Once I have answers, I can move on. I will suck it up and work for Brodie if that's the way my cards are dealt.

Is it ideal? No.

Is it what I want? Fuck no.

Do I have a choice?

Not if I want to continue working for Edward Rummens Watches.

I'm startled when there's a knock at my door, and I see Brodie behind the glass. I need this bullshit dealt with so that I can get back to being a brooding bitch-ass boss. Quinn's words, not mine.

"Mind if I take a seat?" Brodie asks, pulling out the chair before I can answer.

"Have at it." I tilt my head towards the leather chair his ass is only seconds from sitting on.

"That was a pretty fantastic retreat, right?"

I nod. "You could say that."

"Look, I wanted to say, I know we haven't always been..." He's searching for the word, so I offer a suggestion.

"Friendly?"

"Friendly, yeah, right." He crosses his leg on top of his knee and gets comfortable. A little too comfortable for my liking, and this awkward conversation like we're besties at brunch.

I think Quinn is wearing off on me. Besties, bitch-ass boss. I let out a small chuckle, thinking of Quinn.

"Everything okay?" Brodie asks as if I'm losing my damn mind.

"Just thinking of something Quinn said this morning."

He nods. "Yeah, she's something."

My forehead creases at his statement.

"What are you implying?"

"Whoa, chill, Jaxon. Quinn's great. It was nice to see you let go of some of this uptight shit you hand out."

I stand and make my way to the window, my back towards Brodie.

"You got the promotion, didn't you?" I ask him, not bothering to comment on his statement about my personality.

I wonder who the hell this uptight fucker is that I've become. I was proud of who I was. I worked my ass off, and it showed, not only in my work but in my demeanor. Everyone took me seriously. Boundaries were respected, and deadlines were met. But was it necessary to close myself off for so many years?

My revelation is put on hold as Brodie stands and joins me by the window.

"The promotion? Why would you think that?"

I turn to him, trying to read the bullshit he might be handing me. At only an inch or two taller than him, we stand almost face-to-face.

"Edward didn't announce the promotion on Saturday, and then you two were all buddy-buddy, clinking glasses at the bar.

He runs a hand down his face. "Julie's pregnant. We're having another baby."

"What?"

"I told Edward on Saturday that Julie's expecting. He insisted on a celebratory drink."

"Shit." I turn back to the window, what a piece of work I am. "I mean, sorry, congratulations." I turn to shake his hand.

"Thank you." Silence fills the space between us. "I didn't put my name in for the promotion, Jaxon."

My heart stops. "What?"

"The promotion is yours. It always has been."

"What about all the rumors about Edward wanting a family man to run his company?"

Brodie shakes his head.

"Office gossip, I guess." He nods at my desk. "Can I use your phone?"

"Go for it."

Brodie picks up the receiver and punches in three numbers. "Jenny, can you come to Jaxon's office, please?"

He places the receiver back down and turns to me. "We'll see if we can get to the bottom of this. In the meantime, the promotion's yours. I'm sure Edward will talk to you about it today. He probably would have earlier this week, but I heard you took a few extra days' vacation. Good for you, buddy."

I shake my head and sit back behind my desk. I can't believe the lengths I went to for this promotion, and it was mine this whole fucking time.

Brodie sits back down across from me. He leans back in the chair and clasps his hands together.

"I really thought it was yours." I run my palm down my face. I'm stunned. This was not what I was expecting.

"I'm not ready for a job like CEO, and with another baby on the way, that's the last thing I want to add to my plate."

I nod in agreement.

"But look at you—you're a married man, and now you're going to be CEO. What more could a man ask for, right?"

"What?"

"You're the happiest I've seen you in five years. You willingly socialized at the retreat instead of being cooped up in your room like every other year. Quinn's good for you."

"I know she is," I agree.

"I think we need a fresh start, you and me."

"I couldn't agree more." And I mean it. I've pegged Brodie as the villain for the last five years, and it's been nothing but my insecurities feeding it.

There's a knock at the door, and Jenny peeks her head in. Brodie motions her inside the room.

Jenny stands beside the unused chair next to him. "What can I help you with, sir?"

"You heard that Edward was looking for a family man to promote? Where did you hear that?"

"Well, from you, sir."

Brodie squints at her response. "I never said that."

"You did, on the phone. I heard you talking to someone. You were talking about being a family man, and how Edward was looking for a CEO."

"Jenny, you can't start gossip like this." Brodie stands, shaking his head. "This is unacceptable behavior. What is said in my office is confidential. If you hear anything, business or otherwise, it's off the table for discussion. You signed a non-disclosure agreement."

Jenny looks like she might start to cry, and I feel slightly guilty.

"I'm sorry, sir."

"We'll talk more about this later." He nods towards the door, and Jenny excuses herself. He turns to me. "I can't believe my own assistant started the rumor. She must have heard me talking to Julie on the phone. We were talking about trying for another kid, and then the conversation changed to the promotion, since Edward had just declared he wanted to take a step back. I can't believe she put those two conversations together and started that rumor."

"I've misjudged you, Brodie. I've wasted five years hiding because of my own bullshit. A true lack of judgment. I hope we can start over."

"I'd love nothing more." He gets comfortable again in the chair. "Now, first things first. How the hell did you get a woman like Quinn to marry your sorry ass?"

We both laugh at that, and I decide to hold the whole fake marriage thing close to my chest. It doesn't matter how Quinn came to be in my life. What matters is that she's here with me now, and I won't ever let her go.

By the time Brodie leaves the office, we've made plans for him and Julie to come over for dinner next week so we can start over.

Work's been steady all day, so I haven't had time to make my way up to Edward's office until now. I had Lester set the meeting up.

I have no idea how Edward is going to take this meeting, but I need to talk to him about the promotion.

Betty lets me into Edward's office. He lifts his hand, motioning for me to come in, but I can see he's on a call. I look around the room. It's a corner office facing the water, just a few floors above, but the space is twice the size as mine.

I take a seat on the oversized brown leather sofa and cross my leg, leaning into the thick cushion behind me. I glance at the side table where a picture of him and Carole are standing, smiling in front of his boat.

Edward's been a man who loves the water ever since I've known him. They spend every chance they get on their sailboat. I look around and notice a few other pictures. They never had kids. Edward's baby was this company.

"Jaxon," he greets me, and I stand, shaking his hand. "You beat me to it. I was planning on calling you up here this afternoon."

I raise my eyebrows in question.

"Is this about the promotion?"

"The job's yours if you want it. There's no one else I'd rather take my baby to the next level."

"Thank you, sir. That means a lot." I sit back down, and Edward follows suit, sitting beside me.

"What is it? Isn't this what you've always wanted?" Edward asks when he sees that I'm hesitant.

"More than you know." I wipe my palms down my thighs.

"Jaxon, what is this about?"

## CHAPTER FORTY

"There were rumors," I start. "You may have heard."

"Can't say that I have. Shed some light."

"Gossip was you were only going to promote a family man as CEO."

"I don't understand."

"I just figured you were giving the promotion to Brodie, truth be told."

"No, not at all." Edward shakes his head. "The job's yours—on one condition."

"What's the condition?"

"Quinn, you marry that woman again. You give her a proper wedding, with guests who care about you both, and take a goddamn honeymoon. Quinn's a sweetheart, and you need to cherish her and treat her like the queen she is. Plus, I'm not over the fact that I wasn't invited."

I grin. "I have no problem with that, as long as Quinn wants it too."

"So, do you want the job or not?"

"Yes, I do." I stand tall and confident. "I look forward to showing you I can handle your company as if it were my own."

"That's why the job is yours, Jaxon. I have no doubt about that. Not a single doubt."

# Chapter Forty-One

*Quinn*

The slit on my dress lands right at the center of my right thigh, showing off quite a bit of skin. I've paired the red dress with four-inch lace-up heels. The soft ties wrap around my ankles three times, and I shift to see the look from the back.

Picking up my black purse, I head to the front door, expecting that Jaxon will be home any second. I fix my lipstick at the front hall mirror while I wait. When I hear the car pull up, I throw open the door.

Jaxon texted me a few hours ago saying that he had some news and that he wanted to take me on a proper date.

We're going on a real date.

I laugh, thinking back to how we got here. I married a man without ever having gone on a single date with him. Mom would be beside herself. But look where it's got me. I am going on a date with my husband, a man who is successful, kind, caring, who loves and cherishes me.

And of course, I feel the exact same way about him.

## CHAPTER FORTY-ONE

I'm standing in the doorway when Jaxon gets out of the car and makes his way up the walkway.

The smile on his face grows when he sees me, so I do a little spin and giggle. He's radiating desire, and it sends a flutter through me, right down to my lace panties.

He's wearing a tailored classic navy suit. The shirt underneath has tiny checkers, and his tie matches both. His brown shoes finish the look.

He takes my hand in his.

"Mrs. Baker," he greets me, pulling me in and giving me a light peck on the cheek.

His facial hair prickles my soft skin. "Mr. Baker."

"Are you ready for our first real date?"

He steps off the stoop and waits for me to meet his step.

"Where are we going?"

"It's a surprise."

I watch Jaxon shake his head at Henri, letting him know he doesn't need to get out of the car.

Jaxon pulls open the door behind the driver's side and waits for me to crawl in. He whistles when the slit of my dress moves higher up. I wiggle my bum into the seat, crossing my legs at the ankles.

"Those legs, those shoes. It's going to be hard keeping my hands off you."

My cheeks hurt, I'm smiling so much.

Jaxon comes around to the other side and buckles himself in. The ride takes about forty-five minutes. Jaxon won't tell me the news; he said he wants to wait until we're at dinner. My only guess is that he got the promotion, but with him not saying anything, I'm having doubts. Still, I don't know what else it could be.

We step out into the early evening air as the sun is starting to set, a soft breeze fluttering the leaves in the trees. We walk into the restaurant to the sounds of jazz.

"Jaxon Baker," Jaxon tells the hostess who nods and picks up two menus.

"Of course. Follow me."

I follow her to a small table at the far end of the restaurant. I can see the performer on stage from my seat, but we're far enough away that the music isn't quite as loud. "You look beautiful, Quinn."

"You look very handsome," I return the compliment. His eyes are sparkling in the dim light. "Now tell me the big secret. I can't wait anymore."

"Someone's impatient."

I roll my eyes playfully and lean back in the chair. "Fine. I can be patient. Tell me now, or later, or even tomorrow. I'm fine with that." I'm pretending to be nonchalant, but he sees right through me.

"I got the promotion," he declares in one breath.

"I knew it! Of course you did, Jaxon." I'm so delighted, I get up from my seat and make my way around to hug him. "Congratulations."

"Thank you."

I come back to my seat as the waiter arrives with two glasses of water. We pause our conversation while he tells us the specials, and I let Jaxon order for me, trusting I will like whatever he chooses.

"I want to hear everything," I tell him after the waiter leaves to put in our order.

"Brodie came into my office, and we had a talk."

"Oh, no. How did that go?"

"Julie's expecting."

My eyes widen in surprise. "She is? I had no idea."

## CHAPTER FORTY-ONE

"No one did, except Jenny had an idea, Brodie's assistant." I look at him quizzically, knowing there's more to this story. "She's the one who inadvertently started the rumor about Edward wanting to promote a family man."

I shake my head. It was all a misunderstanding. I can't help but feel a little tinge of uncertainty if this affects my being here with Jaxon. But I look at his bright smile, and I know that I have nothing to worry about. Jaxon made it clear that he loves me, and I'm not going anywhere.

"Turns out she heard Brodie on the phone and put two conversations together, then she told someone else what she heard. Brodie had a sit-down with her after, and an email went out at the end of the day from HR about non-disclosures and no tolerance for gossip."

My hands fly up to my mouth. "What will happen to Jenny?"

"Nothing right now. Just a warning. Edward takes this stuff seriously."

"So what happened after that?"

The waiter returns with two glasses of red wine. I take a sip and let the liquid circle my tongue before swallowing.

"Turns out Brodie is a pretty decent guy," he admits, but I see a hesitation.

"What is it?" I ask.

"I've let my childhood insecurities get the better of me." I place one hand on top of his. "I really fucked up." He tells me about smoothing things over with Brodie. "I met with Edward too."

"And?"

He pauses to take a sip of his own wine. "He wanted someone he knew and trusted with his company."

"So, it all worked out?"

"It did. But there's something else Edward spoke to me about, and I couldn't agree with him more."

"What is it?" I'm literally on the edge of my seat.

"He told me to give you a proper wedding, with friends and family."

"But I don't need that," I tell him, and I try to convince him of that. "I love you, and I'm happy with where we are and where we're going."

"Quinn, you turned my life around. I am so happy to have met you, no matter how unconventional. I owe this happiness that I'm feeling to you. You made me see what was missing in my life."

I feel my eyes beginning to water, and I dab at the corners before it can ruin my makeup.

Jaxon continues before I can say anything, taking both my hands in his.

"I want to marry you again. I want to take you wherever you want to go for a proper honeymoon, if you'll let me."

I notice his eyes are glossy as he tells me this.

"I would love that."

When we've finished our meal, and Jaxon has paid the bill, Henri drives us to the pier downtown. Couples are walking hand in hand under the glow of the lampposts. The sun has set, but the night sky is bright from the moon. A few teenagers run by joking with one another, and their laughter spills around us.

When we've finished our walk and we fall into a slow kiss under the moonlight, he tells me he has one more surprise.

I follow him off the pier and through a walkway that leads into a garden. Flowers are blooming, and there are trees casting privacy, so I'm surprised when we take a turn and there's a large sculpture of a faceless couple intertwined, their heads bowed, and foreheads touching. Just to the left of the sculpture is a wall built to look like a bridge. It starts low to the ground and rises at the center before dropping lower on the other side. It's made of metal and has hundreds of locks attached to it. I run my hand over the top of the made-up bridge and turn to Jaxon.

"It's a lover's wall," I say.

Jaxon pulls a gold lock from his pocket and holds it up for me to see. When he twirls it around, I see it's engraved with "Jaxon and Quinn" on the back and the year we met. "Want to do the honors?"

"Let's do it together."

He places himself behind me, his arms coming around to my front, and together we clasp the lock tight on the bridge. When it's locked, Jaxon holds up the key.

He turns to the fountain that surrounds the sculpture and tells me to make a wish.

I close my eyes and think about the love blooming between us. With a kiss to the key, I raise my arm and throw the key into the water.

# Epilogue

## Quinn

*Six months later*

"Stop moving," Nicky tells me for the third time.

He's twisting my hair with his fingertips and spraying enough hairspray to last a month, but I'm a ball of excited energy.

"I think you should wear pink lipstick," Alysha says from the sofa across from us.

We're in a suite at the Bella Villa where the corporate retreat was held.

Jaxon flew Alysha down to be here with me, and we've spent the last week together, shopping and picking up last-minute things.

When Edward suggested we get married at the villa, I knew it would be perfect.

Since Jaxon is about to start his new role in the next three to four months, Edward thought it would be perfect timing to have friends and family together, have a proper wedding, and for Jaxon to take some much-deserved time off for our honeymoon.

The wedding wasn't difficult to plan since Manuel and his staff took care of almost everything as part of the wedding package. Manuel was on it right away, just as excited as we were. He filled our email inbox daily with questions and pictures, asking for us to choose the color scheme, flowers, meal, and everything down to the nitty-gritty of place settings.

It's a small wedding. Our guest list is under a dozen, but the people who have come to matter most to us are here to witness our special day. We didn't have to go to all the trouble of getting a marriage license seeing that we're already married, but the ceremony will be as if it's our first.

Nicky's been hounding me to get a new dress, but I chose to wear the one I did at city hall and the shoes to match. The only difference will be my bouquet, and the fact that Nicky and Alysha will be by my side up at the altar.

Jaxon's parents flew down a couple of weeks ago, and I've had some time to get to know them. I understand a little more about Jaxon now after having met them. They're great people, just possibly not the best parents, but Jaxon's seeing a therapist to work on some of his childhood issues, something we both agreed to do.

It feels good talking to a third party without judgment. Telling them all about Mom and Granny and the weight that I carried for so many years on my own, and of course the fact that I chose to fly across the country to marry a man I knew so little about. The therapist was concerned for my safety at first, but I insisted that I've fallen head over heels in love with Jaxon.

When Nicky's finished my hair and Alysha's done my makeup, we all get dressed.

Alysha is in a stunning pale pink dress that compliments her skin tone, and Nicky insisted on wearing a suit to match. Nicky couldn't wait to meet Alysha, and I'm so happy the two of them are getting along, so much so that Nicky is trying to convince Alysha to move here. She hasn't said yes, but she also hasn't said no. In time, who knows? Maybe I'll have my two best friends here with me.

When it's time to walk down the aisle, I wait for Nicky and Alysha to walk up ahead of me.

This time feels different. I'm in love with the man I'm about to re-marry. There won't be any awkward eye contact or worrying about what will become of my life after committing to a stranger. I know what I'm getting myself into this time around, and I can't wait for it.

I notice Jaxon's eyes are shiny with tears when I stand before him.

"You look stunning." He plants a kiss on my cheek as I shift next to him.

"Thank you."

We take each other's hands, and I see Lester and Brodie standing close behind with their own wide smiles.

Brodie and Jaxon have been spending time together outside of the office. Turns out they both love billiards, so every couple of weeks they go out to play for a few hours.

Edward and Carole are sitting with a very pregnant Julie in the second row. Behind Jaxon's parents is Vinny.

I don't have family of my own here with me, but Edward and Carole have taken me in just as they did with Jaxon. We may not be filling up the villa with a hundred guests and a whole entourage of bridesmaids and groomsmen, but we have everyone here that matters.

A little yap has us turning towards the chairs where Luna is sitting by Vinny's side.

# EPILOGUE

The ceremony was more beautiful than I expected.

We wrote our vows this time, instead of reading a standard set from the internet, and I find myself holding back tears of happiness as we slide the rings on. Jaxon surprised me with a second band that matches the engagement ring and wedding band I was already wearing. This one sits at the base of the ring and is covered in tiny diamonds.

When we say I do and our lips meet for our second official kiss as husband and wife, a surge of love soars through me.

There's a private dinner set up in the dining hall, the same fairy lights twinkling overhead like during that last night at the retreat, and we're all seated at one long table that has been lined with a pale pink tablecloth. The chairs have been wrapped in a cream-colored fabric, and flowers line the table runner.

Chatter and laughter fill our hearts between bites, kisses and thigh squeezes under the table as we have our meal. When we've all finished eating, music begins to fill the air. Jaxon and I have our first dance together, the one we missed out on the first time around.

His arms are wrapped around me, holding me close, and I know in this moment that this is exactly where I was meant to end up.

In the arms of Jaxon Baker.

I open the bathroom door to our hotel room as quietly as I can, wanting to surprise Jaxon.

We arrived late last night at the hotel where we'll be for the next two weeks while we explore Europe. After traveling all day, we fell into bed, our eyes closing as soon as our heads hit the pillow.

Jaxon is still sleeping, but I woke up early, showered, and put on something blue. The same blue lace bodysuit from our first night as husband and wife. The one that proved Jaxon was a true gentleman. But a lot has changed, and I am fully expecting that Jaxon will have no issues being less than gentlemanly this time.

I clear my throat, and he stirs, but his eyes remain closed.

I do the same again, but this time with a more exaggerated sound, which has him rubbing his eyes and sitting up.

"Good morning, Mr. Baker."

"Fuck me," Jaxon mutters, his eyes darkening, and I know he's growing under the sheet that's barely covering him.

"I plan on it," I respond.

I walk towards the bed slowly, allowing his eyes to wander over the lace that leaves little to the imagination. By the time I reach the bed, Jaxon's sitting on the edge, waiting for me.

I place my palm in the center of his chest.

Our mouths collide, and we spend the rest of the day tangled up between the sheets.

The end.

# Discussion Questions

1. How did you feel when you finished the book?

2. What did you think of Jaxon's decision to find a wife just to get a promotion?

3. Which activity at the corporate retreat was your favorite? Have you ever been to a retreat of a similar nature?

4. How did Quinn grow throughout the story? How did Jaxon? Can you relate to either of them?

5. Quinn loves reality TV. What's your favorite reality TV show?

6. Quinn signed up to be on a matchmaking site. Have you ever been on one yourself? What was your experience like?

7. If Benefits Included was a movie, who would you cast for each role?

8. Quinn took a huge leap of faith flying across the country to marry Jaxon. Did you ever take a big risk?

9. Quinn adopted Luna without talking to Jaxon first.

Do you think this is something that should be talked about between partners first?

10. If you could have dinner with one character, including Alysha or Nicky, who would it be?

# About the author

Erin Lisbeth is a Canadian romance author with a diploma in creative writing and a love for happily ever afters. When she's not curled up with a good book or watching Hallmark movies and reality TV, she's writing quirky, relatable characters. Outside of writing, Erin enjoys meditating, practicing yoga, and hitting the road for her next adventure. If you enjoyed reading *Benefits Included*, consider leaving a review!

You can follow Erin on the following social media platforms:

Instagram: Erinlisbeth_
Facebook: Erin Lisbeth

# The Dating Debacle

# The Dating Debacle
## Chapter One

I look to my right as I hear Jake sigh over the sound of a hockey stick hitting a puck. He's wiping a layer of sweat off his brow with the sleeve of his blue jersey. The sight of the darkened material turns my stomach. I don't know when it started, but all those traits of his that I used to think were adorable now make me cringe. Those kissy noises he used to make from across the room, as he called me, or the red ball cap he used to wear, which smelled like feet. Why does it even smell like feet?

I take a sip of my drink and turn back to the game. The scoreboard reads 2-1. Last month, I bought Jake these tickets for his birthday. Hockey is more his thing, but I don't mind going to a game or two. I look around, hearing people shout out the names of their favorite players. Crossing my arms, I tug my sweater tighter around me to block out the cool air from the ice below.

Two players body check the guy with the puck into the boards, and I hear Jake sigh again, raising his arm and checking his watch. I ignore him and turn back to the game.

Jake and I have been together for two years. We met at a little diner one night after a few too many drinks and a lot of karaoke. My friends and I had been out celebrating a friend's birthday.

Lucy, Briar, and I have been friends since college. Lucy and I had shared a tiny dorm room that barely fit more than our two single beds and a desk each. You can say we had no choice but to be up in each other's business.

I studied English literature while Lucy focused on communications and media. We met our friend, Briar, during our second year when we teamed up one night at the on-campus pub, where a heated game of trivia was taking place. The theme of the night was TV sitcoms and movies. You can say we had it in the bag, and after that, the three of us became inseparable.

After our night of karaoke, we walked out into the brisk, frigid air and followed the crowd of people on the street, all in desperate need of some greasy food. We saw a diner across the street with its glowing sign advertising that it was open 24 hours, and we knew they had a reputation for making amazing pulled pork poutine. We made our way through the crowded diner until we found a large booth occupied by two guys with room to spare.

The moment our eyes met, I felt a spark with Jake. He had crystal blue eyes and thick blond hair. The kind you want to run your hands through. Lucy slid right into the booth and motioned for the guys to move over and make room for us. We ordered lots of food and water and laughed until the sun rose.

When we left the diner that morning, Jake and I exchanged numbers, and by that afternoon, I had a text from Jake asking me out on a date. It didn't take long before I was spending all my time at his apartment.

He lived in a much larger place than mine, and although he had two roommates who were a bit on the messy side, I was head over heels for Jake. I wanted to be around him as much as possible. He was an obvious sports fan, who not only loved to watch hockey but also played a few times a week. I was in awe of his amicable but loud personality and the confidence he exuded, something I sometimes lacked.

As time went on, that loud personality became obnoxious, and the confidence seemed a bit more egotistical than I was comfortable being around. Things just changed. The rose-colored glasses were off, and I was having second thoughts. We had gone from spending most of our weeknights together to once or twice a week in the last few months.

Jake glances at me as I sip my drink a little too loudly, trying to get the last few drops of it through the paper straw that is now starting to deteriorate. I place my cup under the empty seat next to me.

The crowd is cheering as the scoreboard changes to 3-1. The noise level is rising, and people are getting up from their seats and singing along to the music. I can feel the bass vibrate through the bottoms of my feet. Jake, who usually loves this sort of thing, is still sitting, looking nervous. I turn to him, crossing my arms to stay warm, wishing now that I had not left my oversized puffer coat in the car, but it would hardly fit in the chair with me.

"What's going on? Are you not feeling well tonight?" I ask, seeing sweat appear on his forehead once again.

He wipes it with the back of his hand, turning to me with a nervous grin. How is he sweating, and I am here shivering? My toes feel like ice cubes as I look down towards my feet, wiggling them in my gray faux-suede ankle boots.

"I'm good, Sof. I kind of wanted to talk to you."

I lean into him, not sure if I heard him right. The crowd is clapping and singing to the music, drowning out the sounds of the skates gliding across the ice.

Jake turns in his seat to face me directly. As though he is trying to find his keys, he places his hands inside his pockets. Jake's gotten a little OCD about his keys since last winter when we got locked out of his car after a movie one night. It had been -15, and we had to wait outside for a cab to come and help us break into his car. The keys had fallen on his seat. It had kind of turned into a romantic night. Jake embraced me under the light post, shielding me from the cold. Snow was falling from the sky, and I nestled into his neck, breathing in his musky scent. Those moments were few and far between now. Maybe Jake was starting to feel the distance between us as I have. I know I should have spoken to him about this sooner. Life just kind of got busy, and we were familiar.

I spend most of my days at this cute shop where I work. Plants, Pottery & Books is sort of like my second home. I work in the back, in the tiny used bookstore. We have a lot of regular customers who I have grown to love, and of course, there's Ben.

Ben's uncle owns the shop. His uncle took him in when his parents passed away, so the shop is sort of his second home too, I guess. I like to call him my work BFF, but he usually just grins and ignores that statement. Work is always more fun with a friend.

I've been working at Plants, Pottery & Books for just over two years. I found the job in the last few months before graduation, when I was running out of my student loan and needed some extra money. Working at the shop allows me time to freelance. I guess I sort of put work and my friends ahead of Jake these days. We just have little in common anymore, and I can't see him being the one.

I guess this is it. We're probably breaking up. The thought isn't making me feel overly sad. I feel myself frowning while I think about this. Shouldn't I feel sad? I guess that is probably a good sign that this is the right thing to do.

"What's going on?" I raise my voice so he can hear me, leaning in closer. I can smell the face cream I bought him. It took me forever to get him to use a cleanser instead of washing his face with shower gel.

"Score!" someone yells behind us. I turn to see a group of guys with their arms raised above their heads, laughing and cheering.

"This isn't the best place or time to talk, Jake. Maybe we can talk after the game?" I ask, turning back to him.

Jake looks at me, shaking his head. "I can't wait any longer. I need to do this." He plays with the zipper on his coat, moving it up and down on its track, my eyes following the movement.

I get the whole pulling off the Band-Aid, but this is hardly the place to do it, I think to myself, wiggling my toes more, trying to build some heat in my boots.

"Why don't we take off early, then? I can barely hear you," I say loudly, pushing my hair aside as I lean towards him once again.

People are getting up from their seats as the intermission begins. I turn my legs to the right of me to let a few people pass by. Someone steps on my frozen toes as they squeeze past me. I squint, feeling it radiate up my foot. Ugh, I could use a warm bath right now, with a good book and a glass of Pinot.

Jake shakes his head again, grabbing one of my hands with his. I look him in the eyes and notice the look of happiness that has settled across his face.

Well, that's weird. I mean, yeah, it's for the best, but could he pretend to be sad just a bit?

We were together for two years. It's not like a casual dating situation. I have a whole drawer at his apartment, as well as many pairs of shoes and some of my best face creams. I'll have to go back to his place. I can't live without my eye cream and lip gloss. Plus, Jake has a few things at my place too. He could probably live without his sweats and a hoodie or two, but it makes little sense to keep his stuff, either.

Okay, maybe I shouldn't judge him for feeling some type of relief since I am now more worried about my abandoned beauty products than the breakup itself.

Jake is gazing at me. I am suddenly thinking about the cute little clutch I left there last week.

Oh. My. God, Sofia. Pay attention. This dude is about to break up with you, and all you can think about is your inventory at his place.

I try to focus on Jake, bringing my awareness back to him and placing my hand on top of his. If being dragged to yoga once a week by Briar has taught me anything, it is to be present. I'm a work in progress. Rome wasn't built in a day. I look up at Jake again as he lets go of my hand. I see him take something out of his pocket, and the next thing you know, he's on the ground.

"Geez, Jake, get up from there. Do you know how gross these floors are?" I say, utterly disgusted. "What are you doing?" I feel my eyes roll before I can stop myself.

Jake looks like he has no intention of getting up. I see him get into a comfortable position that looks vaguely familiar.

*Oh, hell no! What in the actual fuck is happening?*

Jake grabs my hands once again and smiles shyly. I am going to throw up. Yes, I am going to throw up right here, right now, for everyone to see. With my luck, the Kiss Cam will come on, and everyone will see it. I will be known as that girl who threw up on her boyfriend as he proposed.

I try to pull back from his grasp, and I pull so hard that my hand whacks me in the forehead as it lets go of his grip. I rub the slightly sore spot above my right eye.

Perfect, this is going simply great. I look around to see if anyone has noticed Jake down on his knee. A few people are looking this way. I feel my cheeks flush.

I am so embarrassed. We have never, not once, spoken about getting married. We aren't even living together. There are steps you must take. Everyone knows it! First, you date, then you're a couple, then you move in with each other, then you get married. Plus, I thought he was about to break up with me! I stare at him in disbelief.

"Sofia, you mean so much to me," Jake starts.

Oh, God, he is going there. I feel so bad. I force myself to turn away, looking down at the floor.

"Sofia, please look at me."

I turn back to face Jake, feeling a lump in my throat, not quite sure if that is the vomit that is about to come up or if I am going to burst into tears. Either one would not be ideal right now. I'm a crier. Stressed, embarrassed, sad, or even hangry, yup, I cry. I would say that I'm quite stressed right now. I can feel my underarms sweating profusely, and I no longer notice my frozen toes as heat creeps up my body.

"Do you remember the night we met?" Jake is still staring, now waiting for a reply.

"Uh, yes, Jake, I do..." I start to reply, but Jake cuts me off mid-sentence.

"I felt an instant connection the moment our eyes met. You have become not only my best friend but my soul mate," Jake continues.

A small laugh escapes me. My hand flies up to my mouth to cover it as if I can take back the laugh or stop the words that are about to spill out.

"Jake, come on. You know I don't believe..."

"Yes, yes, Sofia, I know you don't believe in soul mates, and that's okay. I do. I know we are perfect for each other, and I want to spend the rest of my life showing you that we are." Jake lets go of the one hand that didn't manage to escape his grasp earlier.

Oh, here it comes. I swallow hard as the lump moves its way up my throat. I cringe at the sour taste in my mouth.

He looks down at the silver box in his hand. I hear a gasp and turn to see where it came from. I notice there are now quite a few people watching us and pointing. They don't appear to be turning away anytime soon.

Who proposes at a hockey game during intermission, anyway? I'm not even a hockey person! People are standing and squeezing by, making their way through the rows, coming back from the washroom, or filling up their nachos or drinks. The music is blaring. This is hardly a romantic setting in front of all these strangers.

"Jake, listen," I start to say. "Let's get out of here and go talk," I plead with a look in my eyes, willing him to catch that I'm not exactly feeling his vibe—this vibe.

Jake doesn't appear to notice. If we were soul mates, wouldn't he catch on?

Opening the box, I see a small princess-cut diamond sitting high on a simple gold band. It is pretty. *Wow, look at that thing sparkle.*

No, stop it, Sofia! Don't let the bling blind you! I blink a few times and gather myself.

He raises his voice slightly to be heard over the music. "Sofia..." Jake is taking the ring out of the box.

"Jake, I'm serious. Please stop," I say as my voice starts to quiver.

I grab the front of my sweater and start to pull it away from my skin as I suddenly feel hot and clammy. Jake doesn't appear to be taking in any of what I am putting out. He is pulling the ring out of the box and holding it up to my ring finger.

Jake has a huge smile on his face. "Sofia, will you marry me?"

How can he be so oblivious?

Do I look happy right now?

Do I look like someone excited about what is happening?

Jake starts to slip the ring on my finger before I can even open my mouth to reply. I hear clapping coming from behind me and someone shouting, "She said yes!"

"No." The word comes out harsher than I intended. Jake looks up at me as he finishes sliding the ring onto my finger. "I don't want to get married, Jake," I say a little softer. Jake's eyes meet mine. I see a flash of pain cross over his face. "I'm sorry, Jake." I start to pull off the ring.

A man is standing right behind Jake, carrying more than he seems capable of holding.

"Excuse me," he says.

Jake turns around, still with one knee on the ground. I see one of the two drinks the man is balancing with what appears to be three slices of pizza start to waver.

The man's eyes widen.

Before anyone can react, the drink falls from his grasp, landing on the floor right beside Jake and splashing him down his left side. Jake jumps up quickly from the shock of it.

He looks towards me, and I see anger setting in.

"I'm sorry, man, my bad." The man shrugs. "But you're not exactly in your seat now, are you?"

Jake slumps next to me to let the man pass, turning his legs away from me. He closes the ring box and puts it back into his pocket. The man walks past. I look down at the ring in my hand. He gets up and makes his way towards the aisle.

"Jake!" I yell after him, grabbing my purse that I had stuffed under my seat.

The bottom of the bag is damp from the drink that was just spilled. I get up and follow him out. He pushes his way through the people coming back from intermission.

"Jake!" I yell at him again, not knowing if he even heard me the first time.

He keeps walking. I break into a little jog, coming up behind him as he makes his way onto the escalator going down. I step on and start walking down the moving steps, ignoring the uncomfortable feeling of walking on a moving escalator.

"Sof, just stop," I hear him mutter.

"Look, Jake, I love you, but I just don't think we're working anymore, you know?" I say as I steady myself on the step beside him, grabbing onto the railing.

"No, Sofia, I don't know. I just asked you to be my wife. I thought we were working." Jake stares straight in front of him. I see his jaw clenched, his face hardened. We reach the ground floor and step off at the same time.

I grab his hand. "Jake, wait." He stops, not turning to face me. Making my way in front of him, I place the ring in the hand I'm holding. "I'm sorry, Jake. I thought you were going to break up with me tonight, and I started thinking that maybe that was a good idea." He winces, so I soften my voice. I feel my shoulders relax a little. "I just think we've grown apart. Can you really say you're happy?"

Jake looks down at the ring he's now holding, then back up to me. "Yeah, Sof, I was." He's walking again towards the exit. "Don't follow me."

I stop as the door closes behind him. My heart sinks as I wipe the tears that have started to fall with my sleeve. This was not how I thought today was going to go, although it's probably for the best. Jake and I were not meant for each other. It'll be okay. Jake will be okay when he realizes he is better off. We're both better off.

I pull out my phone from my bag and request an Uber.

I push open the door and step into the frosty night air, once again wishing I had on a coat. The parking lot isn't very busy since the game is still going on. I put my phone back into my bag and waited for my ride to show up.

Manufactured by Amazon.ca
Bolton, ON

53966196R00187